Learning the Hard Way

Tamsin was confused about Jamie's behaviour and her own reactions to it. Jamie was a man; he wasn't supposed to sit back and let a woman tie him up. Somehow the fact that he liked it made it even more incomprehensible to her.

And yet she had *liked* having him on that leash. Furthermore, she wanted to do it again. She started exploring her feelings about it and found herself becoming excited. She thought about how meek, how abject, he'd been. It was all a game, she told herself. He was physically stronger than she was. She didn't have any real power over him, only the power he chose to give her. And she liked the thought of that very much.

Learning the Hard Way
Jasmine Archer

BLACK LACE

Black Lace books contain sexual fantasies.
In real life, always practise safe sex.

First published in 2003 by
Black Lace
Thames Wharf Studios
Rainville Road
London W6 9HA

Typeset by SetSystems Ltd, Saffron Walden, Essex
Design by Smith & Gilmour, London
Printed and bound by Mackays of Chatham PLC

ISBN 0 352 33782 6

1

'Last Friday night Jamie came in his pants,' Tamsin said, almost inaudibly.

Gina hooted. 'He came in his *pants*?' she shrieked, so loudly that people at the nearby tables started turning their heads. 'I wouldn't have thought Jamie had it in him. How did that happen? Tell me!'

'We were dancing at the club. Slow dancing. I pressed up against him and felt – my God, he must have been wearing a codpiece! It was so –'

'Men don't wear codpieces any more, Tamsin. They haven't for centuries. That was his cock you felt. His *cock*!' Again Gina's voice had risen as she spoke. The people at the neighbouring tables turned their heads again and seemed to give up all pretence of minding their own business.

'I know that, Gina. I was making a joke. And would you mind keeping your voice down? We're entertaining the whole restaurant. It's embarrassing.'

'Sorry. Do go on with your story.'

'OK. I was wearing that sexy little black silk minidress that makes my breasts look bigger and shows nearly everything else I've got. I was hoping that, finally, Jamie would make a move. He didn't. But his body certainly did, in spite of him.'

'You mean he got a hard-on?' Gina's response was quieter this time, but the people were still staring.

'Well, yes. He pulled me closer to him. Then he groaned and thrust at me. I felt a dampness, too high up to be me. I was turned on and wet, but this was in the wrong position. Then it seemed to flatten out. He pushed way and covered his crotch with his hands.'

Gina giggled. 'And?'

'I finally got it. He'd come in his pants. I looked at his crotch and saw stains spreading out behind his hands. He ran for the loo and stayed there about fifteen minutes. When he came back to the table the stains were bigger. Poor boy, he'd obviously been trying to mop himself up with water. It didn't work.'

'Did you say anything?'

'No. I was too embarrassed. But I wanted to tell him that he could have dried his trousers with the hand drier.'

Gina hooted again. 'And then what happened?'

'We danced some more. No more slow ones, though. Then he walked me home, but he didn't come in for his usual cuppa. Said he had a headache.'

'A headache!' Gina roared, and this time Tamsin joined in.

For a few minutes they ate in silence, busy with their salads. Finally Tamsin broke the silence. 'I've got a big favour to ask. I want to learn about sex toys before I leave for the States. You're the only friend I'd dare ask. You know how shy I am. I don't want to be this mousy creature forever. I want an active sex life – like you. And I don't want it to be all vanilla, either.'

'What are you going to be doing in the States, anyhow? I thought it was a business trip. Photography, not sex. With that woman – what's her name? Leandra, is it?'

'Yes. We're doing a book, *L.A. From Other Eyes*. She's invited photographers from all over the world to go to L.A. and photograph whatever they fancy. When I won that award, she contacted me. It's a perfect opportunity.'

'For photography or sex?' Gina teased.

'Photography, of course. Professional development.

But I'm hoping I can get some sexual experience, too. You know I want to branch out and become a photographer of nudes, and I don't think I can do that well unless I'm active sexually. I think my inexperience would show in my work.'

'You've got a point. I could teach you myself,' Gina said, 'but it would probably be a waste. You've never shown even the slightest lesbian tendencies. But – do you remember my friend Marcus? He'd be delighted to help out.'

'You mean the chap I photographed with you? The dancer you work with? I assumed he was –'

'Not all male dancers are gay, Tamsin. I can tell you from personal experience that Marcus isn't. At least he's straight when he's with me. Shall I make the arrangements?'

Tamsin assented, rather shyly, and they made a date for the following week. This done, they declined dessert and hurried off on their separate ways.

The next week was a frantic one for Tamsin. She spent all her free time running errands, preparing for her long summer in California. In addition, she had extra work to do for her boss and mentor, the photographer who had recognised her talent when she was still at school. He seemed anxious about losing his assistant for a while. His anxiety manifested in nitpicky requests and constant demands on her attention.

Nevertheless she had time to think about her upcoming session with Marcus. She'd met Marcus only once, when she was photographing the dancers, but they hadn't had much time to get acquainted. She planned to remedy that when she met him again at Gina's.

Gina hadn't said much about him, except that he was the best dance partner she'd ever had. When Tamsin had photographed him, she'd been expecting the cocky arrogance that she'd too often noticed in men who know they are the best at what they do. But he hadn't been like that at all. In fact, she'd liked him. She hadn't pursued the friendship, though, because she'd lacked both time and opportunity.

Now that she was going to meet him under rather unusual circumstances, she wished she'd spent more time getting to know him. Oh, well. She'd do that when they got together next week. In the meantime she needed to put him out of her mind and focus on getting ready for her trip.

On Thursday Tamsin arrived early for her date with Gina, and chose a table on the patio. Watching the jutting fountains reminded her of the scene with Jamie. Replaying that evening had lent fire to her fingers whenever she pleasured herself during the ensuing week. She elaborated upon it endlessly, changing the scenario slightly each time. The truth was that she'd always got off on the idea of a man coming in his pants. This, of course, wasn't something she could share with the average date who was focused on slipping his cock into her. Male friends with whom she had discussed the topic were appalled. Come in your pants when there was an available woman? This simply wasn't done.

She hoped this was a British phobia. Maybe American men would be more willing. Since she had no American man handy to check it out with she was, for the moment, left to her own imagination.

Now she was glad that Jamie was going to the States with her. As her best friend (not counting Gina, who was as close as a sister), he could provide moral support in a high-pressure, unfamiliar environment, even though he was hopeless in the sex department. Too bad she found him so attractive.

She played the scene with Jamie once again. What if

4

she'd been wearing a miniskirt with a thong instead of a sheath without panties? And what if he'd placed both hands firmly on her bum, hiking up her skirt in the process? What if he'd then pulled her firmly against his throbbing erection, thrusting himself against her sopping panties? She could almost feel the final push, the tightening of his balls, his breathless, 'Tamsin, I'm . . .'

'. . . coming.'

Tamsin jerked her head round and realised the waiter had been speaking to her. 'Excuse me. What did you say?'

'I said your friend just rang up and said she'll be late but she's coming.'

'Oh. Of course. Thank you.'

Blast! That had been a bloody good fantasy, before it was interrupted. She'd been so lost in her thoughts that she'd completely forgotten she was meeting Gina here.

Turning heads alerted her to Gina's arrival. Gina was drop-dead gorgeous and created a commotion wherever she went. Today she had obviously raced over from her dance studio. She'd flung a leather micromini on over her tights. Her leotard top revealed only a hint of her tiny breasts. Her auburn hair was pulled back in a dancer's chignon, and her translucent skin was devoid of makeup except a lip gloss that matched her hair.

The two women greeted each other as Gina sat down. She refused Tamsin's offer of a drink. 'Let's get along to my flat. Marcus is waiting for us there.'

For a moment Tamsin had the urge to cry off. She was terrified at the thought of a strange man showing her how to use sex toys. But she needed to learn somehow, if she wanted to appear more sophisticated than she really was. She was afraid her new friends would laugh at her if they realised how inexperienced she was. The truth was that her idea of wild sex was using a vibrator instead of her fingers. She decided to treat this experience with Marcus as if she were visiting a sex therapist; that way she could deal with it and perhaps not be so embarrassed.

Gina's flat was only a block from the café. Entering it, Tamsin looked round in awe. The flat always affected her that way. Tamsin lived in a bed-sitter and professed no interest in her surroundings. The main part of her life was lived in the studio, where she worked for her mentor and was allowed to do her own work during her free time. Gina's flat, in contrast, was a real home. The walls were lined with photographs of Gina in provocative poses. Tamsin had taken some of those pictures herself, including the ones of Gina and Marcus together. There was also a large display cabinet that contained all of Gina's dancing awards.

The women greeted Marcus, and Gina left Tamsin alone with him while she went to make tea. Marcus was tall and deceptively slender. His build hid the fact that he was extremely strong, as a dancer must be in order to lift his partner over his head several times in each rehearsal and performance. Tamsin found him attractive, so of course she felt shy. Fortunately Marcus didn't have that problem. He kept up a running commentary until Tamsin forgot her nervousness and laughed at his wit. By the time Gina returned with the tea, Tamsin and Marcus were sitting side by side on the sofa like old friends.

'Marcus is going to be in California this summer, too, Gina. He was just telling me about his plans.'

'Really? You beast! Why didn't you tell me? I'm going to be lonesome.'

'I seriously doubt that, Gina. You'll have all the other chaps – and the girls – in the ballet corps to keep you company.' He stood up and drew Gina to her feet. 'Gina, my love, don't be sad. Life will still be worth living without me. Promise you won't do anything stupid. I'll be back, I promise, *mon petit chou*. He executed a grace-ful pirouette, then lifted Gina over his head and twirled her while continuing to speak. 'I don't want you to suffer because of my absence. Please don't suffer.'

'Marcus, you're outrageous. Put me down!' Gina flailed her arms but couldn't reach his head. 'Now!'

'I don't believe you're serious, my love. Do you know why? Because you're laughing so hard while you call me these cruel names. Outrageous, indeed. However, I'll put you down, but only because I'm afraid that if you keep up this unseemly mirth you'll wet yourself, and I'm in a dangerous position if that happens.'

After depositing an indignant Gina on her bum, he sprawled on the floor beside her and leaned against Tamsin's knee. 'Are you cruel too, Tamsin?' he asked, gazing up at her with a soulful expression. 'Would you call an old friend a beast and outrageous? Please tell me you'll be kind to me. I'm a sensitive creature, and Gina has wounded me beyond repair.'

'I'll be kind, Marcus,' Tamsin said, falling into the silly mood of the other two. 'I won't call you a beast. Unless, of course, you do something to deserve it.'

'Oh, my love! I'll adore you forever! You're the woman I've been waiting for all my life.'

'Enough of this,' Gina said. 'Tell me about it, Marcus. Are you really going to California?'

'Yes, I am. I'm not scheduled for any rehearsals until autumn, so I'm taking advantage of the hiatus to go help my friend who has a motel on the beach near Santa Monica.'

'Work in a motel? *You*?' Gina dissolved into laughter. 'Why, except for your dancing, you're the laziest chap I know.'

'You're about to hurt my feelings again, Gina. I happen to be a very competent handyman. I do electrical work, fix air conditioners, that kind of thing. I have practical as well as artistic skills, unlike some people I know. My father made me learn. He could never believe that his son would make it as a ballet dancer.'

'What about your dancing? You can't go an entire summer without a class.'

'I don't intend to. I'm going to train with a local ballet company every day. It will be a good change of pace for me, and it never hurts to make connections in the international ballet scene. But that's enough about me. Now I want to talk to Tamsin, since she's promised to be kind to me.' He leaped to his feet from the floor and, in one fluid motion, landed on the sofa beside Tamsin.

Tamsin had almost forgotten why she was there. The clowning around had relaxed her to the point where the situation seemed like any casual conversation among friends. Now, remembering, she tensed up again.

'Relax, love. I'm harmless.' Marcus draped a friendly arm around her shoulders and pulled her over until her head was resting on his chest. He buried his nose in her hair. 'Mmm. Nice.'

'It's just my shampoo.' Brilliant. Why couldn't she ever think of anything clever to say like other women, Tamsin thought in disgust. Sometimes it seemed to her that others were born knowing things that she'd never be able to understand.

'Whatever it is, I like it,' Marcus said. They all sat in silence for a few minutes.

'Don't get all romantic on me now, you two.' Gina got up and rescued the teapot, which was in imminent danger of being kicked off the coffee table. When she returned from the kitchen, Tamsin and Marcus had moved to a reclining position with their arms around each other, and were necking like teenagers.

Tamsin felt quite at ease, which surprised her. She'd thought this whole afternoon might be awkward and embarrassing. But it wasn't. The talking had helped; she felt as if she'd known Marcus for a long time. When Gina suggested that they all adjourn to the bedroom, Tamsin was most willing to go.

Marcus rose and led the way. The bedroom walls were filled with nude paintings of Gina dancing. Tamsin was not surprised to see that the bedspread had been turned down, revealing black satin sheets. On top of the sheets were a paddle, a large dildo, and a set of clamps.

'What's that?' she asked, pointing to the clamps.

'You'll see,' Gina said, 'in a moment.'

Gina unbuttoned the waistband of her leather skirt, letting it drop to the floor. She wriggled out of her leotard and then out of her tights. She was naked underneath. Her shaved sex was as smooth as a baby's skin. Her tiny breasts had never known a bra.

She stared impatiently at Tamsin. 'Well? Aren't you going to undress?'

'Oh ... sure.' Tamsin had been daydreaming again. Hurriedly she began undoing buttons and zippers, leaving her clothes in a heap on the floor beside Gina's. She felt oddly self-conscious. Of course she and Gina had been naked together before, in dressing rooms, but this was entirely different. She hadn't realised just how different an afternoon of playing with sex toys would be. The presence of a man made a difference, too.

Marcus shucked off his leather trousers, shirt, and shoes, leaving him in only a white silk jockstrap. He pointed to the bed. Tamsin obediently clambered up. She tried not to look at Marcus's crotch, but she couldn't help herself. His jockstrap was filling up in a most enticing manner.

She felt herself responding to the sight. She had begun to feel damp while they were making out on the sofa. Embarrassed, she covered her crotch. One of her questions had been answered, at least. Marcus's cock wasn't as slender as the rest of him. On the contrary.

She stared, fascinated, as the thin material of the jock-strap threatened to split with its burden.

'Now,' Marcus said, 'lesson one. This is a dildo.'

'I can see that!' retorted Tamsin, feeling patronised.

'This is what you do with it,' Marcus continued, ignoring Tamsin's ill-tempered protest. 'Oh! Wet already?'

Tamsin blushed. She lay back on the satin sheets, succumbing to the magic Marcus was working with his fingers.

'You don't just shove it in,' Marcus continued instructing. 'You have to make sure your partner is ready. Like this.' He placed his thumb on Tamsin's slippery clit and rubbed it gently.

'And like this.' He gently inserted a finger into Tamsin's sizzling sex and scooped up some juice. 'You've got to lubricate the dildo, but I can tell you don't need much of that.' Nevertheless, he smeared the juice from Tamsin's pussy all over the dildo.

'Now!' he exclaimed, as he worked the dildo into her. It went in easily.

'Oh!' was all Tamsin could manage. It felt just like a penis – not that she'd experienced many of those, either. She couldn't believe she was reacting this strongly. How could this be? She barely knew Marcus.

Marcus eased the dildo back out, leaving Tamsin feeling empty. He picked up another item from the pile of toys.

'This is a harness for the dildo. I could strap it on and do you that way. See, the dildo is hollow inside so a man can wear it over his cock. I thought of putting it on before I came to meet you, but I didn't want to freak you out. But now at least I'm sure *this* won't freak you out any more.' He slid his jockstrap slowly down over his hips, wriggling to free his imprisoned cock.

'Oh, please! Let's try it again!'

'Chill out, girl. I have a few other things to show you first.' Marcus bent over Tamsin's stiffening nipples and took one in his mouth. As he rolled his tongue around it, it got harder. While his tongue was busy, his hands groped for the nipple clamps, which Tamsin fortunately hadn't recognised as such. Marcus removed his mouth and quickly put the clamp on the long, erect nipple. Tamsin moaned.

Marcus followed the same procedure with the other nipple. He waited for a minute, gently stroking Tamsin's hair. Her breathing slowed a little and she relaxed. When it was clear that she wasn't going to come immediately, Marcus put his mouth on hers and forced her lips open with his tongue. Tamsin's tongue met his instantly. The two tongues fenced, savouring each other.

Marcus picked something else off the pile and reached behind Tamsin's ample bum. His fingers found the little puckered hole. He slowly inserted the butt plug, a difficult job because of Tamsin's squirming. He played with it until she relaxed and the plug popped in. She moaned into Marcus's mouth and writhed lasciviously. Marcus backed off one more time. He cradled Tamsin in his arms, murmuring to her until she calmed down, then gently he ran his hand over her sex hair, barely touching it. Tamsin thrust her mound up at his hand and Marcus cupped it in his palm, carefully avoiding her clit. Tamsin's juices continued to ooze. She kept on thrusting, more frantically now.

'Easy, girl. I don't want you to start coming too soon.'

Marcus pulled his hand back and Tamsin futilely tried to writhe against it. Her thighs tried to trap his hand, but Marcus was too quick for her.

'Soon, Tamsin, soon.'

He fumbled for the dildo, which was now strapped

into the harness, and eased the tip of it into Tamsin's sex. Straddling her thighs, he thrust his pelvis forward. The dildo slid in another inch or so.

'Hold still, hon. I can't get it in if you wiggle like that.'

Tamsin was beyond listening. She wanted the dildo to fill up her whole cavernous empty space. Her thrusts became more frantic.

'If you don't hold still, I'll have to restrain you,' Marcus said. His cock inched closer to Tamsin as the dildo continued to penetrate. He reached around to feel her bum and she moaned with pleasure again. Her occasional groans turned into a continuous low keening sound. She tossed her head from side to side. Her chest was beginning to flush. There would be no holding back now. Marcus flipped the switch on the butt plug, activating the vibrator.

'Oh, oh yes!' Tamsin gasped. The surge began, radiating out from her depths, zapping her clit. She forgot about the nipple clamps until Marcus reached up and fumbled for her breasts. With a practised hand he removed both clamps. Tamsin sobbed with pain as feeling rushed back into her nipples. Then she was overcome by a wave of the most intense pleasure. Sensation shot from her aching nipples right down the front of her body to her clit.

She wanted, she needed, to be closer to Marcus. Splaying her legs, she opened her sex wider and flattened it against his. She rode the dildo, grinding her pelvis into Marcus's.

Tamsin lost all track of time as she rode her orgasm out. Finally it subsided. With a shock Tamsin realised that she'd bitten Marcus's lip almost hard enough to draw blood. She sucked on the lip and tenderly kissed it. Then they lay back in each other's arms, exhausted.

'The butt plug,' Tamsin managed to say.

'What? What about it?'

'It's still vibrating.'

'So it is. Sorry.' Marcus turned the vibrator off.

After a few minutes of contented silence, Tamsin said, 'I never knew it could be like that, especially with a man I don't even know well. I guess I'm a bit of a whore at heart.'

'Aren't we all?' Gina chimed in, to Tamsin's surprise. She'd forgotten Gina was in the room. 'That was quite a show for such a shy girl, Tamsin. There's hope for you yet.'

'Too bad you're going to the States next week. I've got lots more tricks I could show you,' Marcus said.

'What's wrong with the rest of this week? Neither one of you is in rehearsal right now, and all I'm doing is packing for my trip.'

'What's wrong with right now? We can have a nap, order in some Chinese, and experiment with Gina's other toys,' Marcus suggested.

It was a good plan, but it didn't work out quite that way. The nap was the first to go. Lying together in such close proximity only stirred them up again rather than lulling them to sleep.

'Marcus, are you awake?' Tamsin asked.

'Of course! How could I be otherwise, with you tugging on my cock like that? You win. No sleep for us. Come on, let's go take a shower and then come back and play.'

Getting off the bed was difficult because Marcus had inserted a finger in Tamsin's sex and refused to remove it. Gina was blocking Tamsin's exit on the other side, as Tamsin had ended up in the middle when they all curled up together on the king-sized bed.

'What's that?' asked Tamsin, when they finally made it to the shower.

'It's soap, silly. You are familiar with soap, aren't you?' Marcus teased.

In answer Tamsin swatted his bum with a flannel.

'I know that! What I mean is, is it what I think it is?'

'Shaped like a penis? Of course. It's Gina's, remember? What did you expect?'

Marcus picked up the soap and aimed it at Tamsin's bush. She laughed, then took a sharp intake of breath as the penis-shaped soap touched her clit. She nibbled at one of Marcus's tiny nipples. He slid the soap down a bit until it rested at the opening of Tamsin's slit. She laughed and grabbed it away from him; it slipped to the floor, and they both dived after it. They tussled over it while the water poured down on them. Tamsin found herself positioned so that a stream of water landed directly on her clit. She cried out, momentarily distracted, while Marcus seized the opportunity to grab the soap. Once again he placed it on Tamsin's tender opening and began to insert it, while she wriggled to keep the water playing on her clit.

'Mmm. Nice and slippery,' Marcus said. 'I don't think it's just the soap either.' He continued to tease Tamsin, alternating between her clit and her now sizzling opening.

Tamsin panted and moaned. She lifted her head to lap at Marcus's nipple.

'Bad girl! No, no!' Marcus said as he pulled back. 'I'll have to punish you.'

With a final swipe at Tamsin's clit, he pulled himself up off the shower floor.

'Come on, get up. I can't punish you properly in here. Stand up so I can finish washing you.'

Tamsin obeyed. Marcus soaped her thoroughly, steering clear of her clit (which had already been soaped) but lingering a bit over the delectable space between her buttocks. Tamsin began writhing and sighing with pleasure.

'Don't even think about it, my dear! I'm not touching you again until we're back in the bedroom.'

True to his word, he dried himself off and marched out of the bathroom. Tamsin quickly did the same. She couldn't wait to see what Marcus had in mind as her punishment.

Gina had already tied silk scarves to the metal rings at the head and foot of the bed. Oh, so that's what those are for, Tamsin thought. She'd seen them before when she'd visited Gina's flat, but she had thought they were merely decorative.

'Punishment time! Get up on the bed. The longer you keep me waiting, the worse it will be for you,' Marcus said.

Tamsin resumed her position on the bed. She watched with interest as Marcus placed each wrist in a soft cuff, each of which he tied to a silk scarf. She felt a tingling in her sex at the thought of being helpless. Spreading her legs, she waited while he cuffed her ankles. The tingling increased as she realised that now Marcus could do anything he wanted with her.

That thought almost sent her over the edge.

'Marcus, I'm going to . . .'

'No, you're not. I haven't even touched you yet,' Marcus said. 'Just wait until I do!' He leaned down to blow on Tamsin's exposed clit.

'I don't dare touch you. You'll come again, and I don't want you worn out for what I've planned. I'm going to the kitchen with Gina for a minute. Don't you dare come while I'm gone.'

Tamsin closed her eyes and tried to recoup her strength. All too soon Marcus was back with a jar of chocolate sauce and a can of spray whip.

He dipped a finger into the chocolate and smeared it around Tamsin's left breast. When it was well coated he did the same thing to the right one. She wriggled with pleasure.

'Here. Lick.' Marcus waved his gooey finger in front of Tamsin's mouth. 'No, wait.' He reached down and scooped some juice from her sopping sex. 'Chocolate come. Eat up.'

While Tamsin sucked Marcus's finger clean, enjoying the novel sensation of smelling and tasting herself at the same time, his other hand was busy with the whipped cream spray. He laid out a perfect circle of white cream on top of Tamsin's chocolate-covered areolas.

'Perfect. Now all we need is cherries on top. Oh, there they are!'

Tamsin's engorged nipples, fully erect now, suddenly popped up through the chocolate, creating a cherry-like illusion. Marcus laughed.

'Beautiful. Wait. I'll get a mirror and you can admire them too.'

Tamsin was awash with sensations. She had never thought to check out her own juices; nice girls simply didn't do such things, but she found her own smell to be rather nice, actually. It reminded her of the sea. But the taste! The taste and texture reminded her of delicate mushrooms. It seemed strange that she'd swallowed men's come but had never thought to taste her own. She vowed that, beginning tonight, she was going to make up for all the opportunities she'd missed.

Gina brought a hand mirror, and Tamsin gazed with pride and wonder at the sight of her thrusting breasts. They were gorgeous! She'd never considered that she had pretty tits; this was a revelation to her. Of course, she'd never seen anybody's bosom decked out like a hot fudge sundae before, either.

Gina stepped aside while Marcus pounced on Tamsin's right breast. 'Dinner time!' he announced between slurps.

'Too bad you can't reach them. You could join me.' He rolled a chocolaty tongue around Tamsin's nipple.

She felt another orgasm building. She wanted to grab the nipple Marcus wasn't using and rub it between her fingers. She struggled against her bonds. Her sex was dripping again; being reminded that she was tied up made her inner turmoil more intense.

Marcus finished his first chocolate sundae and moved onto the other one. His fingers remained on the right breast, pinching the nipple as he sucked on the left one. Tamsin's hips bucked; she thrust her mound as high as she could, considering that she was restrained. She moaned again.

Marcus kept on lapping as Tamsin writhed beneath him. When he finished the chocolate, he moved his head down to Tamsin's aching sex. She cried out when she felt Marcus's tongue on her clit. Her sex gushed, coating his mouth. Once more she cried out, louder this time.

With Tamsin still bucking and moaning, Marcus reached between his legs and felt his swollen cock. One touch was all it took – he, too, exploded in ecstasy.

Finally both of their orgasms subsided. Marcus crawled back up and lay next to Tamsin, his hand gently cupping her sex. He felt the steady post-orgasmic pulsation of Tamsin's clit. Totally relaxed, he almost dozed off. Tamsin's voice roused him.

'Aren't you going to untie me, Marcus?'

'Sorry. I almost forgot.' Slowly and carefully, Marcus freed Tamsin from her bonds. Then he climbed back onto the bed and resumed his former position, his hand covering Tamsin's soaking bush. Gina, who had given herself an orgasm while watching the other two, crawled up beside Marcus. They all fell into an exhausted sleep. Worn out from their activities, all three of them slept the night through.

They never did get their Chinese food.

2

The phone was ringing when Leandra opened the door of her house. She debated about whether it was worth hurrying to answer it in time. It was too hot to rush, especially in her business clothes, and at this time of day it was probably only a telemarketer. On the other hand –

She picked up the phone just as it emitted that peculiar dead squawk that signalled the last ring. 'Hello?'

'Leandra? This is Tamsin in London.'

'Tamsin!' Good thing she'd picked up. This was important. 'What a pleasant surprise!' Pleasant unless the little twit was calling to cancel. A couple of Leandra's photographers had done so and completely wrecked her schedule. This Tamsin person hadn't better be backing out. 'Is anything wrong?'

'No, not at all. I'm just calling to confirm that the flight information I gave you is still correct. Will you be fetching me, or shall I hire a taxi?'

'I'll pick you up, of course, Tamsin. I'll be delighted to.' Thank you, Muse! And forgive me for thinking of her as a little twit, even for a moment.

'Thank you. I can't wait to meet you. I have one question, though. Your speciality is urban anthropology, I think you said. Tell me, is there anything special I should know about photographing for urban anthropology? I'm not familiar with the discipline.'

'No. It's just routine street photography – architecture and quirky compositions and stuff, though I hope it'll be artistic, of course. I'm turning all of you photographers loose in the L.A. area to photograph whatever strikes your fancy. So far it's been very successful, and the people involved have enjoyed it. I'm sure you will, too.'

When she rang off, Leandra went to her desk and picked up a portfolio of Tamsin's photographs and thumbed through it. Tamsin had a gift for turning the photographing of buildings into a sensuous act, and she seemed unaware of it. Leandra wondered what she would be like as a person.

In the meantime the afternoon stretched ahead of her, to do with as she wished. With only one fleeting regret that her partner Nigel was out of town, Leandra decided to go running. There was a trail in the woods behind the park that she'd been meaning to check out.

She ran up the stairs, shedding her clothes as she went. When she reached the door of her bedroom she was clad only in a gossamer wisp of a white lace bra, matching thong panties, and four-inch black heels. The thong barely covered her luxuriant blonde bush, which she'd trimmed into the shape of a heart. Her bra miraculously held up her jutting abundant breasts, her nipples and areolas visible through the lacy material. Crossing to the bed, she ran her hands lightly across her flat belly, which was partially covered by the thong. She lay down on the bed and massaged her long, firm, runner's legs while she appraised her tiny waist, boyish hips, and firm buns. Pretty good for thirty-three, she decided, not for the first time. Damned good, in fact. Runner's body, except for the tits. But those hadn't kept her from running her first marathon in under four hours last year. Her tits were OK. Besides, Nigel liked them. He loved to mash them together around his cock and fuck them.

Enough of that, she told herself. Nigel will be home

tomorrow, and Tamsin will be here next week. This is your day, for yourself, your unexpected afternoon off.

She stood up and hooked her thumbs into the string of her thong, slid it over her slim hips, and let it drop to the floor. She smiled to think how horrified her students and colleagues would be if they knew what she wore under her conservative business clothes. They'd be even more horrified if they knew she acted in beach movies, and that she'd been hired because of how she looked in a bikini.

Leandra liked sexy lingerie and wore it every chance she had. But today she didn't need panties under her running shorts. She eased the shorts up over her hips, checking to be sure that nothing peeked out under the flared legs. These shorts were skimpier than the ones she was used to wearing, but that made her feel all the freer.

She liked the feel of the lacy bra, so she kept it on instead of changing into a sports bra. She threw on a white T-shirt and her running shoes and then left the house.

The leather car seat was hot under her bare thighs. She squirmed, trying to find a cooler spot and, as she did so, the silk of her running shorts rubbed against her mound in a most pleasurable fashion. She squirmed some more, not entirely because of the heat. If this kept up she might forget about running entirely. And she *wanted* to run.

Leandra was glad when she got to the park but, once there, she realised she didn't feel like having an all-out sprint. She jogged for a few kilometres, enjoying the sensation of the slight breeze that slipped inside her shorts and played with her sex. Her tits bounced with each step, and her long, curly blonde mane flew behind her in the breeze. She really should have worn a sports bra; this one wasn't made for running. Her nipples gradually stiffened with the rubbing of the material against them.

When she stopped to rest, she realised that she hadn't seen anybody since she'd started her run. This thought made her feel vaguely horny. She had complete privacy. The whole mountain was hers. She could do whatever she liked.

She stepped off the trail, walked through a thicket, and found herself in a sunny meadow. She lay down in the grass and spread her legs until her tendons creaked, the way she'd imagined the tendons of those girls in adventure movies creaking when she'd watched them in junior high.

Long before she ever thought of having sex, those bound girls had made her panties dampen. Watching the women being tied up in preparation for being eaten by space aliens, she'd squirm uncontrollably in her seat. The boy she was with would inevitably think it was his inept pawing at the front of her jacket with his sweaty hands that had caused this effect. Because of this, Leandra was a popular date. The truth was that Leandra didn't identify with the helpless maidens at all, but with their captors.

She could only dream about playing such games until she was old enough to go to university. There, her sorority initiated her in more ways than one. The initiation itself was a true awakening.

'Paddles? You're going to paddle the pledges?' Leandra had asked.

'Hush, Pledge. Don't speak unless ordered to do so.'

'But isn't it against university . . .?'

'Who's going to complain to the university, Leandra? Now hush!'

Already the first girl was screaming as the paddle

thwacked across her helpless bum. Fortunately the girls were being paddled fully clothed. Leandra would have died if she'd had to expose her sopping panties.

She accepted her paddling without making a sound. She felt humiliated. She ought to be the paddler, not the paddlee. Her hands twitched with the need to wrap them around a paddle and wallop somebody else's quivering ass. Next year it would be her turn. Next year she'd be participating as a fully initiated member, telling the new pledges, 'Hush! Don't speak unless ordered to do so.'

The next year she had been most creative in her paddling of the pledges. The year after that the sorority had put her in charge of the ritual. Remembering her discomfiture at her own paddling, she developed slightly more elaborate rules for her own ceremonies. For one thing, the pledges were ordered to wear white cotton panties.

'I want us to be able to weed out the girls who don't fit in,' she said, without bothering to explain her 'fitting in' criteria. What she meant, of course, was that she wanted to see who among the group ended up with damp panties. She would schedule those girls for private sessions with their 'Big Sister' (Leandra, of course) after the initiation.

There was always at least one. The first year it was a girl who, defying orders, had worn a white satin thong instead of the mandatory cotton panties.

'I d-didn't know anybody was going to see!' she quavered.

'Why would we tell you to wear white cotton if we weren't going to make sure you did?' Leandra asked reasonably. She leaned back in the sorority president's leather chair, staring at the hapless pledge who stood trembling before her. 'Just look at you. There's pussy juice oozing down your thigh. Cotton panties would have soaked that up. You should have thought of that.'

'But I wasn't expecting to get turned on!' the pledge wailed. 'When you lined us up and had everybody flip her skirt up to show her panties, I started to get hot.'

'No real harm done,' Leandra conceded, 'but I'll have to punish you just the same. Take this key, unlock that file cabinet over there, and bring me what you find in the bottom drawer.'

'The only thing in here is a ping-pong paddle.'

'Bring it to me.'

Understanding slowly dawned on the girl's face.

'You're going to . . .?'

'Yes. Lie across my lap, face down. Good. Now pull up your skirt at the back. It's so short I can see the crotch of your thong, but I need your whole bottom.'

The quivering girl did as she was told.

'If you ever tell anyone about this, I'll see that you're expelled from the sorority. You are to tell the others simply that you had a chat with your Big Sister. Understood?'

The girl nodded, hiking her skirt up all the way to her waist.

'Very well. Now I'm going to give you six strokes. After each one you are to say the number and "Thank you for correcting me, Mistress Leandra." If you forget or lose count, we go back to one. Ready?'

The girl nodded again.

'What did you say? Speak up! I didn't hear you.'

'Yes, Mistress Leandra.'

'That's better.' Leandra gave her a light swat. The girl jumped.

'One. Thank you for correcting me, Mistress Leandra.'

The paddle swished down again, a little harder.

'Two. Thank you for correcting me, Mistress Leandra.'

By the fifth stroke the girl's bum was a fiery red. On number six she made her first mistake.

'Five. Thank you for correcting me, Mistress Leandra.'

'That was six, not five. The next one will be number one.' Leandra's thighs felt wet from the girl's copious love juice. She hit the girl again, harder than before.

'One. Thank you for correcting me, Mistress Leandra.'

On the sixth stroke she made the same mistake as before. Leandra got suspicious.

'You did that on purpose, didn't you?'

'Busted.' The girl tried to suppress a grin.

'Then I'm not going to paddle you any more. This is supposed to be punishment.'

'Please, Mistress Leandra?'

'Not now. No.' At the expression on the girl's face, Leandra relented a bit. 'Maybe some other time. It depends on your behaviour. Now go join the others.'

'OK.'

'What?'

'I mean, yes, Mistress Leandra.'

'See that you don't forget again.'

But the girl was already gone.

Leandra stretched in the soft grass. The wind was still playing with her sex, drying the drops of moisture that had begun to form. Enjoying the feeling, she resumed her train of thought. Why couldn't she ever remember that wretched girl's name? It hadn't been that long ago, although there had been many others since. She remembered everybody else's name. It was only that one that eluded her.

'What are you doing in here? Nobody comes in the pledge mistress's office without permission. Get out!'

'But, Mistress Leandra, you sent for me.'

'I never ... no, wait. You're right. I did send for you. But how dare you assume I'd remember you? Do you think you're that important to me? You're just a dreary girl who needs punishing far too often.'

'Yes, Mistress.' The twinkle in the girl's eye belied the respectful tone of her words.

'This time what did you do? Oh, I remember. You broke a cup.'

'But I paid for it, Mistress.'

'That doesn't matter. You're clumsy and inconsiderate. Some other girl might have needed that cup before you replaced it.'

'But ...'

'Don't argue with me. I'm going to punish you. Today I have a special punishment planned. Go to the filing cabinet.'

'Yes, Mistress Leandra.' The girl hurried to get the paddle.

'Mistress? The paddle isn't here. There's only a ... it looks like a whip!'

'It *is* a whip, you silly goose. Breaking a cup is a serious offence. It requires special punishment.'

'But ...'

'Two extra strokes for that "but". Now bend over and grasp your ankles.'

Leandra watched as the girl bent down, exposing pale yellow silk panties. This was the part of the job that she liked the most.

'Your skirt isn't high enough. Pull it up.'

The girl obeyed. Leandra hit the inside of her thighs with the whip handle.

'Spread your legs.'

'But ...'

'Two more strokes.' Then Leandra saw why the girl was reluctant. A tiny stream of juice oozed under the leg band of the panties and was starting its slow trek down her thigh. When her legs were held together Leandra hadn't been able to see this.

'You're disgusting. I always have to deal with your body fluids in some form or another. Aren't you ashamed of yourself?'

'Yes, Mistress Leandra,' the girl answered with a broad grin.

'Well, then?'

'I can't help it, Mistress. Every time you punish me I get wet.'

Leandra couldn't resist. She cupped her hand over the girl's sex, gently massaging her clit. Her hand instantly got sticky. Her other hand crept to her own crotch and started rubbing her clit. She felt as if she were on fire. She was glad the girl couldn't see what she was doing. Reluctantly she removed her wet hand from the girl's panties and picked up the whip again.

'Ready? Ten strokes. You know the drill.'

In response, the glutinous trickle on the girl's thigh was joined by another gush of fluid. Watching, Leandra pressed harder on her own clit. She flicked the whip so it landed between the girl's legs.

'One. Thank you for correcting me, Mistress Leandra.'

Leandra continued to rain down blows, with the girl making the appropriate response after each one. By the seventh stroke the backs of her thighs were bright red. Leandra was sure her bum was red too, though she couldn't see it through her panties. The girl had wetness spreading clear down to her knees. Leandra felt her own juice ooze out of her panties. She was glad she was wearing black pants. The girl would never know. She aimed the ninth stroke directly, but softly, between the girl's nether lips.

'Nine. Thank you for ... oh, I'm coming! I'm sorry. I can't help it. Oh!'

Leandra watched in amazement as the girl fell to the floor, writhing in orgasm. She lightly whipped the girl directly across the clit and was rewarded with another orgasmic flood. Feeling her own orgasm building, Leandra pressed the end of the whip handle onto her own bulging clit.

Her orgasm racked her whole body. She leaned back against the edge of the desk and shuddered with ecstasy. Holding both hands over her clit, she fingered herself into another spasm. Then another. She was astounded: never before had she come when she was disciplining one of the girls. Now three years of wanting was exploding in a mind-shattering orgasm. Her juices trickled further down her thighs. She held herself, feeling the dampness through two layers of material, and tried not to moan out loud.

Alerted by the sudden silence from the floor, Leandra looked down and saw that the girl was spent. She lay there limp, barely breathing, with closed eyes. A tiny snore escaped her.

Good. She didn't notice anything. Leandra diddled her clit again, and was rewarded with another spasm. She allowed herself a small, audible moan.

Gradually she finished herself off, with the spasms getting weaker and weaker. Finally she felt sated.

She rested against the desk for a minute, catching her breath. When she could trust herself to speak, she nudged the girl gently, with the toe of her boot.

'Wake up! You've got to leave now.'

The girl opened one eye, then seemed to realise where she was.

'Oh, no! What happened, Mistress Leandra?'

'You came while I was whipping you. Must have knocked yourself out with the intensity of it. But I need you to leave now.'

'OK.' The girl scrambled to her feet. 'You won't

tell, will you, Mistress? That your whipping made me come?'

'It's not the kind of thing I'd like to advertise. If I did, girls would be lined up outside my door at all hours and I'd never get any studying done. You and I will meet again, never fear. For one thing, I need to punish you for coming without my permission. Now go.'

Leandra locked the door behind the girl and adjusted her clothing in front of the mirror on the supply-cupboard door. As she did so, the door began to swing open. She watched in horror.

'Jolly good show!'

Leandra would have known that clipped British accent anywhere.

'What are you doing here, Nigel?'

'I got trapped. I came in to get some toner for the copying machine. When I heard somebody at the door, I shut myself in. Obviously I couldn't leave while you two were having your *tête-à-tête*.'

'Why didn't you just leave when she came in?'

'I hadn't found the toner yet. Keeping the copier in good working order is part of my job description. You wouldn't want a poor, hard-working foreign student to get sacked, would you?'

She certainly didn't. Nigel was the sorority's general fix–it man and piano mover. In addition, it wasn't unheard of for him to be a surrogate lover for members who hadn't had a man in a while. He was indispensable to the running of the organisation. Leandra had had a crush on him for the last two years, though it would have been beneath her dignity to admit it.

'I don't need to ask you to forget what you've seen, do I?'

'If you pay the price.'

'Price? What price?'

'Go out with me. Just once. If it doesn't work out, you're off the hook. But my price is one date.'

That had started it all. They had gone to the cinema, then spent the night in the marina aboard a houseboat that Nigel had said belonged to a friend of his. Leandra had been introduced to new heights of sexual sophistication. That was twelve years ago, and they were still together, still exploring.

She smiled as she thought back on the night she'd discovered that the houseboat actually belonged to Nigel. It was about six months after they'd started dating.

One evening, the phone rang at a crucial moment in their lovemaking.

'Get it, will you, love?' Nigel panted. 'I can't . . .'

As Nigel's cock exploded all over her hand, Leandra grabbed the receiver and listened for a moment.

'Justin wants to borrow the houseboat. What does he mean? It's his houseboat, isn't it?'

Nigel continued to pump sperm into her hand. Ignoring his condition, she shoved the phone in his face. 'You talk to him!'

The ensuing conversation (after Nigel was able to speak) left no doubt as to the ownership of the houseboat. Leandra demanded an explanation.

'I didn't want the girls at the sorority house to know I didn't really need the job. I was new in this country, and having a job was an easy way to make friends. Then I lied to you about it, and before I knew it, it was impossible to tell you the truth. Can you forgive me?'

'Forgive you for owning a houseboat?'

'No. For not telling you I did.'

'Only if you'll accept your punishment. It will be a long one.'

At his nod, she extricated herself from the sodden sheets and stood over him. Her clit stiffened as she sniffed the smell of their mingled juices, as well as his latest outburst on her hand.

'Bad Nigel! Look what you did to my hand! Lick it off!'

He pulled her hand to his mouth and began to lap off the sticky, fresh sperm.

'Faster! I haven't got all night!'

When he had cleaned her hand to her satisfaction, she straddled him, with her sex positioned over his mouth.

'You got me all sticky there, too. Clean it up!'

Leandra felt new floods of love juice threatening to seep out as Nigel did a thorough job of cleaning her sex with his tongue. Damn, she was hot! For a moment she was tempted to forego the punishment and let him tongue her to another shrieking orgasm. Fortunately she regained her senses. She knew that she'd have even better orgasms if she punished him first.

'All right. That's clean enough. Now stand up!'

He hastened to obey. Leandra noticed that his cock was rising again. The man was insatiable. That was one of the things she liked most about him. She rearranged herself so she was sitting on the side of the bed, her feet on the floor.

'Hand me a shoe.'

Nigel searched the tangle of clothing on the floor, finally emerging with a toeless, black, stiletto-heeled pump. He handed it to her.

'Bend over my lap. Face down.'

As he hurried to obey, she felt his stiff cock nudging her thigh. Maybe she'd better prolong this a little bit. She grasped the shoe by the heel and aimed it at his bum.

Just as it made contact with his flesh, he juddered

and groaned. A hot gush of spunk bathed Leandra's thighs.

'How dare you? I hardly touched you! I didn't give you permission to come!'

'Sorry, Leandra. I couldn't help it.'

'That's Mistress Leandra to you. And I don't care what you can help or cannot help. You came without permission!'

She felt a letdown; she'd experienced a rush when she thought about punishing him, and now he'd ruined her fun by coming. Not only that, but he'd come all over her. Unthinkable. What was worse still was the heat she felt in her sex, the orgasmic explosion that threatened her. She couldn't let him know.

'Leave! Now!'

'Uh, Mistress Leandra, that might be a bit difficult.'

'Why, pray tell?'

'It's my houseboat, that's why! I'm not going to leave you alone with it.'

'Oh. Right. Well, uh . . .'

'I'll call a cab for you.'

This was not at all how she'd planned for the evening to end. Waking up in the morning on the houseboat would have been much more to her taste, especially now that she knew it belonged to him. It was time to make peace.

'Nigel, I'm sorry, I got carried away. Please don't send me away. I won't punish you if you don't want me to.'

'You've already punished me, I think.' He was smiling as he said it. 'And I just found out that I like being punished. I'd always thought I'd hate it – I'm a punisher, not a punishee.'

'So am I. But you taught me that I enjoy both roles. Just don't tell the girls at the house. It would destroy my image.'

'And you, Mistress Leandra, get to keep my secret too. Now let's get back to what we were doing before we were interrupted.'

Leandra squirmed as she relived that night. Her hand crept under her running shorts and her fingers were grazing her sex before she realised what she was doing.

'No. Not now,' she told her hand as she reluctantly pulled it back. 'Nigel is coming home tomorrow. We're going to save it for him.' She adjusted her sticky shorts and spread her legs wide to the sun. There was no way she could leave with her shorts this wet in the crotch. Anybody who saw her would know what she'd been doing.

The sun was setting her sex on fire. She stretched and spread her legs, allowing the sun easier access. The wind reached under her shorts and brushed across her sizzling sex. Lazily she reached down, almost touched herself again, and stopped; she had never liked solo orgasms. For her sex was a waste unless she had someone to share it with.

When the sun and wind had done their work, she jumped to her feet and brushed herself off. Then, before she could change her mind, she trotted back across the meadow to the trail.

Loping down the mountain to the trail head, she sensed that Nigel was going to have the homecoming of his life.

3

Some five thousand miles away, in an unassuming London residence, an elegant woman called Vanessa methodically flogged her client Harry's bare bottom with the back of a hairbrush while he wriggled on her lap. Finally he began to blubber.

'Ow! Don't! Stop it! It hurts!'

'Be quiet, bad boy, or I'll turn the brush over. Then you *would* have something to cry about.'

Harry continued to squirm, muffling his sobs. At last it was too much for him, and he blurted, 'But I've been a good boy today!'

'I said to be quiet.' Vanessa didn't miss a beat with her brush. She could tell that Harry's ordeal was coming to an end, judging from the stiffness of the rod that was imprisoned between her thighs. She stepped up the pace of the beating, hitting first one red cheek, then the other.

'Oh, Mistress, you're so cruel!' Harry raised his bum and succeeded in freeing his cock. He flopped back down, with his cock trying to poke a hole in Vanessa's thigh.

Vanessa didn't respond. Instead she switched to a small but deadly whip that was conveniently lying on the coffee table. In spite of her threat to use the other side of the brush, she knew the bristles would turn his bum into hamburger. The whip was better. Besides, she enjoyed using the whip.

It had the desired effect. After two strokes, Harry cried out with joy and exploded all over her leg. When his release was complete, he climbed off her lap and tripped on the trousers that were bunched around his ankles.

'Harry, you fool, one of these days you're going to break your silly neck.' Vanessa got up from her chair and took Harry by the arm. 'Come on, let's get you cleaned up. And me, too. You came all over me again.'

'Sorry about that.' Harry sounded anything but sorry. 'Can't be helped.' He allowed himself to be led into the bathroom.

Vanessa normally didn't help her clients clean up afterwards. Most of them preferred her to stay in her role and coldly walk out the door after she'd done what she had gone there to do. Harry was different. He had been a client for so long that he had become almost a friend. She didn't mind doing for him what she usually wouldn't even do for her boyfriend, when she had one. Or girlfriend, of course; she tended to have more of those. Since men were her business, she found she could relax more easily in the arms of another woman.

Right now Harry needed some TLC. He usually did, afterwards. She took a wet, soapy cloth and cleaned off the sticky mess he had made. Then she rinsed the cloth and gently bathed his bright red bum. When she patted it dry with a warm towel, his penis began to twitch.

'No, Harry, you bad boy. You've had your punishment for today.' She ignored his slowly rising cock and handed him a clean pair of underpants. 'I'll wait for you in the other room.'

In a few minutes Harry emerged fully dressed, looking as if he were walking into a board meeting – which was exactly what he was going to be doing in about an hour. Vanessa was putting on her coat.

'Vanessa, could you stay for a few minutes? I have a job proposition for you.'

Curious, Vanessa took off her coat. What could he

want of her? Her services were specific, not likely to be termed a 'job proposition'. She sank down into a wing-back chair and waited.

'You don't know much about me on a personal level, except that I can well afford your services as often as I wish. That's as it should be. I've been making discreet enquiries about you and have learned that you can be absolutely trusted to keep a confidence. I should certainly hope so, given the nature of your profession. Anyhow, I've decided to offer you full-time employment for the next several months. It's a matter that requires the utmost discretion. Could you make yourself available?'

'I don't really know, Harry. It depends on what it is, as well as how lucrative it would be. Then there's the problem of my other clients; I don't want to lose those gentlemen. Besides, it would be unethical to just drop them.'

'You'd be able to fly back here as often as you wish to accommodate them. Please, at least hear me out before you decide.'

Something in Harry's tone allowed for no argument. He was every inch the commanding CEO. Vanessa wasn't used to seeing him like this. She waited for him to continue.

'I need a surveillance job done. Don't worry, I wouldn't ask you to do anything illegal or unethical; it's perfectly legitimate. However, due to its nature, I'm more comfortable asking you than I would be hiring one of the agencies that exist for such purposes. You will be well compensated for your work – extremely well compensated. And there's a certain amount of flexibility. As I said, you'll easily be able to fly back and forth to attend to your other gentlemen.'

'But, Harry, why me? I have no experience in tailing people.'

'True. However, you are an expert in what I need done. Your vast experience will be most useful to me.'

Harry sounded as if it were a done deal. This made Vanessa a bit nervous, since she hadn't a clue what he was talking about.

'Harry, I really need to know more. I can't commit myself to such an uncertain ... For instance, my expertise in *what*?'

'Sex, of course. I thought I'd made that clear.'

Vanessa was no longer intimidated. This was more like the bumbling Harry that she knew and was fond of. The Harry of her experience never made anything clear. She knew he was a wealthy, world-famous architect, with a kinky private life she could only guess at. But to her he was just an amiable, rather ineffectual man who tripped over his trousers and loved to be punished.

'It's not clear at all, Harry. Could we start at the beginning?'

'All right. I'll try. You know I'm writing my autobiography. I told you, didn't I? Never mind. Anyhow, I'm also writing a second version, to be distributed only to my friends and others in the scene. This one will include photos of me in various interesting positions. Finding a photographer is problematic. I need one who can do a professional job both on my buildings and my sex life. I thought I'd found someone, but he ran screaming, as it were, when I asked him to photograph me being whipped while tied to a girder in one of my unfinished buildings. Poor chap.'

'Yes, I remember something about that,' Vanessa said. The gossip had been outrageous, but she didn't want to tell Harry and risk inflating his ego even more.

'I've been studying the work of this young woman who recently won a major award for her travel photography. Tamsin, her name is. She only uses the one name. I like what she does with buildings. It's my other requirement that's a big question mark, and that's why I'm interested in her sex life. She's off to Los Angeles next week to work on a project that may take a few months. I need you to observe her.'

'But why, Harry? This sounds like an invasion of her privacy. What has she done to deserve that? I must say, I'm not comfortable . . .'

'Trust me when I say that the invasion of her privacy will be worth it to her. Besides, I'm not asking you to stalk her. You'll become her friend and try to become her fuck buddy, as the Americans call it. If this doesn't work out, if there's absolutely no chemistry between the two of you, then your job is done. You may come home, and I'll give you a generous bonus for having tried. Then we'll both leave young Tamsin in peace. But if you two connect, as I hope you will, you'll both have a good time. You'll be very well paid, and Tamsin will get a most lucrative photography commission and, depending on how it works out, I may loan her one of my properties and set her up in her own studio.'

'It's beginning to sound interesting. But what kind of a report do you want?'

'I need to know about her sex life. What she enjoys doing, that kind of thing. This offer I mentioned depends upon her sexual proclivities. I won't be more specific than that because I don't want to influence your observations. I need objective reporting, and I promise you that your reports will be destroyed as soon as I have read them. There's nothing about this that could harm the girl. On the contrary, there's a lot that could be to her benefit. If she meets my expectations, she'll be a very happy girl; if she doesn't, she'll never know of my interest in her. Her life will continue as it has. There's no problem either way.'

'I don't know, Harry. You say next week? That doesn't give me much time to get ready. How about if I fly over there in a fortnight?'

'No. Next week. I want you on the same plane as she is so you can make your first connection. Better than that, I'll arrange for you to be in the same row of seats. She's travelling with a male friend. You'll probably need to win him over, too. He's not a romantic interest, and from what I hear, he's rather shy with women. But I suspect he can't resist your charms for long. No man can.'

Vanessa resisted the urge to point out that not all men like to be whipped. In her personal life she'd met plenty of men who found her talents less than irresistible. Fortunately she realised that this would not be a tactful revelation to make to a client. She voiced one last protest.

'Harry, I don't have anything to wear in Los Angeles!'

'I've already anticipated that. Women *never* have anything to wear! Come with me.' He led her to a door that had always been closed when she was on the premises. She hadn't really wondered about it; Harry liked to play in the drawing room, so the closed door had never been of concern to her.

When she saw what was inside, she gasped. Then she shrieked with glee before she could control herself. The bed was covered – literally *covered* – with what seemed like hundreds of dainty undergarments. There were thong and bikini panties, cut-out bras, bustiers, teddies, camis, garter belts, seamed and fishnet stockings. All were clearly designed as play clothes. There wasn't a practical item in the entire lot.

'That's not all, my lovely co-conspirator.' Harry threw open the door of a walk-in closet, revealing minidresses, separate miniskirts and tops, shorts, thong swimsuits, and shoes: demure pumps with four-inch heels, stiletto-heeled sandals, even a pair of trainers. Harry noticed that Vanessa was looking askance at the latter.

'You need one practical thing, love. Those are for when you get tired of indoor exercise and need to go outdoors for a while. You can't wear spike heels to the beach, after all.'

'I can't wear fishnet stockings with those, either,' Vanessa protested.

'How silly of me. I forgot. Voilà!' Harry quickly fished out a pair of sports socks from the pile. 'Now, you stay here as long as you like and try on these things. Put the ones you want in a clearly marked pile, and I'll ship them to L.A. for you. Of course, you may take it all if you want. There's no limit.'

The doorbell rang, followed by loud knocking. 'Margie is here,' Vanessa said – unnecessarily, for the knock was followed by a bellow.

'Harry, come on! You're going to be late!'

Vanessa opened the door, and Margie almost fell into the house. The chauffeuse was stunning in her meticulous uniform, though she was an imposing sight in her own right. Well over six feet tall, she was fifteen stone of solid muscle. She grabbed Harry by the arm and pulled him towards the door.

'Goodbye, Vanessa. It seems that it's time for my board meeting. Make yourself comfortable. Just be sure the door is locked when you leave.'

Vanessa followed them to the limo that was parked in the drive. She watched Margie toss Harry into the vehicle as if he were a bag of garbage. Harry landed on his back on the cross that had been fitted inside and gave a loud groan. Margie lashed his wrists and ankles to the crosspieces.

'I'm not punishing you today, Harry, so don't get your hopes up. We're running late.' Margie got behind the wheel and drove off without a backward glance.

Vanessa went back to the bedroom, savouring what was a rare chance to indulge the other, more traditionally feminine, side of her personality. Since her work wardrobe consisted entirely of leather outfits and stern uniforms, she had no need for frilly underthings. Her clients never saw her out of role, and her private lovers usually saw her naked. When she got home from a client's place, she'd take an extravagantly long bath. Then, clad only in a dab of perfume under each breast and a pair of spike-heeled shoes, she'd open the door for her evening's entertainment.

All this lingerie was a glorious treat. She fingered it lovingly, relishing the texture of each piece. Harry had suggested trying them on. Well, why not? She wriggled out of her tight-fitting black leather jacket and miniskirt. Underneath she wore a black lace suspender belt with black stockings. A wisp of a black lace bra completed her outfit. She stood in front of the full-length mirror admiring herself. Lazily she unhooked her stockings and slid them down her legs. Her chestnut bush stood out in stark contrast to her black suspender belt. Vanessa rarely bothered with panties. That was going to change, though, she promised herself, as she surveyed the frothy confections spread out before her.

She chose a tiny, silk, cream-coloured thong and slipped it on. It felt cool against her sex. She pressed it into her clit, feeling a stirring throughout her whole lower body. Bending over slightly, she enjoyed the way the elastic gripped the fold between her bush and her thigh. She adjusted the thong at the back, tingling with anticipation as she slipped it between her cheeks. Anticipation of what? She had no idea. She was all alone here. Harry wouldn't be back for hours.

She searched until she found a matching bra. Quickly she changed into it. The silk rubbed against her large nipples, making them harden. Cupping her hands under her breasts, she looked in the mirror again. The bra and thong were a perfect fit. She admired the flatness of her stomach and her tiny waist above the thong. She took a step forward. The thong shifted, revealing only the enticing bulge of her sex.

Vanessa was starting to get hot just looking at herself. She rubbed her nipples and was rewarded with more stiffening. They were sitting up and begging. She pinched one through the silk, then twisted it. It was as if an electric shock had run through her body. She tried it with both hands, pinching and twisting both nipples at the same time, and now she had two electric shocks, both running all the way down to her sex.

Abandoning one nipple, she slid her hand down to the thong and cupped her pussy. The thong felt a bit damp to the touch. She petted herself and was rewarded with more dampness. Her other hand alternated nipples: pinching, twisting, and pulling on them. She breathed faster.

She felt weak, as if she were going to fall. Dropping back on the bed behind her, she bent her knees and viewed herself in the mirror. Good, she thought. It was seeing what she was doing that made her so hot. Sighting between her upraised breasts, and framing the mirror between her knees, she was face to face with her thong. As she watched, it grew darker with a spreading stain. She slipped her hand under the silk and felt her slit, now slick with her juice. She rubbed a finger along her clit, then into the opening beneath. Circling slowly, she rubbed her clit with her thumb. The feel of the silk intensified everything she was doing. She whimpered without realising it.

She had no idea how long she had lain there. Rubbing her sex and her breasts had had a hypnotic effect. Gradually she realised that she was moving faster, that her body had taken on a life of its own. One hand was frantically flicking her nipple now. The other was circling faster and faster with both her thumb and her forefinger. She was thrusting up with her pelvis, too, just as if there had been a penis waiting to meet her.

She saw in the mirror that the thong was ruined. She could see the outline of her clit and her cleft as the soaked garment pressed close to her skin.

This felt wonderful, but she wanted to end it now. If only she had her whip in here with her. She could tease her clit with it, give her stiff nipples a few light strokes, and –

There it was! Those thoughts did it. Her orgasm built in a roaring crescendo. Heedless of whether there were servants in the house, Vanessa cried out as the spasms hit. Her body tossed on the carpet of luxurious undergarments, heightening her pleasure. When the spasms threatened to die down, she grabbed a handful of lingerie and pressed it against her clit. When the second orgasm was ending, she wrapped a finger in a delicate silk creation and continued to massage herself.

Her other flailing hand discovered a familiar shape in the pile of clothing. It was long and tapered, just the right size to be ... a vibrator! And it was. Now if Harry had managed to remember the batteries ...

He had. Her finger flicked the button at the end and was greeted with a welcoming buzz. Dear Harry. Too bad he was a client.

She wiggled out of the thong and pressed the vibrator to her opening. It slid in as if it had been made to her specifications. It ought to, as heavily as she was lubricating.

Still orgasming, she turned the vibrator back on. She received a greater jolt than she had expected. The tension built up again, and a new series of waves washed over her. She pumped the vibrator in and out, massaging her clit with the other hand. Orgasmic waves arrived one after the other.

Finally the waves ebbed. Nothing she did would start them up again. She sank back on the bed, sated.

She must have dozed. When she opened her eyes, she was disoriented. Then she remembered where she was. Checking her watch, she was reassured to find that only a few minutes had passed. It wouldn't do for Harry to find her like this – it would destroy her credibility as a professional dominatrix.

Languidly stretching, enjoying for the last time the feel of all those fine fabrics against her skin, she sat up on the bed. After a quick shower in the adjoining bathroom, she resumed her work clothes and brushed her short chestnut hair, smoothing it into its usual cap. She decided not to sort through the lingerie. Harry could send it all. She packed the used bra and panties in her leather toy bag and let herself out of Harry's house.

4

This was the day that Leandra had thought would never arrive. Nigel was due back from Asia after a three-week business trip. Rather than worry about all the beautiful Asian women he'd have met, Leandra planned a few surprises of her own.

She'd spent the morning with Brenda, the girl who did her bikini waxes. Brenda had carefully shaved her bush into a heart shape, leaving her sex extremely vulnerable. As Brenda worked on her, Leandra had felt her clit stiffen and peek out between her newly shaped pubes. Brenda had laughed and given it a quick kiss. One more opportunity lost. Leandra had no time for dalliance today, though normally she found Brenda to be a tasty little morsel. Today she was devoting her energy to Nigel. She was determined to give him a case of amnesia about what he'd seen and done in Asia.

Her heart-shaped pubic hairdo made her feel exposed, even though she had covered it with a pale blue silk thong. Her clit thrust against the silk, becoming even stiffer. She squirmed in anticipation of the evening.

After a leisurely lunch, she ran a hot bath and continued her preparations for Nigel. She popped some Mozart into the CD player and sank back into the tub. The musky bath oil she'd chosen heightened her mood. Her clit expanded before her eyes, as if basking in her approval. She'd considered piercing her labia and inserting a tiny gold ring, but it wouldn't have had time to heal. Better wait on that, do it at the beginning of his next long trip.

She patted herself and was amazed at her quick response. It was as if all her feelings were at the surface now that there was less hair to hide behind.

She was tempted to leave her fingers there for a while. Certainly her sex was willing. Regretfully she pulled her hand away. She wanted to save it all for later.

Leandra finished soaping herself and rose to her feet in the tub. The way the water trickled off her pubes was exquisitely erotic. She patted herself dry and stepped out of the tub. She wrapped herself in a thick white towel and sat on a chair, painting her toenails. Her feet had to be at their best for Nigel. She dabbed a little perfume between her toes. That would surprise him when she commanded him to service her feet.

She had dawdled over her bath but now she needed to hurry so as not to be late at the airport. She inspected a pale green thong, then decided against it. She wriggled into a short, tight, black silk skirt. Braless, she pulled on a black spaghetti-strap tunic top over her full, jutting breasts. Fortunately the tunic covered the blatant display of her heart-shaped charms.

It was too bad they had to stop by Nigel's boss's house to go to a reception. She wanted to wear her new handcuffs at her belt, but under the circumstances she didn't think it would be appropriate. A pair of sinfully expensive black leather high-heeled sandals completed her ensemble.

Leandra made it to the airport in record time and hurled herself into Nigel's arms. A few minutes later she was snuggling up to him while he drove.

They arrived at the reception, and Nigel helped her out of the car. As she got out, her skirt inched up dangerously close to her naked crotch. She leaned forward and whispered, 'Guess what, honey? I'm not wearing any panties!' Giving him no chance to react, she ran ahead of him to greet their waiting host.

All she could think about was Nigel's cock. It was a shame they had to be at this deadly dull party. She hoped they wouldn't stay long. Oh, it was all right, as far as parties went; everybody was dressed to the hilt, making polite, civilised conversation. There was live chamber music, which would usually have enthralled her, but right now she could only think of sex. Her heels sank into a luxurious pile of fine carpeting. White. How could anybody have white carpets? How could they afford to clean them? These were immaculate. But they –

Her mind continued to race while she smiled and nodded politely at the distinguished, prematurely silver-haired gentleman who was lecturing her on the spiritual qualities of practising sumi-e.

'I know the martial arts are considered spiritual practices, but sumi-e suits my temperament much better. If you wish, I can give you my Master's e-mail address . . .'

'Master?' she interrupted. Damn, she'd have to pay closer attention. She'd been obsessing about Nigel's cock again and hadn't heard a word, though she'd been going through the motions of listening. Master of what? What on earth was this old guy nattering about? She was losing her grip.

'. . . and phone number. Yes, of course. Master Brushstroke Sensei. Sumi-e doesn't have belts, you know.'

'No, of course not.' Nigel, please rescue me before I make a bloody fool of myself. 'Yes, if you'd be so kind. I'd like to get in touch with him. I could use some spiritual cock . . . I mean, grounding.' She sipped her white wine and glanced around, desperately looking for Nigel.

Just when she thought she couldn't take another second of this guy and his sumi-e, Nigel appeared as if by magic. 'Excuse me, sir, but I'm going to kidnap this lady. I need to speak to her on a matter of business.'

'Of course.' The gentleman turned to Leandra. 'It's

been a pleasure talking with you, my dear.' He kissed her hand and wandered off to the other side of the immense room.

Leandra waited until he was out of earshot and then turned to Nigel. 'How much longer are we going to stay? It's been three whole weeks, and I need you.' She leaned closer to his ear and whispered, 'I can't stop thinking about your cock.'

Nigel laughed. He fingered the hem of her skirt, then darted his hand under it.

'Something feels different here, other than the fact that you're a tad damp. I can't wait to see if my suspicions are correct, but I can't very well do that here. You must be patient, love. We'll be here for a while, I'm afraid. I can't leave; he's my boss. But to pass the time more agreeably, I'll introduce you to some people.'

Leandra sighed. She wanted to go home, tear his clothes off, and make him suck her toes. However, she knew that it would be useless to plead. When Nigel's mind was made up, it was impossible to persuade him to change it. She resigned herself to staying until he was ready to go, however long that might be. With a forced party smile, she followed him to a door at the other side of the room.

Expecting a continuation of the party crowd, she was surprised to see only a spiral staircase leading downward. Nigel nodded and motioned for her to precede him.

At the bottom of the staircase was another door. As it slid open on silent pneumatic hinges, Leandra walked into a scene from hell.

The room was almost pitch dark, lit only by small fires along the side walls. When her eyes adjusted a bit she realised that they were artificial gas fires, designed to look like the real thing.

The sight was unusual enough, but what really captured her attention were the sounds and smells. She heard the cracking of whips, howls of pain, and the moaning, sobbing sounds that she connected with sexual ecstasy. She knew it must be sex by the smells – the odours of male and female sexual arousal permeated the room. Reflected in the firelight she saw glistening puddles, randomly arranged on the floor, that bore witness to the source of the smells.

Now that she could see more clearly, she made out the shapes of men and women: some in slings, some on racks, one strapped to a cross, others that she couldn't see but assumed to be engaged in similar activities. The ones who weren't immobilised in these positions were wielding riding crops, cats-o'-nine-tails, and similar instruments of torture. She heard the thud of a hairbrush on bare flesh somewhere near her. All of the people at first glance were strangers to her.

'What's all this, Nigel? In your boss's house? I don't believe it.'

'Most of the people upstairs wouldn't believe it either. But George is an OK bloke. He acts like a tight-arse in the office but he has a dungeon in his basement.'

Leandra was getting more excited as she took in the scene. Still, this was the wrong time for this. She wasn't in the mood for a play party. She just wanted to take Nigel home and devour his cock.

There was another problem, too. She and Nigel rarely played together at these events. Since they both were openly dominant, one of them would have to be publicly humiliated if they both played. It was one thing to do a little role-reversal in their own house or on the houseboat; it was quite another to switch roles in public.

They'd probably split up and play with other partners as they usually did. Now that she thought about it, the prospect sounded more interesting. *Extremely* interesting, in fact. By now her eyes had adjusted enough so that she could see the naked backs and bums of some of the chaps who were being flogged. Not bad, not bad at all. Maybe she'd see if one of the Mistresses was into a three-way scene. That would get her warmed up for Nigel, later. She turned to tell Nigel what she'd decided, and found that he was already gone.

Fine. She'd entertain herself, then. She certainly didn't need Nigel in order to have a good time.

She went over to a small umbrella stand filled with whips. Hefting a small leather riding crop, she savoured the aroma of the leather and gave it a couple of practice swings. This would do very nicely.

Nobody paid any attention to her as she strolled around the room seeking a scene that she could join. People seemed engrossed in what they were doing; none of them looked as if they needed company.

Nigel suddenly reappeared at her side, resplendent in full leathers. 'Forgot to tell you, love, there are dressing rooms over by that wall.'

'But, Nigel, I didn't bring . . .'

'Don't worry. Nobody came to this reception dressed to play. Our host has thoughtfully provided everything we could possibly need.' He disappeared again into the crowd.

Leandra strode to the wall he had indicated, happy to have a place to go and a purpose. Wandering around wasn't her style but he'd sprung this on her with no warning; it would take her a few minutes to get adjusted. Already she could feel her mind-set altering. This looked like fun after all.

She was amused to see the signs on the dressing rooms: 'Tops' and 'Bottoms'. For a second she was tempted to peep into the 'Bottoms' room to see what was available for them. Then she decided against it. She didn't know these people, and she certainly didn't want to be labelled as a submissive. She strode into the 'Tops' dressing room.

It was a good thing that she was alone, or else she'd have been embarrassed by the astonishment she showed. As it was, she stood there with her mouth agape before quickly gathering her wits.

The room was filled with leather clothing. Along two of the walls were wardrobes, labelled by size and gender, in which hung leather pants, shorts, chaps, miniskirts, and jackets. The third wall contained shelves full of gloves, leather bustiers, leather suspender belts, and other accessories. The fourth side of the room was a veritable shoe store. There were shoes and boots of every description: thigh-high boots (with and without high heels), stiletto-heeled shoes, cowboy boots, and even a selection of plain, heel-less, sturdy shoes. Along with the shoes were socks and stockings in various sizes. There were masks, too, for those who found excitement in anonymity. The centre of the room contained benches and lockers.

Leandra chose a bustier, a matching suspender belt, leather bikini panties, fishnet stockings, stiletto-heeled, thigh-high boots, and long black leather gloves. She changed quickly, leaving her street clothes in one of the lockers. She picked up her whip and a collar and leash and left the dressing room. Leandra was ready to play.

She walked briskly around the room, getting her bearings. Occasionally she stopped to look at something that caught her interest. Watching and admiring a particularly skilful flogger, she noticed a tall man in a loincloth standing on the other side of the rack, staring at the scene as avidly as she was. Something about him seemed familiar, though she couldn't quite put her finger on what it was. She'd been to so many of these things over the years that she couldn't remember everybody. She'd probably met this chap at a scene somewhere. The fact that he was wearing a mask didn't help her identify him. The mask covered his whole head, so she couldn't see what his hair looked like. Oh, well.

He was displaying the code that identified him as submissive. Perfect. Maybe she'd remember who he was if she whipped him a little. She approached him and invited him to play. He assented.

She snapped the collar around his neck and led him around the room, looking for a play space. Two people were leaving one of the crosses, arm in arm. Leandra seized the cross, staking out her claim. She signalled to her submissive partner to step up on the footrest at the bottom of the cross. She tied him to it hand and foot with ropes the other couple had left behind. She gestured to her partner to honour the whip she was about to use on him. He kissed it and murmured his gratitude.

This was the first time she'd heard him speak. There was something about his voice ... but no, she was imagining things. She put it out of her mind and got down to business. First she gave the whip a few practice cracks. It made a most satisfying snap. Then she flicked it at him.

The whip hit just above his right nipple. Leandra knew she could do better than that. On a good day she could hit the tip of a nipple with the tip of a whip with no effort whatsoever. Maybe she was just out of practice. It had been a while.

She tried again. Bingo. Whip and nipple connected with a loud *thwack*. Good. Warm him up a little bit. She didn't want to hit him full force yet. Let them both work up to it. She flicked the whip again, hitting him in the same spot. He groaned.

She cracked the whip again, testing. He cringed at the sound. Very good. Let him show some fear; she liked it when the submissive was afraid – it made her feel powerful. She cracked the whip again, teasing him. Now she wanted to prolong it, leave him in suspense. She stood back and observed him. He shifted in his bonds as she watched him. Good. She must be making him nervous.

They were here to play, not to have a staring contest. She took a step forward again and raised her whip. *Thwack*. It landed on the tip of his right nipple, a perfect bull's-eye. A bead of sweat trickled below his mask and dropped on his chest. She cracked her whip again, landing on the same spot. She was getting back in practice. The whip was feeling more comfortable, more like an extension of her hand.

She raised it again and aimed it at his left armpit, which was defenceless under the arm that was held straight out, tied to the cross. It hit its target. The submissive man let loose an involuntary howl. Leandra realised she was hitting him too hard for this stage in the scene. She waited until he recovered from the blow, then hit his other armpit. This time he didn't scream. She saw another drop of sweat trickle below his mask. Was it too warm in here, or was this nervous perspiration? She couldn't tell. She flicked her whip at a nipple again and was rewarded with a moan.

Sometimes Leandra talked to the submissive she was playing with, but tonight she didn't feel like it. He couldn't be a novice, or he wouldn't be in this dungeon. She knew that no novices would have been invited to the basement. The man knew what he was getting into. She had no pity for him. She whipped a nipple again.

She noticed that his nipples were stiffening and her own stiffened in response – not that she'd let him know.

She looked at his loincloth. It was beginning to bulge as his cock started on an upward curve. He was getting turned on. This wouldn't do; it was too soon. Intending to put a stop to it, Leandra cracked her whip across both nipples at once. The man groaned and his loincloth bulged out further. The whip left a mark across his chest. Leandra laid another stroke on top of the first one.

She didn't like the look of that loincloth. She went over to him and unwrapped it. He spoke for the first time. 'Please don't.'

She ignored him and slowly drew the garment between his legs. A rapidly stiffening penis bobbed up from a thick salt-and-pepper bush. Clearly, he liked it. He couldn't have meant what he said.

'Please don't uncover me. People will see.'

Of course they would see. That was the point, or part of it, anyway. In Leandra's experience, submissives were exhibitionists at heart. While they would never voluntarily bare themselves, having the dominant take the matter out of their hands was a turn-on for them. But she didn't know this man at all, didn't even know what he looked like. She'd better check with him.

'If I cover you back up, the scene is over. Is that what you want?'

'No, Mistress.'

'Be quiet, then.'

She raised her whip and laid another lash across his nipples. His penis swelled. Good. This guy really liked it. She barely touched him with the end of the whip this time. The tip of the crop landed at the edge of the areola, leaving a small mark. She did the same thing to the other nipple. Then she hit him in the centre, between his ribs, a little lower. The only part of him that reacted was his cock – a clear fluid was beginning to ooze from the end of it. A drop made its way down the side and was lost between his testicles. Leandra decided it was time for a little verbal stimulation.

'You were right not to want to expose yourself. People are looking at you. They're thinking, "Look at that silly fool, with his big, naked, stiff dick. He shouldn't be like that in public. He's a bad man."'

Hearing that, the man squirmed in his bonds. He moaned while his penis rose higher. Then she saw why he was embarrassed about his nudity. It was strange that she hadn't noticed it before, but of course, it wasn't visible until his penis was standing straight up. She stared, and marvelled.

The man had a birthmark on the underside of his shaft. It was a perfect heart, only visible as such when the penis was almost fully erect. She understood his reticence; some dominants would tease him cruelly about it.

Leandra hit him again, across his chest, a little lower. Then she went back to his nipples and gave him another stroke. They were as engorged as his tool. He was moaning non-stop now, his hips thrusting forward.

She hit him again, lower, across the expanse of his chest. In this manner she inched down until the whip was at the top of his bobbing penis. Red welts were appearing on his chest, producing a peculiarly striped effect.

He seemed to know where the next blow would land. His body went rigid in anticipation.

He was right. *Swoosh* went the whip, right over the top of his cock. He yelled. This time his scream was real, not part of the game. He broke into a sweat the whole length of his body.

Leandra laid a stroke right beside the last one. Then she stopped to let him recover a bit. But she could tell that he was enjoying it – his penis grew even bigger, if that was possible.

'Don't stop, Mistress. Please don't stop!'

All right, if that was the way he wanted it. She gave him two strokes in a row, each one a little lower than the last.

The man was sobbing now. Great spasms wracked his body as he tried to stifle his tears.

Leandra hesitated. Was she going too far? No. The man knew how to stop her if he wanted to. He must be enjoying this. She whipped him again, although not as hard this time. The whip landed right across the birthmark.

He shrieked. The birthmark must be tender. She would have to be more careful. But she couldn't resist hitting it again.

His penis exploded without warning. Great gouts of semen shot into the air while he howled his shame. He spurted again, then again. Finally, his dick still erect and twitching, he was spent. He hung his head as if he were drained of any will to hold it erect. His come had splashed all over his chest and pubic hair. Some had even landed on his feet and on the floor. Leandra gazed with satisfaction at the mess she had caused. In her novice days, just thinking about the power she held over such a man would have almost caused her own orgasm. Now, however, she was used to it. It took more than that to make her lose control.

She let the man rest for a minute, then freed him and helped him down from the cross. As she was turning to leave, she heard him say, 'Thank you, Mistress. And do try sumi-e. It's very spiritual.'

Now she knew why he seemed familiar. She'd been talking to him upstairs. Of course. No wonder she hadn't put it together immediately: men looked entirely different in a dinner jacket than they did naked and tied to a cross.

She wandered aimlessly around the room, her sense of urgency gone. Finally she spotted Nigel's dark curls and went to see what he was doing. She found him flogging a tall, leggy redhead, probably one of the thousands of models that inhabited the city. She was in a sling, her bum bared to the lash. From the look of her bum, Nigel had been whipping her for quite a while.

The welts blended together, leaving a bright-red inflamed surface.

The woman was pleading, 'No, Master! Please! I'll be good! No more, please!' Nigel paid no attention and continued to wield his whip.

A crowd had gathered to watch. That was usually the case with Nigel. He was a true artist with the whip, much respected by other tops. Leandra arrived just in time to see him tease the top of the redhead's bum cleft with the tip of his instrument of correction. Then he flicked it down lower, between her cheeks. She cried out again.

Nigel lowered the sling and started lightly chastising her sex. His first stroke landed on her clit. She shrieked with what sounded like mingled joy and pain.

'Again, Master!'

'No. I'll do as I wish. Be quiet.'

Deliberately, he returned to her bum and laid a few strokes, while she whimpered in frustration. Finally he turned his attention back to her sex. He hit the top of her cleft, then a little lower, then the top of her clit. She howled in pain.

'I can't get at you. Spread your legs.'

Looking frightened, the young woman obeyed. Nigel flicked his whip down the length of her clit. It looked as if it would burst.

Leandra saw the telltale signs of approaching orgasm. A flush spread slowly from the woman's neck clear down to her pubic hair. The woman was suddenly quiet. Leandra sensed the storm building. Then the woman spoke.

'Oh, Master!' Her orgasm was upon her, obvious to any onlooker. She exploded. Orgasmic ripples engulfed her as she flooded herself and the sling. It was a long orgasm, a tribute to the skill of a master flogger. Nigel had been working on her a long time before Leandra arrived.

'Let me . . .' Leandra said.

Wordlessly, Nigel moved aside. Leandra approached the orgasming woman and put her hand on her sex. Rubbing in a circular motion, she coaxed out another flood as well as a gush of tears. The orgasm continued. Even Leandra was astonished at its length. It seemed that this woman would go on forever. She ran her finger up and down her slit. The woman sobbed.

'Too much! It's too much! I'm losing myself.'

'Shh.' Leandra sought to soothe her, while continuing to prolong the orgasm with her finger.

Finally it stopped. The woman didn't move. Leandra saw that her eyes were closed. She had fainted from the intensity. She was right, this orgasm was too much.

Leandra slapped her cheeks. The woman opened her eyes and smiled.

'Are you OK?' Leandra asked.

'Sure. Don't worry about me. I often faint when I come. It's no big deal.'

Leandra helped her down from the sling and led her to the dressing room to clean up. Nigel had disappeared again.

After a hot shower, Leandra and the other woman dressed in their street clothes and went back out into the dungeon. Leandra couldn't find Nigel. This was probably fortunate, because she was horny enough to let him whip her in front of all these people. Then she'd have trouble regaining her public image. She found the stairs and went up, back to the party.

Nigel was there, chatting with some distinguished-looking gentlemen. He looked as if he'd been there all evening. Not a hair was out of place. Not a blush stained his cheek. His breathing was steady, calm. But Leandra could see the telltale hint of an erection pushing against his dark trousers. He always wore tight briefs in order to avoid embarrassing displays, but Leandra knew.

Good. It meant he hadn't come yet. Neither had she. Their activities in the dungeon had merely warmed them up for each other when they were finally alone.

On the ride home, Leandra could barely control herself. She didn't think she could make it all the way without getting some relief. Trying to be patient, she waited. Finally she spoke.

'I like your little redhead, Nigel.'

'Really?'

'She's gorgeous. But she's hardly the bimbo you think she is. I talked to her while we were showering. She's an aerospace engineer, in L.A. for a convention. One of her friends knows our host, so he brought her along.'

'I seem to have a knack for attracting the bright ones, don't I?'

'Don't get your ego in an uproar. I think it's those sexy dark curls of yours rather than your genius, love.'

'Whatever. By the way, I . . .'

'I know. You didn't come,' Leandra said.

'How did you know that?'

'Because *I'm* a genius. Now, let's remedy that situation.'

Leandra simply couldn't wait any longer. Nigel had been away three weeks, and this whole evening had been a tease. If she didn't take some action, she was going to come just thinking about it.

She leaned over and buried her head in his lap, then undid the top button of his flies with practised teeth. Then the next button. The white cloth of his tight briefs strained through the opening as his flies gapped open. She worked on the rest of his buttons, enlarging the opening with each one. When she reached the bottom button, the white cloth that encased his erection exploded out of his flies. He groaned as she ran her tongue lightly over the bulge.

'Look, Nigel, I want to show you something.' She scooted up on the seat and spread her legs.

'I can't, love. I'm driving.'

'Stop the car, then.'

They were driving along a deserted road. No traffic had passed them in the last ten minutes. Nigel pulled over to the side and stopped, but left the engine running while he turned to face Leandra. The white of his bulge was visible in the moonlight.

'All right. Show me,' he demanded.

Leandra hooked her finger under her miniskirt and pulled it up, very slowly. As Nigel watched, mesmerised, her cleft gradually came into view, contrasting starkly with the black of her skirt. Her opening was glistening, matting the blonde, heart-shaped bush that surrounded it and framed her engorged clit.

'See? Nobody has even touched me. I wanted you to be the only one tonight.'

Nigel couldn't speak. He opened the door and tumbled out, heedless of the white bulge that was exposed between his flies. He stumbled around to the passenger door, opened it, and wrapped his arms around Leandra, supporting her breasts. He pulled her out of the car and thrust his bulge into the crevice between her cheeks. She squirmed, raised her skirt at the back, and ground her naked flesh back into his tumescence. She couldn't control her urgency; she had been waiting so long. Three whole weeks, and then this evening. She needed him *now*.

Lifting her as if she weighed nothing, Nigel carried her to a flat, grassy space behind a clump of bushes. Before he could lay her down, she had wriggled around until she was facing him. She spread her legs as far as she could so that her clit came in contact with his briefs and the bulge they encased.

'Wait, love. Let me get my clothes off.'

Leandra was beyond hearing. In a frenzy, she rubbed herself up and down on him, riding him like a horse. She wrapped her legs around him and arched her back so that her sex made even closer contact with his.

'Oh my god, Nigel, I'm ... *oh*!'

She felt his erection throb as her orgasm overtook her. She knew his orgasm wasn't far behind. Her spasms were nibbling at his erection, driving him closer and closer to completion.

'Wait, love.' He eased them both to their knees, fumbling with his belt. He jerked his trousers and briefs down with no time to spare. Leandra slid down on his rigid cock just as his testicles tightened and started to contract. A rush of semen flooded Leandra's pussy, then another one. She pressed against him as close as she could get. While he was moaning in release, Leandra fingered herself. As their spasms died down, they collapsed upon the grass.

Leandra lay still, enjoying the throbbing of his penis as it pulsated within her. She moved, and a flood leaked out of her sex all over his.

'We both needed that,' she said. 'Look how much you came.'

'You, too. But damn, Leandra, you nearly made me come in my pants!'

'I'd be delighted if you did, love. That's not as awful a thing as men seem to think it is. If you think about it, it could be considered as quite flattering to the woman, that a man gets that excited in her presence. Maybe some day you'll be able to do it for me.'

'Perhaps.'

When they had recouped their strength, they got back into the car and continued their journey home. Leandra smiled all the way. This had most definitely been worth waiting for.

5

Once again removing Jamie's head from where it lolled against her shoulder, Tamsin closed her eyes in another futile stab at sleep. So far she hadn't been able to stop her mind from racing even long enough to relax, much less go to sleep. The plane was somewhere over the Atlantic, she knew, although it seemed as if they must be almost at Los Angeles by now. She yawned in an attempt to convince herself that she was sleepy. Tomorrow – no, today – she'd be meeting Leandra, and she absolutely had to be at her best. What would Leandra think if she was so groggy that she couldn't focus on the business at hand?

Jamie emitted a soft snore and snuggled against her shoulder again. Tamsin pushed him away once more, reflecting that a few days of this would make all her romantic feelings for him disappear. There was nothing like snoring to quench ardour. That, and lack of sleep.

Beginning to nod off, Tamsin stirred restlessly as a hand brushed against her thigh. She came fully awake with a start. Blast. Just when she'd finally dozed off, too.

She glanced down quickly to make sure the hand wasn't her own. How awful if she were to be caught playing with herself in her sleep! But the hand was one she'd never seen before. As it made its inexorable way up the side of her thigh, she realised it belonged to a woman.

But she'd been sitting by Jamie the whole time. Where had this woman come from?

Then she remembered. She was by the window, with

Jamie in the middle seat. Just before takeoff, while they were congratulating themselves on their luck in being able to spread out over three seats, a young woman had claimed the aisle seat. They'd chatted for a few minutes before settling down for the long flight.

However, that didn't explain why there was a woman's hand next to her thigh. Feigning sleep, she peeked out beneath her eyelashes.

It was obvious that Tamsin's thigh was merely incidental to the main prize. Their seatmate – Vanessa, or some name like that, Tamsin recalled – was sprawled over Jamie's lap, playing with his thigh. She apparently didn't realise that she was brushing against Tamsin's at the same time. Tamsin decided to enlighten her.

'Excuse me, but that's my thigh you're poking.'

'Oh, so it is. I'm so sorry. Do you mind awfully?'

Tamsin found that she didn't mind as much as she thought she did. Since she was wide awake again, the situation intrigued her. Why was this Vanessa person making so free with Jamie's thigh? It was the kind of thing she wished she could do herself but knew she'd never dare. Especially to Jamie, of all people.

'I didn't wake you, I hope. Did I? I couldn't sleep, and I needed some diversion,' said Vanessa. 'Since you told me that you and he are just pals, I thought I'd entertain myself with him for a while. That's all right, isn't it?'

'Of course,' replied Tamsin, trying to sound like the sophisticated libertine she wanted to be. 'I have no claim on him. Besides, I'm curious to see what you can do. He's hopelessly shy with women. As for waking me, there's no way I could sleep anyhow with Snoring Man roaring sweet nothings into my ear.'

'He's not snoring now. Watch this.' Vanessa squirmed on top of Jamie and settled in his lap.

'Hey, what's happening?'

Startled, the two women turned to see Jamie's eyes, wide with amazement, staring at them.

'I was dreaming that you ... Oh, my God, it's true!'

'Keep your voice down, Jamie. Do you want to wake the whole plane?'

'I forgot. Sorry.'

'Besides, I think you've been pretending to be asleep. The proof is poking my right tit,' Vanessa said.

Blushing, Jamie grabbed at his offending cock.

Vanessa focused all her attention on Jamie. 'I never gave you permission to get an erection.'

'A chap can't help it, you know. Your breasts are rubbing against it. And it was your hand on my thigh that woke me up.'

'I *said* you don't have my permission.' Vanessa glared at him, assuming the queenly role that came so naturally to her.

'Quite right. I don't. Sorry,' Jamie acquiesced.

Vanessa wiggled her tits, deliberately massaging Jamie's erection with them. Jamie groaned.

'I'm warning you, don't get any nasty ideas. I shall have to punish you if you do. Now close your eyes and go back to sleep.'

That was about as likely an event as if he were suddenly to leap up from his seat and belt out an operatic aria. Tamsin was aware of this, but she wasn't sure that Vanessa was.

Tamsin had listened in amazement to this whole exchange. This was not the Jamie she knew. She recalled Jamie fleeing the dance floor in shame because of an erection. Now he was proudly defending himself to the mysterious Vanessa for having one. And this talk of permission – what was that all about? She would have to ask the woman about it later, when Jamie wasn't around. In a few short minutes Vanessa had established a power over him that Tamsin didn't understand. The thought excited her.

'Tamsin? Are you going to sleep on me? I was asking if you have a boyfriend.'

'Oh. No, I'm not going to sleep. And no, I don't have a boyfriend.' Tamsin felt a twinge of self-disgust. Why was she telling this stranger that she didn't have a lover? It was none of her business. And Tamsin thought it made her look like some pathetic creature who couldn't even attract a man.

Vanessa's reaction was just the opposite. 'Oh, so you haven't settled down to just one, eh? You're a woman after my own heart. There are too many fine men out there to limit oneself to just one, don't you think?'

Tamsin hadn't thought of it quite like that, since she tended to see her sexual inexperience in a negative light. But now she began to reflect on what Vanessa was saying. Yes, that was right. She was discriminating, not unlucky. She didn't have a boyfriend, not because she was hopelessly devoid of sex appeal, but because she didn't want to confine herself to just one man. She liked the new interpretation this put on things.

'. . . women? Tamsin?'

Oh dear. She really was going to have to pay more attention to the conversation. For a second there she'd thought that Vanessa had asked her . . . but no. She was exhausted. She wasn't hearing right. Vanessa couldn't have said what she thought she'd said. She'd just pretend she hadn't heard.

Vanessa herself made it clear that Tamsin wasn't imagining things. 'I asked you if you've ever been with a woman.'

That's what Tamsin thought she'd heard, and it was something she didn't want to discuss with a stranger. But in spite of herself she found herself blurting out the truth. 'Well, yes, I guess. I have this friend. We're like sisters. We've fooled around a little bit. She's bisexual, but I'm not.'

'You're not? That's what a bisexual is, Tamsin. A person who enjoys sex with both men and women.'

'Oh. Right. Well, I like men better.'

Jamie made a snorting noise, reminding both women that he was still there. Vanessa studied him thoughtfully.

'Watch this,' she said.

Vanessa needed to do something for herself, and soon. Playing with Jamie's cock and thigh while chatting with Tamsin had aroused her almost to breaking point. She squirmed on Jamie's lap and looked up at him.

'Open your eyes, big guy. I know you aren't asleep.' Indeed, his erection was nearly poking a hole in her shirt. 'It's your turn now.' Your turn – and *mine*, she thought.

She nuzzled his erection against her cheek. She felt it twitch. Slowly she eased her hand back from his thigh until she was cupping his cock. Carefully, so as not to scare him off, she rubbed it through his trousers. He didn't push her away, which she found encouraging. She continued to massage his bulging crotch while he began, ever so slowly, to thrust.

Her body was in an extremely awkward position, though. She'd lain on his lap while she talked with Tamsin. Now she found it impossible to reach him in the way she wanted to. Without losing contact with his crotch, she raised herself up until she was once again sitting in her own seat. This gave her all the manoeuvring room she needed.

Unfortunately she hadn't come totally prepared. All her toys were in her luggage. She could pretend that he was tied up and powerless. But would he go along with it? Sometimes these shy chaps could surprise one. Still, she'd go slowly. She didn't want to scare him.

Continuing her hypnotic massage of his crotch, she leaned over and placed a chaste kiss on his lips. No response. Just about what she'd expected. She'd have to warm him up.

She kissed him again, lingering this time. She extruded her tongue and gave a tentative lick. He responded, his lips parting slightly. Seizing the advantage, she plunged her tongue all the way in. Suddenly he relaxed, opened his mouth, and pushed his tongue forward to meet hers. They remained this way for a while, the tips of their tongues lightly flicking against each other. Her hand felt a stronger stirring in his crotch.

She wished they were in a bed instead of in an airplane seat. It was hard to get at him and do the things she wanted to do without the other passengers noticing. She had never encountered a man who was this passive, and it was driving her wild. He wouldn't have needed restraints even if she'd had them handy.

With her free hand (she wasn't going to let go of his crotch. No way!), she slowly unbuttoned his shirt. She took an agonisingly long time with the top button, although she wanted to satisfy her curiosity about what he wore underneath it. Her questing fingers were met with a soft, silky down. Good. No vest. That made things easier.

He didn't resist anything she was doing. She might have thought he was asleep if it weren't for the obvious activity at his crotch and mouth. His tongue kept flicking back and forth, never missing a beat. And his erection! Vanessa had never dreamed he would be this large. The thought of having it inside her made her even hotter. That would be hard to do on an airplane, though.

And she wasn't sure yet that he'd even want to. That made the challenge all the more exciting.

She undid another shirt button. There! She could finally spread his shirt open, baring his chest. Her free hand found a nipple, which she gently twisted. He moaned.

Vanessa moved her mouth to his other nipple, which was stiffening. She lapped at his little love button, then sucked on it. His crotch responded.

Then she felt a hand on top of hers. Tamsin! She'd almost forgotten about her in her own need. If Tamsin wanted to play too, this would solve the problem of not enough hands. She eased her hand out from under Tamsin's. Tamsin pressed down on Jamie's crotch without further instruction. Vanessa used her freed hand to undo the rest of the buttons and pull his shirt out of his trousers. Then she unbuckled his belt and the top button. She reached inside and pulled the waistband of his underpants away from his crotch, allowing his penis to expand and straighten out. He sighed with relief.

The tip of his cock peeked out above his trousers, and again Vanessa marvelled at its size. What a beautiful cock! It was both long and thick. At the moment it was as hard as a length of pipe. The end glistened with a droplet of love juice. As she watched, another one appeared.

Vanessa reached to undo the next button, only to find that Tamsin had beaten her to it. She went for the next one, Tamsin for the next. In no time, between the two of them they'd freed his happy cock from the confines of its denim prison. Now they were treated to the sight of a huge white Jockey-shorts bulge rearing up through his open flies. The top of his underpants was damp with the colourless fluid that was now oozing from his cock hole in a steady stream. Vanessa wanted to ride that cock more than she'd wanted anything in her life. Her sex was screaming to her, and she felt the wetness spreading in her panties. Only Jamie's cock could put out her fire.

She hiked up her skirt. With one practised yank she had her panties down to her knees. She kicked them off, not caring that they landed in the aisle of the plane where people could see them. All she cared about was the juicy, irresistible cock that was twitching and jumping in front of her eyes.

Pushing Tamsin's hand aside, she flung a leg over Jamie's lap and hoisted herself up so she was straddling him. With legs spread wide, she plastered herself against the iron ridge of his cock. She rubbed her clit up and down over his underpants, getting more frenzied by the minute.

It wasn't enough. She needed him inside, needed to feel him thrust up and down inside her as she rode him. She raised herself up a bit, and he came up with her. Supporting herself on her knees, she tugged at his trousers, succeeding in slipping them down below his bum. That was a little better, but his underpants were still a barrier. Driven by her need, she groped ineffectually at his underpants, succeeding only in twisting them.

Tamsin came to the rescue. Placing one hand on each of his hips, she hooked her thumbs under the waistband and pulled the garment down. Jamie raised his bum at the crucial moment. His magnificent cock soared into the air.

Vanessa seized it joyously, but she was too far gone to be able to do anything with it. It was Tamsin who effected the match, placing her hand over Vanessa's and helping her guide Jamie's cock into her desperate sex. Vanessa was so hot and so wet that it slid right in, in spite of its size. Weeping with bliss, Vanessa sank down until she felt the hairs of his sex plastered against hers.

She was beyond rational thought. Fortunately Jamie's instincts took over and he began to pump his cock in and out: in until their crotches joined, out until Vanessa could see almost the entire length of it. Vanessa just sat on it and let him do the work. Her silent tears became soft whimpers, then loud gasps and moans as her desire escalated. She needed him to touch her clit; she could come if he touched it. She leaned over him, trying to rub herself on his hair, but she couldn't quite do it.

Tamsin reached around Vanessa and began stroking her clit. Vanessa moaned as her orgasm built within her and threatened to explode. She moaned again as the orgasm broke the surface and the contractions caught and released Jamie's cock. Finally the contractions subsided and she collapsed in exhaustion, her head on Jamie's chest.

Jamie was still pumping. He didn't make a sound, nor did he move any part of himself except his magnificent cock and his pelvis. It was as if he'd been tied up after all.

Tamsin slipped her hand under Vanessa's bum and felt for Jamie's balls. When she found them, she cupped them in her hand and gave a gentle squeeze.

That was all it took for Jamie to erupt into orgasm. Now the rest of his body moved, too. As he continued to flood Vanessa's willing receptacle, he wrapped his arms around her and pressed her closer to his chest. They probably would have fallen asleep in each other's arms, if it hadn't been for the voice of the captain.

'Ladies and gentlemen, we will be landing at LAX in about fifteen minutes. Please fasten your seat belts.'

Tamsin hurried to help Vanessa and Jamie untangle themselves and become presentable before the cabin lights came on. Their timing was perfect. They got

Jamie's flies buttoned just in time. When the lights came on, they looked like any three sleepy passengers who had had to rouse themselves for the landing.

One of the flight attendants stopped by their seat and announced, 'Don't be alarmed. We're expecting a little turbulence, but it's normal, nothing to worry about.'

Turbulence! Tamsin, Vanessa and Jamie hooted with laughter. If the flight attendant had appeared sooner, she'd have seen some *real* turbulence.

The three co-conspirators sat patiently in their seats until the plane had landed and the seat-belt sign went off. Still giggling, they collected their belongings and filed off the plane into the terminal, where Leandra was waiting for them.

6

Tamsin gave Vanessa Leandra's phone number and made their remarkable new friend promise to ring them up. Blowing a kiss in farewell, she sent her on her way. Tamsin and Jamie headed for the 'Welcome, Tamsin' sign that was being held aloft by a strikingly beautiful, well-endowed blonde who, in her four-inch heels, towered over all of them. As they introduced themselves and shook hands, Tamsin noticed that Leandra was eyeing Jamie with interest. It seemed as if she could hardly wait to get better acquainted with him.

'Jamie is my assistant,' Tamsin explained. 'He carries the heavier equipment and helps me set up my shoots.'

She could hardly keep a straight face as she uttered these words. She needed a man to carry the heavy equipment about as much as she needed a third tit. In fact, she liked to think that she never needed help from anyone for anything. But she'd needed an excuse to bring him along to L.A. This one was as good as any.

'He'll stay in a hotel, of course,' she added.

'Of course not!' Leandra was quick to respond. 'I have plenty of room in my house. You'll stay with us, Jamie . . . unless, of course, you have other plans.'

'Well, uh . . . all right. Thank you very much.'

Leandra shepherded her guests through the bustling airport to the parking lot, talking non-stop with Tamsin about her plans for her project. She ignored Jamie as he followed along like a well-trained pet.

'. . . a couple of days, until you get over your jet lag.

Then we'll go to various parts of the area and you can shoot whatever strikes your fancy.'

Only half listening, Tamsin darted her eyes all over, attempting to absorb the brilliant light of the Southern California sun. This place was a photographer's paradise, no doubt about it. She couldn't wait to begin. She was sure she wasn't going to suffer from jet lag.

To her surprise, Leandra stopped at a white stretch limo. The driver hurried to open the doors for them, and then went to retrieve their luggage.

'No, it's not mine,' Leandra hastened to assure them. 'I just hired it for the day. I knew you'd be bringing a lot of equipment, and I didn't think it would fit in my car. Besides, it's fun to ride in a limo once in a while.'

In a short while they had reached Santa Monica and were heading up the Pacific Coast Highway. Tamsin and Jamie gawked out the window like the tourists they were. Leandra continued her running monologue, to which Tamsin and Jamie made no response. Finally she realised that they weren't listening to a word she said.

'Hey, you guys! Hello? Hello? Earth to Tamsin? Jamie?'

'Sorry. I didn't mean to be rude. It's just that ... the ocean, the mountains, the sun ... I can't wait to start getting it down on film.'

'Sure. I forget. Living here, I take it for granted, which is a shame.' Leandra gave Tamsin's knee a friendly pat. Tamsin finally pulled her eyes away from the window and looked at Leandra. As she did so, a slow blush suffused her face.

Leandra was sitting in the seat that faced them. Her legs were spread, her skirt had hiked up, and – she wasn't wearing any panties.

Following Tamsin's gaze, she smiled and closed her legs. She pulled her skirt down and was, once again, the proper university professor.

Jamie had been watching this scene, too. For the rest

of the drive, through the Palisades and then into Brentwood, he didn't take his eyes off Leandra.

Tamsin wondered at this. This wasn't the shy Jamie she'd known in London. So far she thought she liked him much better this way. But he still didn't seem to see her as anything but a friend. And she, after seeing what he'd given to Vanessa, wanted a repeat performance soon. Maybe Leandra – but no. Her relationship with Leandra was to be business. What had just happened must have been an accident. She knew how easy it is to forget you're wearing a skirt and let your legs gape open. Still, with no panties you'd think a woman would be more careful. But perhaps . . .

Stop it, Tamsin, she chided herself. You're here to do a job, not to be intimate with your colleagues.

Leandra's legs gradually opened again. Both Tamsin and Jamie stared hopefully, but this time their eyes went unrewarded. Leandra's miniskirt was pulled down just far enough so that they couldn't see what they both knew was there, tantalisingly out of reach of their eager gaze.

Leandra dropped the pen she'd been waving to punctuate her comments. She bent over to pick it up. As she returned to a sitting position her skirt once again crept up a bit higher, but what Tamsin wanted more than anything to see was still covered, if only just barely.

So fascinated were the two guests that they didn't notice when the limo left the road and wound up a long, curvy, palm-lined driveway to Leandra's house. Leandra dismissed the limo driver after he had carried the luggage into the foyer. She led the way up the stairs, with her two guests eagerly looking up her skirt like a pair of teenage boys. Though Leandra's skirt flicked back and forth as she climbed the stairs, Tamsin and Jamie got no further glimpse. Tamsin began to think she'd imagined the whole thing, that it was a mild hallucination brought about by the stimulation of the experience with Vanessa and the jet lag that she denied having. She'd have to do a reality check with Jamie later.

The day passed quickly. Leandra changed into a pair of baggy shorts and a clingy tube top. She and Tamsin spent most of the afternoon discussing photography and, specifically, Leandra's *L.A. From Other Eyes* project. Tamsin learned that the other photographers, chosen from all over the world, had already done their part.

'How did you get interested in this project, Leandra? It's fascinating, but somehow I wouldn't have expected it to come from an anthropologist.'

'Good point. I just got lucky, I guess. When I was in grad school I had this classmate from Finland who used to spend every spare minute exploring the city. He usually took his camera, and he got some most unusual photos, even though he wasn't that great as a photographer. I got fascinated with what this city looked like to someone from a different culture, and, well, you know the rest. It took me a few years, but finally I applied for the grant and got started.'

'I don't suppose you'll tell me who the other photographers are,' said Tamsin.

'You're right. I won't. It's only because I don't want any of the photographers to be influenced by any of the others. That is, I don't want any unconscious bias to creep in. You see, Tamsin, I wanted to see Los Angeles through the eyes of strangers. All the photographers chose what interested them the most about the city and its environs. Then they did a series of photos. They had total artistic liberty. I'm writing the accompanying essay for each series, subject to the photographer's approval. That's what I plan to do with your work, too.'

'It sounds like a lot of fun, actually,' said Tamsin.

'This is the perfect working holiday. I can't wait to get started.'

'That's settled, then. Come on, let's go see if that lazy boy is conscious.'

They roused Jamie from his jet-lagged nap and went to a trendy restaurant by the ocean for dinner. As they relaxed on the restaurant's patio, sipping their drinks and enjoying the sight, sound and smells of the ocean, Leandra interrupted the murmur of their conversation.

'Oh, blast! I've dropped my pen. Jamie, would you be so good as to . . .'

Jamie was already on his hands and knees under the table. Leandra leaned back, pushing her bum forward. Her hands were busy in her lap. Jamie quickly backed out from under the tablecloth, blushing, and scrambled into his seat. When he handed Leandra the pen, Tamsin noticed a bulge in his trousers. A shadow crossed Leandra's face as she thanked him. Tamsin pondered this all during the ensuing dinner. It seemed most odd.

Upon their return to the house, they retired to their separate rooms. Tamsin found that she couldn't sleep, in spite of her sleepless night on the plane. She read for a while and was just feeling drowsy enough to doze off when she heard a commotion down the hall. The words were almost indistinguishable, but she managed to make them out.

'Bad boy! Bad! I'm going to punish you!'

'But, Leandra –'

'That's *Mistress* Leandra to you!'

'– *Mistress* Leandra, then. I picked up your pen, just as you asked me to.'

'Stupid boy! Did you really think I was asking you to find my *pen*? What's the matter with you? Did you notice anything, shall we say, out of the ordinary?'

'Well, Mistress, I thought I saw . . .'

'Yes? Go on?'

'I thought I saw . . . your privates.'

'You *thought* you saw? Boy, are you blind? What else could it have been? And do you have any idea why?'

'No.'

'No, *Mistress*. I don't want to have to tell you again.'

'Yes, Mistress.'

'I'll explain it to you, then. I wanted you to crawl between my legs and put your face in my crotch and *eat my pussy*! But did you, you cretin? When what I expected should have been so obvious? No. You had to get the *pen*!'

'I'm sorry, Mistress Leandra. I didn't know . . .'

'I'll make sure you know for next time, because I'm going to punish you.'

Tamsin had heard enough. She jumped out of bed, covered her nakedness with her white silk robe, and headed down the hall towards Jamie's room. The conversation had stopped. Now there were other sounds. *Smack*! *Thwack*!

Surely she couldn't be doing this! Tamsin stationed herself outside Jamie's door and listened. There was a new sound, too soft for her to have heard from a distance. It sounded like the deep groan of pain. Or was it pleasure? She couldn't tell. The sound came again.

Pain, she decided, and pushed open the door. Jamie was her pal, and if he needed help –

As her eyes took in the scene, she slowly realised that he didn't need any help. Not from her, anyhow.

He was tied face-up to all four posts of the bed. Leandra was sitting on his face. He lapped at her pussy while his penis bobbed straight up in the air.

Leandra held a small leather crop. She lashed at his penis, making it even stiffer. Just as he seemed about to explode, she stopped. When the danger had passed she whipped him again. Each time she stopped, he begged her to continue. Tamsin couldn't help but notice the cruel smile on Leandra's lips as she refused him.

The sight of all this was causing restless stirrings in Tamsin herself. She thought she'd learned from Gina all that there was to know, but she now realised that she was wrong. This was more far out than anything Gina had attempted.

What surprised Tamsin more than anything else was Leandra's choice of clothing. Instead of being naked or in nightclothes, she was dressed almost entirely in leather. She had on a black leather bustier, which served to emphasise her prominent breasts and tiny waist. A leather suspender belt held up black, silk, seamed stockings. She wore studded leather bracelets at her wrists. A pair of black leather boots, with five-inch heels, was on the floor by the bed.

And was that...? Yes, it was. Tamsin could hardly believe her eyes. Over the suspenders, Leandra was wearing a pair of black leather bikini panties. And they were crotchless! In Tamsin's wildest imaginings she'd never visualised anything like this. She continued to watch in stunned wonder.

Leandra and Jamie were oblivious to their audience. Jamie had eyes only for Leandra's pussy, while Leandra's eyes were fixed on Jamie's cock.

Now there was a longer than usual pause between whip strokes. Jamie's cock began to deflate. Leandra watched dispassionately.

'Good boy! Look what Mistress Leandra has for you now.' From some mysterious place inside her cleavage she produced a studded leather cock ring.

'I couldn't put this on you while you were so big and bad,' she said. 'Now I think you're small enough so it will fit.'

Jamie's cock, though it had shrunk a bit, was still a

considerable size. Quickly Leandra snapped the ring around the base of it.

'That's better!' she said. 'See how big you still are!'

Jamie groaned at her touch but was powerless to do anything. Drops of clear liquid oozed from the tip of his penis.

'Now I'm ready to sit on it,' Leandra announced. She lifted herself off his face and crawled down to his stomach. Turning around, she straddled him again. She enveloped his cock, while he moaned his need.

'No, no. Not there!' She raised up and back, positioning his cock at the tip of her opening. Slowly she slid down to a sitting position as his cock filled her. Jamie moved as if to thrust, but Leandra pushed him back down.

'No! Bad boy! Lie still!'

'I – I –,' was all Jamie could manage.

'Be quiet! If you can't keep silent, I shall have to force you to.' She raised and lowered herself, up and down, up and down, on his ever-stiffening cock. Frantically Jamie struggled to free himself.

'Do you remember your safe word?' Leandra asked.

'Yes, Mistress Leandra.'

'Do you need to say it?'

'No, Mistress. Please, no.'

'Then lie still! I don't want to have to tell you that again.' She resumed her ride, using him as if he were a mere joystick.

Tamsin was spellbound. She couldn't have taken her eyes away from this scene even if she had wanted to. Jamie's glistening cock, appearing and reappearing as Leandra pumped up and down, had a hypnotic effect upon her. Without her realising it, her hand crept between the folds of her robe and groped towards her dampening sex. Her fingers found the familiar crevice and lingered there. Slick with her juices, her fingers began to circle her clit. She was imagining herself as Leandra, impaled on Jamie's cock.

Leandra increased her speed, galloping towards orgasm. Her hands covered her crotchless panties and rubbed herself faster and faster. Even with her lack of experience, Tamsin could see that Leandra was about to come. A flush was seeping above her cleavage. Leandra tossed her head from side to side and seemed to be stifling a moan.

Jamie started thrusting in spite of having been forbidden to do so. As his thrusts increased, it became obvious that he wouldn't be able to come with the cock ring on. He groaned helplessly.

Leandra rose up without losing contact with his cock. In an acrobatic feat that made the watching Tamsin marvel, she turned around with his cock still in her. Now she was straddling him backwards, giving him an excellent view of her most delectable bum.

Leaning back, she braced her hands on his shoulders, thrusting her full breasts into the air. She rested in that position for a moment, then began once again to slide up and down on his cock.

Leandra seemed to be completely in charge. Tamsin whimpered aloud at the thought. How she'd love to have somebody do that to her.

Instead of being in charge, however, for once Leandra was out of control. Her orgasm hit just as Tamsin was starting hers. Both women cried out as Leandra collapsed back on top of Jamie. She recovered quickly. She lifted her head and looked directly at Tamsin, who was still overcome by her orgasm.

'Come here, Tamsin, and help me free his hands. That's the one disadvantage to tying a man up – you don't have the use of his hands.'

'You knew . . .'

'Of course I knew you were there! All that noise you

were making, how could I not? Now come and help me out.'

Shyly, Tamsin approached the bed. She'd never done anything like this before. She reached out and fumbled with the knots on Jamie's bonds. When she'd succeeded in freeing a hand, Jamie reached for Leandra's crotch.

'Not your hand, silly! Your mouth! I want to come over your face.'

As Leandra spoke, Jamie began his struggles once again. Leandra picked up her crop and swatted him on his unruly cock. 'Stop that, now!' she ordered, as if he were a disobedient dog.

Having dismissed Jamie, Leandra turned her attention back to Tamsin. 'Yes, I came. But I need to come again. Once is never enough for me.'

Tamsin knelt by the bed and moved her head closer to Leandra's blonde bush. She noticed that Leandra had a musky smell, similar to her own and yet different. She wished that Gina had taught her about this. Gina was comfortable with both genders, but she herself was hopelessly heterosexual. True, she'd played a little bit with Vanessa on the plane, but that was a one-time thing. It certainly didn't make her even bisexual, much less a lesbian. Still, she wished she could be freer. Intellectually she had no problem with it, but emotionally –

Leandra grabbed Tamsin's hand and pressed it to her crotch. 'Oh, that's good, baby. That feels so good. But take it easy, OK? I don't want to come until Jamie has done one more thing.' She slid up Jamie's body, arriving at his face with her bum almost covering his eyes.

'Eat it, Jamie. Now.'

Jamie lapped at her crack, worming his way with his tongue into her. His free hand pushed Tamsin's away and took its place.

'Just around the rim, dear boy. Ah, that's it.'

Tamsin fingered herself under her robe while she

watched Jamie and Leandra. The thought of the formerly shy Jamie rimming Leandra's bottom-hole while he fingered her at the same time caused her pussy to gush all over her own hand. She imagined herself in Leandra's place, imagined that Jamie was doing these things to her instead of to Leandra.

It was hard to focus on Leandra now with her own need so intense. She hoped she wouldn't lose control again.

Leandra began to moan and wriggle.

'Oh, yes! That's it! Oh, I've got to come! Just a little more . . . please! Don't stop. I need –' She convulsed, with soft moans and whimpers.

As soon as she could speak, Tamsin asked about Jamie.

'Doesn't he get to have fun too?'

'He *is* having fun, Tamsin. You don't understand these things yet. I have so much to teach you.' She turned back to Jamie.

'Hold still, Jamie. You can close your mouth now. I'm finished. I'm going to bed.' She got off the bed and left the room without a backward glance.

Tamsin stared at Jamie, lying there with his hands and legs spread, naked except for his cock ring, his free hand making no effort to untie the other one. She couldn't believe what she had just witnessed. What kind of a person was this Leandra? How could she leave Jamie there in that state? She had come here on a photographic assignment that was turning into something from a porn movie.

'Jamie, I could help you. Do you want me to?' At his mute nod she started to untie one of the foot tethers. Jamie shook his head violently.

'You don't want that? Tell me, then. You can talk.'

Still not speaking, Jamie pointed to the cock ring. His cock was still engorged, with no means of relief. Tamsin unsnapped the strap and eased it off his swollen member. Jamie exploded immediately. Tamsin held his cock while he spurted and spurted again.

'Ah, that's so much better.' Jamie groaned with relief. 'I don't know how much more of that I could have taken. Now you'd better put the ring back on, or Mistress Leandra will wonder.'

'She'll wonder anyhow, when she sees what you did.' Tamsin went into the bathroom and brought back a towel. As she mopped up the evidence, she asked, 'Why don't you want me to untie you?'

'Because I'm supposed to stay like this all night. That's what Mistress Leandra wants. But I desperately needed a good come. Thanks, Tamsin.'

'What's going on here? What's this "Mistress" stuff?'

'It's a game we're playing. You wouldn't understand, Tamsin.'

Tamsin was a little miffed. This was the second time in fifteen minutes that she'd been told she didn't understand. She apparently was expected to remain in ignorance. Nobody seemed inclined to enlighten her. What did they think she was? She wasn't as innocent as they seemed to think. After all, she'd played with those sex toys with Marcus and Gina. And look what had happened on the plane – that was the height of wildness. Or was it? Jamie and Leandra seemed to be far beyond that. She didn't understand what had happened to Jamie, for sure. It seemed as if in a way he had come home. He was so much more relaxed about his body, so much more sure of himself, than he had been in London.

'Anything else I can do for you?'

Jamie didn't make a sound. Tamsin saw that he was sound asleep. She dimmed the light and tiptoed out of the room. Then she remembered that she had forgotten to replace the cock ring. As quietly as she could, she returned to the bed and snapped the ring around his now-limp penis. She tiptoed out again and returned to her room.

Leandra hoped Nigel would still be awake, because she couldn't wait to tell him about their guests. She found him reading in bed while he lazily stroked his penis.

'They're perfect, Nigel, absolutely *perfect*! The boy is a natural submissive. Totally natural. He's inexperienced, but I don't think he'll require much training. I'd almost bet he refers to me as "Mistress Leandra" when I'm not even in the room.'

'And the girl?'

'Tamsin? She's nowhere near as submissive as Jamie. I found her very willing, though. She's not averse to a little girl–girl fun, I think. I'm not sure. I think maybe underneath all her innocence she may have the instincts of a dominant. It'll be fun to see what develops, but I have to take it easy with her. She did come here as a business colleague, after all.'

'How about your *Naked in L.A.* project? Think she'll do?'

'It's too early to tell. I don't even know if she likes to do nude photography. Besides, I have a contract for *L.A. From Other Eyes*. I need to have her work on that first.'

'Where are they now? What did you do to Jamie?'

'I left him tied up overnight. He'll be OK. It's good for him. But – oh my *god*! I forgot to take his cock ring off!'

'You left him in a cock ring?'

'Sure did. A cock ring and a raging erection. It's the first time I've ever done that. I'd better go –'

'No. Stay here. I'm sure Tamsin will take care of it for him. You're the only woman in the world who could just walk away from a chap in that condition. Tamsin will take care of it, and both of them will think you don't know.'

'What will you give me if I stay?' She began to strip off her clothes.

'I'll give you ... this!' He waved his penis at her. 'Make him sit up and beg!'

This was an old game with them, one that they both enjoyed very much. When she had peeled down to her suspender belt and stockings, she lowered her bush to his face.

'Will this make him sit up and beg?'

'Definitely. So will this.' He unhooked her stockings, deftly rolled them down, and eased them off her feet.

Leandra was ready to go again. Although tired from her earlier activities, she got a fresh burst of energy just from being with Nigel. Clad only in her suspender belt, she lowered her mouth to his rising cock.

'No, no, little girl. You've been bad. You've been playing with our guests, and you didn't invite me. I'm going to punish you.'

'Oh, please, Master, don't punish me! I'm sorry! I'll be good!'

'You've said that before. I'm going to punish you so you remember this time.'

'Oh, please, no!'

'Oh, please, yes,' he mocked in a high falsetto. In his normal voice he said, 'You know the drill. Over here. Face down.'

Leandra crawled across the black silk sheets into the middle of the king-sized bed. She buried her face in a pillow.

'Bum in the air,' ordered Nigel.

As she obeyed, she heard the clank of metal and knew he was going to use the handcuffs. She pulled her hands out to the sides to make his task easier. It was with a sense of relief that she felt the cold metal on her wrists and heard them snap shut. Her hands were suddenly raised up. She knew that he was slipping a rope under the chains so he could fasten her to the bedposts. She turned her face to the side so she wouldn't smother.

She felt him prodding her legs apart. Oh, good! He was going to chain her ankles, too. She'd hoped that he would. When he brought the gag for her mouth, she was in ecstasy.

Then he blindfolded her.

She struggled, more from excitement than from need. Part of the game was to pretend the cuffs hurt her. Nigel always thought they really did.

Being blindfolded made her acutely aware of every sensation. Now she was feeling a light touch on her back, too light to be Nigel's hand. It felt like a silk scarf brushing delicately along her rib cage and then to the hollow before her buttocks began their ripe swell.

No, it wasn't a scarf. What, then? There seemed to be little ridges. A feather? Yes, a feather. Oh, luxury. She wriggled with pleasure.

Fingers – yes, definitely fingers – brushed against the top of her bum, insinuating themselves into the cleft. They were encased in something. Leather? Perhaps. She wished she could smell whatever it was; then she'd be able to tell. Her face was turned away from Nigel and whatever he was doing. She couldn't move it without getting hopelessly stuck in the pillow. She concentrated on willing him to pass his hands in front of her nose.

It worked. He did, for a brief moment. It was enough for her to verify her first guess. Leather gloves. He gently stroked her cheek. This was a fine, soft leather, one she hadn't been aware of before. He must have brought these gloves back from his recent trip.

Now she felt his hot breath in her ear. She shivered. She felt a familiar dampness begin between her legs. He licked her ear, alternating the licking with blowing on it; his tongue moved down to her neck. She surrendered to the experience and knew she was at his mercy, that everything that would happen depended on him. She stopped thinking.

He moved his tongue to her shoulder, nibbling his way down her back. Suddenly he bit her. She gasped and felt more dampness.

He turned her body sideways, facing away from him. He reached around her, and pinched the nearest nipple. She gasped again. He twisted it, feeling it go erect. He pulled it out as far as he could, then let it snap back. The second time he pulled it out, Leandra felt a new sensation. A clamp! Oh, that felt so good. She waited for him to do the same thing to her other nipple.

He didn't. Instead, she felt the glove again at the opening to her secret place. The gloved fingers felt slippery this time. He must have dipped them in lube.

Her right nipple was tingling, aching for a clamp. She begged for one, her words muffled by the gag. He paid no attention.

The gloved finger probed, and succeeded in entering. Slowly it moved up until it encountered her guardian sphincter. With an inaudible pop it slid in. It turned and twisted, massaging her inside. He slid a second finger in, then a third. The pinkie followed. He was in up to his wrist.

Leandra felt him closing his fingers into a bunch. She forgot about needing another nipple clamp. Her whole being was focused on what was happening within her. She felt impaled on his arm. Her sex suddenly got wetter.

'Bad girl. You're making a mess. I shall have to punish you more for that.'

'Sorry, Master.' The gag muffled her words.

'Quiet. I'll do with you as I will.'

Realising that he couldn't hear her words, she nodded.

'Hold still, or I'll have to immobilise your head.' He pushed his arm in further and began a slow pumping motion.

Leandra was so aroused that she wanted to turn over and take him inside her. Although she couldn't see him, she knew he would be fully erect by now, his huge cock bobbing in the air. She wanted to see him, knowing that if she did she'd probably come instantly. That would make him furious. She tried, unsuccessfully, to stop thinking about his stiff dick.

A moan escaped her. She tried to stifle it, but it was louder than she thought.

'I said, "quiet"!' With his free hand he fumbled for the crop that was always close at hand. He turned her sideways as far as the restraints would permit. Then he cracked the crop across her tender nipple. As the clamp mashed further into her nipple due to the force of the blow, she yelled. Desperate, she got herself under control. She didn't know what he'd do if she disobeyed him again. She was afraid he might withdraw from her, which would be the worst punishment of all.

Leandra had never been fisted with a leather glove. She wasn't sure she liked it as well as his naked hand. Still, it was far from unpleasant, judging by her exceedingly damp sex. She wished she could reciprocate in some way as her nature was much more dominant than passive. But when Nigel was in the mood for a scene, he had to be the Master. She had to admit she did enjoy the occasional change of pace.

His fist moved faster. While he was plunging in and out, Leandra gave herself over to pure sensation. She felt as if her whole body were being massaged by that leather glove.

Now the crop was beating a tattoo against her breast. Revelling in it, she hoped he'd remember she had a film shoot in the morning. It wouldn't do to appear in her thong bikini all marked up from her scene with Nigel. Fortunately this shoot was on the beach, so she'd have to dress more modestly than when they worked in the studio naked. Surely he'd remember. He always did. There was nothing to worry about.

She'd been concentrating on thinking these thoughts to keep her orgasm at bay. This was becoming extremely difficult. Her sex was oozing, and the sheet beneath her felt damp.

Nigel was paying no attention to that. He'd already punished her for her messiness when he lashed the whip across her nipple. Now he was uncurling his fist and withdrawing his hand. That meant he was going to ... she hoped he was going to replace it with his erection.

For a moment she felt empty. Then she felt a familiar stiffness replace the leather glove. He was going to fill her again, her favourite way. She quivered in anticipation.

He started tentatively. Then thrust his whole length inside her. He was so rigid, so hard, more like a piece of metal than a man – except for the soft skin. She raised herself up to meet him as best she could, hampered by her fetters. Wriggling with joy, she felt his balls against her bum. Her orgasm reached for her, brushed against her consciousness. Oh no, too soon. She had to wait for him, had to –

'Master!' she screamed into her mouth gag. 'Now!'

She knew he couldn't hear her words. It was futile to try to talk. All he could hear was incoherent mumbling. Still, instinctively, she cried out her words.

He paid no attention, as she'd known he wouldn't. But his thrusting quickened as if he'd heard her. His whip hand reached for her clampless nipple. He pinched it harder than he had before, then twisted it. The pain brought tears to her eyes. It also brought something else.

'Now, Master!' she gasped. 'I can't wait! I'm coming now, *now!*'

As she moaned incomprehensible words, her orgasm surged up from the centre of her being. She was carried away as it exploded through her. She bucked and rocked, in spite of her bonds.

She felt Nigel's balls tighten as they slapped faster against her bum. Soon he joined her with his own orgasm. Three times his semen spurted into her. She squirmed, rubbing her clit against the sheet.

Nigel, spent, collapsed against her back. His weight pressed her clit harder into the sheet, initiating another, smaller spasm. Then it was over.

After a few minutes she felt his hands fumbling with her mouth gag. Finally she could talk.

'Thank you, Master, for correcting me.'

He didn't respond. Instead he busied himself with unlocking the hand and the ankle cuffs. She lay passively while he worked, enjoying the feel of his semen oozing out into the cleavage of her bottom. It seemed unusually copious, which pleased her.

Then she felt him turn her on her side. Pulling the top sheet over them, he wrapped his arms around her.

The scene was over. Nestled together spoon-fashion, they fell into a deep, satisfied sleep.

7

The next morning Tamsin got up early and slipped out for a swim in the Olympic-sized pool. She threw off her flimsy robe and slid into the pool naked. Tall hedges protected her privacy from any passers-by. Enjoying her solitude, she turned over on her back and floated, her breasts reaching skyward. Looking down, she could see drops of moisture on her nipples. Further down, the rising sun made miniature rainbows of the droplets that glistened in her pubic fur. She began a lazy backstroke, her breasts rising and lowering alternately with the motion of her arms.

When she made her turn at the end of the lap, she was horrified to find herself almost at eye level with a strange man. His tight, muddy jeans hinted at his occupation. He must be the gardener.

Oh, no. She hadn't known that Leandra had any employees. This was so embarrassing. She contemplated escape, then realised that that would leave her even more vulnerable. She would have to climb out of the water, inevitably exposing her bum in the process. Then she'd have to bend over to pick up her robe. He'd probably be able to see everything, unless she kept her legs tightly together. In that case she was likely to overbalance and fall right in front of him. If she did successfully cover herself with the robe, she wasn't covering much. The robe, more a peignoir than a robe, was made of a transparent, gauzy material that was thin enough to reveal everything.

Her only option was to brazen it out. She could

pretend that she hadn't seen him. Alternatively, she could act as if she were used to swimming naked in front of men she didn't know. Besides, he wasn't important. He was only the gardener.

Or could that be a problem? She knew these Americans had strange ideas about equality. Maybe it wasn't any more acceptable to be naked in front of one's gardener than in front of one's banker. She'd have to ask Leandra later. In the meantime, she was naked in this pool and this man was grinning and staring at her with no sense that he was acting above his station.

It didn't help that he was so bloody attractive. Even though he was kneeling by the pool, she could tell that he was tall. He had dimples when he smiled, as he was doing now. His jeans, though muddy, had clearly been put on clean that morning.

She decided to pretend she didn't see him. But that was not to be.

'Good morning! Beautiful day, isn't it?'

He didn't even address her as 'Miss'! How rude. She'd have to speak with Leandra. Leandra needed to know how her employees behaved with her guests.

To her astonishment, the man slipped out of his jeans and climbed into the hot tub. Tamsin could see the beginning of a bulge in his bikini trunks. This man was a rude gardener, but a most interesting one.

'Why don't you come and join me?' he called from the hot tub. 'It's chilly in the pool.'

This last observation was true enough. Tamsin was covered in goose bumps, which she hadn't noticed while she was swimming.

She decided that she might as well. Her swim was already ruined. She couldn't continue swimming naked with him watching her. He seemed a little odd, but nothing bad was going to happen. She was in Leandra's back yard, and he worked for Leandra.

She lunged for her robe, not wanting to expose herself any more than necessary. Her feet slipped in the wet grass and she fell headlong. The soft grass cushioned her fall. She was more embarrassed than hurt.

As she struggled for a foothold, she felt strong arms under hers, lifting her to her feet. Before she could protest, he tossed her over his shoulder and strode back to the hot tub. Tamsin thought about how she must look with her bum in the air and her breasts flapping against his bare back. Then she realised he couldn't see her. Then she realised she didn't care if he did. She had come to the States for a photographic adventure; she seemed to be in the middle of sexual one now.

He slid her off his shoulder, then lowered her into the tub. The hot water was welcome after the chill of the pool and the morning air. She sank down onto the seat, basking in the warmth. She was feeling more comfortable with him, though she was glad the steam shielded her from his scrutiny.

Modesty didn't stop her from looking at him, however. Since she didn't want to be obvious, she started at his mop of curly dark hair, cut long. She gradually directed her gaze downward, past his startlingly pale blue eyes to his full, sensuous lips, to his dimpled chin cleft. His shoulders, torso and upper arms rippled with muscles. Lower down, she saw the washboard abs of a body builder. All of this was interesting, but it was the part below the washboard abs that attracted most of her interest.

He wore a tiny black bikini that revealed the outline of everything he had – and what he had was a lot. The hint of a bulge that she'd seen before now blossomed into a most interesting protuberance indeed. It seemed to have a life of its own, bulging and twitching, seeking to escape the confines of its tiny prison. For a moment Tamsin thought it would actually burst through the fabric, so fierce was its struggle.

She was confused. How could she be having these thoughts about a man she didn't know? How could she even be sitting here naked in a hot tub, staring at a strange man? Where was her shame?

When she thought about her shame, she realised it was gone. She hoped this was a permanent condition. Shame and shyness had been her constant companions ever since she'd been old enough to recognise the feelings. That's why she was so embarrassingly inexperienced for a woman of twenty-two. The last few days had improved her situation considerably. She smiled as she thought about how much fun it was to be downright wicked. Now there was a delicious man with a delectable bulge sitting across from her in a hot tub.

'Like what you see?' He grinned, dimpling again, and spread his legs while adjusting his bikini. For the first time she noticed his British accent. 'This thing is so tight it's bloody uncomfortable.' He continued tugging as he spoke.

'Why don't you just take it off?' Tamsin surprised herself by saying.

'I didn't want to shock a nice young lady like you. But if you really don't mind, I think I'll –'

'Let me do it. Please.' The words were out of Tamsin's mouth before she could reconsider. But having said them, she was happy. No more pretending. She wanted nothing more at this moment than to relieve this lovely man of his restricting garment.

She crossed the space between them and reached for his trunks. Before she could reflect on what she was doing, she hooked her thumbs on the sides of the garment and tugged it down. It didn't move very far. His erection was holding it in place. Oh, dear. She grasped the front of the bikini and pulled it out from his body. A huge erection sprang up to its full length and climbed up his belly. Tamsin watched in amazement. She'd never seen a penis this big. Of course, she hadn't seen many penises. Still, this looked like a penis to be proud of. Forgetting about the bikini, she sat back in admiration. The man noticed her awed expression and chuckled.

'Nice, isn't it? But it's uncomfortable with that bikini constricting it. Would you like to finish doing the honours?'

'Certainly.' She worked the trunks down to his hips, then stopped. 'Would you mind . . .?'

'Oh. Guess you can't get it off with me sitting here, can you?' He raised his bum so she could wriggle the garment all the way off. 'That's better. Thank you. It's much nicer with you doing it.'

Tamsin was amazed at her own behaviour. She'd just peeled the swimsuit off a totally strange man, and she wasn't even blushing. Now she didn't know quite what to do. The etiquette she had learned when she was growing up didn't cover how to behave while sitting in a spa with a naked stranger. Especially a gorgeous one. Well, *any* naked stranger. Suddenly feeling insecure, she backed across the spa and resumed her seat. The man watched, his lips twitching, clearly amused by her discomfiture.

'Relax,' he said. 'I don't bite. I may nibble sometimes, but I most definitely don't bite. Come sit by me,' he said, patting the seat beside him.

Since Tamsin felt completely at sea in this situation, she followed his lead. When she reached him, he caught her knees between his own.

'On second thoughts, *don't* sit by me. I like this a lot better.'

Poor Tamsin didn't know where to look. Too shy to meet his eyes with hers, she looked down and made eye contact with his penis. The hole in the end of it, by now beginning to glisten with moisture, looked as if it were staring her in the eye. She didn't want to seem to be staring at his erection. It didn't seem polite, somehow.

He was a stranger and the gardener to boot. Not that she was in the habit of staring at the erections of acquaintances, either. Not even Jamie's. She'd known him for years, and she hadn't seen him erect until the flight to the States. She solved her dilemma by closing her eyes.

'Can't decide where to look, eh?' The man was amused, but he sounded kind. At least he wasn't laughing at her. Tamsin reminded herself that she was safe, that this was Leandra's home, that this was Leandra's gardener. Nothing would happen that she didn't want to happen.

That was what was scaring her. She knew that she wanted all sorts of things to happen, none of them covered in etiquette books for proper young ladies. What she really, *really* wanted was for this man to rise from his bench, embrace her in the water, and fuck her senseless. But she couldn't, she just *couldn't*. What would he think? And what would Leandra think if she got it on with her gardener? Leandra was obviously a free spirit, but even Americans must have their limits.

'You're wondering what I would think of you if we made love.' His voice startled her.

'How . . . how did you know?'

'I can see it in your face. You have a most expressive face, you know. It changes every second as you consider your options. It's a beautiful face, if I may say so. As beautiful as some of your other charms.'

This made Tamsin blush. She'd actually forgotten that she was naked too. Instinctively she covered herself with her hands.

'It's a little late for that, my pet. I've already seen enough to know that I want more.'

'I do too,' she quavered.

'You don't sound too sure. It sounds as if there's a conflict between what you want and what you think you *should* want. I promise you I won't do anything without your consent. I'm also sure that you and I want the same thing. Now I'm going to kiss you.' He rose from his seat, maintaining his grip on her knees. His mouth covered hers, while his tongue forced an entrance between her willing lips and teeth. She met his tongue with hers. Their tongues feinted and danced, each trying to pursue the journey to the other's throat.

His arms went around her, drawing her close. His nipples rubbed against hers, which were already erect. His stiffened on contact.

She pressed her groin against his, feeling his erection press into her cleft as the warm, honeysuckle-scented water swirled around them. She stroked his back gently, then more urgently. She felt herself starting to lose control as her nails raked his back. She was wet and ready. The sensuality of the warm water on her skin, and the outrageousness of doing this outdoors, in full daylight, with a stranger, all contributed to intensify the sensations for her. And there was this kiss that wouldn't quit.

She moaned into his mouth. She wriggled her sex, trying to capture him between her legs. He backed off, but only to sit down and pull her on top of him. She knelt, straddling him, and pointed his erection toward her slippery opening. As big as he was, she had no problem lowering herself onto his stiffness. She moaned as he filled her. It seemed aeons since she'd been filled to this extent.

Now she was no longer in a hurry. She could have sat there forever, enjoying the pulsing of his cock and the water lapping around them.

Suddenly he pinched a nipple, forcing her to cry out with the sudden pain. He pulled the nipple out as far as it would go. Then he stopped. The sudden cessation of pain made her sex flood around his stiff cock.

He did the same with the other nipple. This time, forewarned, she didn't yell. The combination of the pain and the bubbling water was giving her sensations she'd never felt before. It was almost as if the water were making love to her, stroking her soft skin and murmuring endearments. The water was as gentle as a woman's hand. Possibly it was as gentle as a man's, too, though she had no basis for comparison.

As if reading her mind, the man began to caress her. His hands lovingly traced their way down her back. Slowly, gently, he massaged her into mindless bliss. His erect penis filled her inside and his embrace surrounded her. She didn't move; she passively accepted what was happening to her. This was heaven. Nothing she had ever done sexually could approach it.

He stroked her thighs. She shivered. This was delicious, even if it was naughty of her. She remembered the night before, with Leandra and Jamie: all those whips and bonds. They drove her wild, but she mustn't scandalise this nice man by mentioning it. He'd probably never heard of such behaviour. She wanted him to think she was nice too, as nice as he was.

He slid his hands to her thighs and caressed them. When his hands reached her knees, he massaged his way back up her inner thighs. She whimpered as he edged closer to her sex. She was impaled on his cock, her legs were splayed, and everything was bared to him. She waited passively as his hands brushed her pubic hair. Suddenly she started moving. She mashed her sex against his, grinding her clit against his bush. Then she moved back to give him access. He took his direction from her motion and inched his hands ever closer to her clit.

She caught her breath, waiting for it to happen. She desperately wanted his fingers on her. She forgot he was a stranger, forgot he was the gardener. All she could do was experience the indescribable sensations. The swirling water was gently brushing her clit, working it into a frenzy. His hands moved closer, almost imperceptibly. She couldn't tell where his hands ended and the water began.

Then he touched her. She gasped. His finger rested on her clit for a second that seemed an eternity. Now that it had finally happened, she could easily tell which was the water and which his fingers. She willed him to continue.

He did. His finger traced the outline of her bud as it swelled in response. While he was doing this, his other hand tweaked and pinched her nipples. Tamsin moaned as the pain intensified and ebbed.

The man's cock began to thrust, slowly and gently. Tamsin had never experienced anything like this, either. She'd been getting used to pounding towards a quick release. Now there was a slow arousal. She was hardly aware that she'd been getting aroused until this moment. The swirling water, the pinching of her nipples, the gently thrusting erection inside her, and his finger rubbing her clit, all combined to create an incredibly intense feeling. Yet she could wait, forever if need be. She was willing to remain passive until the time was right.

She had forgotten that the man was a stranger, just as she had forgotten all the other factors that had inhibited her earlier. She focused on the new sensations: the gradual increase in speed of his penis, the slapping of his testicles against her as he thrust.

Without warning he pinched her clit between his thumb and forefinger. The pain was intense. Tamsin cried out. After a few seconds he let go, which created even greater pain. She thought she'd pass out. As the pain ebbed, she felt a wave of pure lust. At that moment she could have devoured the man. Instead, she bent over and took one of his nipples in her teeth.

It was his turn to cry out. Incredibly, his erection got

even bigger. He pumped faster while increasing the speed of his fingers on her. Tamsin began to meet his thrusts, riding him as he pumped up and down. She felt her orgasm building. It wouldn't be long now. She found his hand and placed her hands on top, pressing him onto her clit. She rotated her hands, causing him to massage her just the way she needed it. Frantically she ground her pelvis close to his, imprisoning both their hands.

She didn't see how he could possibly resist this. He had superb staying power. Most men would have lost control a long time ago. Instead, she was the one having a problem with control. She wanted to wait and come with him, though she wasn't at all sure she could. With her lack of experience, she didn't know how to prolong her pleasure. It wasn't the kind of thing that one asked one's friends, after all. She thought that eventually experience would teach her; however, that didn't help her now.

The man slid his hands out from under hers and placed them on her bottom. He pulled her closer to him, so that she felt her pubic hairs entwining with his. She tried to think about other things to delay the inevitable, but to no avail. Her mind was firmly focused on her body and what was happening to it.

She spread her legs as far apart as they would go, mashing herself even closer to his groin. His testicles continued to slap her as he increased his thrusting.

A stab of pain surged through her. He had grabbed one of her nipples between his teeth. Turnabout. But he wasn't letting go. He tugged at it, stretching it to its utmost. Tamsin felt as if she were going to pass out. The pain was exquisite but, just when she could bear it no longer, he stopped.

For a second the pain was unbearable. Then, as before when he'd merely pinched, the pain turned to ecstasy.

She ground herself against him, moaning and sobbing. There was no stopping her orgasm now. As her contractions reached the surface, his cock thrust faster and faster. She exploded with a gasp just as he emptied himself into her. His moans mingled with hers as he released yet another load. Her fingers flew along her clit uncontrollably as her orgasm continued.

They clung to each other while their spasms subsided. Tamsin was once again aware of the water swirling around her. She tilted her head back and looked him in the eye. He smiled at her. She felt his hands move up her back to embrace her in a gentle hug.

She became aware of a voice, and it wasn't his. It wasn't male, either. Leandra!

What was she going to do? She was about to be caught in a most compromising position with Leandra's gardener. There was no way out of it. She was naked in the spa and so was the gardener. The least she could do was quit riding his cock before Leandra saw them.

Tamsin launched herself off his wilting penis and scrambled back to the other side of the spa. Not that this would help. The situation would be clear to Leandra, whatever Tamsin did.

'There you are! Did you finish the weeding you were going to do? Or did you get distracted first? Oh, sorry. Good morning, Tamsin.'

Tamsin muttered a bewildered 'Good morning.' Apparently Leandra didn't care what her gardener did. She just wanted to make sure he had finished the weeding. She couldn't imagine having an employee and not being angry if he spent his paid time having sex with her guests. Oh well, these Americans. Tamsin would never understand them.

'Hope I'm not interrupting anything,' Leandra said as an afterthought.

'Not at all. We were just finishing up here.' The man

climbed out of the spa and wriggled into his jeans; the sight almost gave Tamsin another orgasm. She watched in awe as that beautiful cock, magnificent in repose, disappeared from her sight. She hoped it wasn't forever.

'I got most of the weeding done, but I needed a break. Let me show you.' He and Leandra set off down the path. Tamsin stroked herself and watched their retreating backs, straining to hear what they were saying. Fortunately for her, their voices carried quite well.

'I see you've met our Tamsin,' Leandra began.

'Well, I wouldn't exactly say I "met" her. We didn't introduce ourselves,' the man said.

'You didn't "meet" her, but you "knew" her in the biblical sense.'

'That describes it precisely.'

'What did you think?' Leandra asked.

'She's shy, doesn't take the initiative much. But she's willing. And courageous. I had a definite feeling that she's not accustomed to dallying with strange men in outdoor hot tubs.'

'I'm surprised you didn't tie her up.'

'And scare her off? Relax, my sweet. There's plenty of time for that later. She has a lot to learn first. But if we play it right, she'll soon be joining us in group scenes.'

Tamsin got up and slowly put her clothes on, all the while pondering what on earth the man meant by 'group scenes'.

8

Tamsin ran downstairs, dressed in a tiny white thong bikini and matching beach sandals, just in time to hear Leandra yell, 'Come on! Anybody who wants to go to the beach, come with me now!'

It was early afternoon. Jamie poked a sleep-tousled head out of his room.

'Five minutes! Or you get left behind!' Leandra called.

Jamie disappeared to scramble for his clothes. He was the only one not yet ready.

'Here! Have some sunscreen. We can't burn our English rose.' Leandra tossed a bottle to Tamsin. 'Hurry up, Jamie!'

Jamie emerged from his room dressed in jeans, a sweatshirt, and hiking boots. Leandra looked exasperated, but she kept her voice patient and friendly.

'We're going to the beach, Jamie, not on a wilderness trek. It's summer. California is hot in the summer, especially in the sun. Didn't you bring any swimming trunks?'

'But, Mistress, you told me not to display my body outside the bedroom.'

'True. I did. But you're not going to show off your family jewels. That's what I was referring to. You may wear swimming trunks to the beach. You have my permission.'

'Thank you, Mistress.' Jamie ducked back into his room, only to emerge a minute later still fully dressed.

'I can't find my trunks. I must have forgotten to pack them.'

'Not to worry. I'll get you a pair of Nigel's. You can buy some when we get to the beach.' She left the room and returned with a pair of leopard-print bikini trunks. 'Here. Put these on. No, don't go back to your room. Take your clothes off and put the trunks on here. After all, I haven't seen your cock in a few hours. I don't want to forget what it looks like.'

'B–but . . .'

'What's the matter? Are you shy in front of Tamsin? She's seen everything you own, too. Come on, strip off.'

Jamie obeyed. When he got to his underpants he hesitated.

'Don't you *dare* get an erection. Jamie! I can see it's starting to twitch a little. Don't let it get any harder, or I'll have to punish you.'

Poor Jamie's cock started inflating in earnest when he heard the word 'punish'. He hurried to tug down his underpants before Leandra noticed. By the time he slid into the leopard-print bikini he was well on his way to a full erection.

Leandra noticed. 'I don't have time to punish you now, you bad boy. It'll have to wait until we get to the beach.'

Tamsin sat in the front seat of the convertible with Leandra. Jamie was left in the back seat to deal with his unruly cock. The women, oblivious to Jamie's problem, were chatting about Leandra's movie.

'I'm the producer, so I get to act in it if I want to. I enjoy making adult movies; it's a quick process. The movie is done before I have time to get bored with it. Of course, I act under a pseudonym. University professors are not expected to parade around in a thong – or less – in an adults-only movie. It's undignified, or some such.'

'Have your students ever recognised you?'

'Oh, sure. But I lie to them. I say, "Yeah, she does look a little bit like me, doesn't she?" They really don't know the difference, and of course they don't press the point. My movies are XXX-rated. The students can't very well accuse their professor of being a porn star. Which is exactly what I am, of course.'

'I'm surprised they admit to you that they watch these movies.'

'We're urban anthropologists. Some of us specialise in pop culture, of which adult movies, books, magazines and web sites are a flourishing part. Once I actually assigned one of my movies to a class. Had to quit doing that, though. Too many of the students noticed the actress's resemblance to me.'

'Why do you do it, if you're jeopardising your university job?'

'Frankly, I like displaying my body. I inherited good genes. My body turns on both men and women. Since I'm bisexual, it feels good to know that I can create sexual feelings in others, both women and men. Speaking of which, Tamsin, I have another project in mind that I want to sound you out about. After we finish *L.A. From Other Eyes*, I'm thinking about doing another book entitled *Naked in L.A.* This one would be photographs of L.A. and its environs, much in the style of our current project, with one exception. We'll have nude models in every photo. This will showcase just you, if you're interested. I'll write the copy, of course, but you'd be the only photographer.'

'Leandra, that would be a dream come true! I'm getting known as a travel photographer, and *Other Eyes* will give me exposure as an art photographer. But my real dream is to photograph nudes. Mapplethorpe is my idol. I just hadn't a clue how to get started. For one thing, I'm too shy.'

'I hadn't noticed,' Leandra teased.

'Oh, stop it! I *am*! Shy, that is. Until I met you, I'd

have been too embarrassed to take a nude photo. But that's really what I want to do, eventually.'

'What do you like so much about Mapplethorpe, apart from the obvious sexual licence he lived by?'

'He was a master of black and white work. His prints are sublime. Most of my work is in colour, but I'm working on my black and white technique in the hope of someday getting really good at it. That's why I admire Ansel Adams so much, too, in the nature area. Populist, but still perfection.'

'I'm glad we had this discussion, Tamsin. I wasn't sure whether you'd want to do it or not. We'll talk more about it later, OK?'

She put her hand on Tamsin's thigh and gave it a little squeeze that hinted at exciting things to come.

The warm sun lapped at Jamie's trunks, arousing him further as he sprawled in the back seat half listening to the women's conversation. He contemplated taking his cock out and having a good wank, but he didn't dare. Mistress Leandra would know. How could she not?

Now, hearing Leandra's last words, Jamie was pushed beyond his endurance. He had been getting hornier while the sun shone down on his erection. Mistress Leandra was creating sexual feelings in others, all right. Specifically, him.

He pulled the elastic waistband of his trunks out from his body. His cock jumped right up and gave him a one-eyed stare. He slipped his hand under the elastic and cupped his balls. Ah, that felt so much better. He slid down in his seat so that his cock lay on his belly. He began to stroke it through the swimsuit material, still mindful that Mistress Leandra might catch him in the rear-view mirror.

So far the women seemed to be paying no attention

to him. Perhaps he could manage to relieve himself without their knowing about it. It was Mistress Leandra's fault that he was in this condition. If she hadn't ordered him not to get hard – no, if she hadn't mentioned punishing him.

Yes, that was what had struck a nerve: punishment. Just thinking about it made his erection grow. Now he no longer cared what the women thought: he needed a wank. He told himself it was necessary, because he couldn't walk up and down the beach with a full erection. At least, that was what he would tell Mistress Leandra if she caught him at it.

Bolder now, he slid his hand into his trunks and gripped his cock. There was already enough lubrication; the end of his cock had been oozing all over the rest of it. Tentatively at first, then more assertively, he slid his hand up and down his shaft.

The trunks were in his way. He pulled them down, hooking the waistband under his testicles. Now he had full access to himself and could still yank his trunks back up if there was an emergency. He forgot about the women, forgot about everything but his own need. He closed his eyes and gave himself over to daydreams of punishment.

Gradually he became aware that the car had stopped. He loosened his grip on his cock and opened his eyes.

They were in a beach parking lot. Horrified, he stared around, too embarrassed to meet the fascinated gaze of the crowd of onlookers who surrounded the car. He groped for a towel with which to cover himself. He couldn't find one. Then he remembered that he'd left his trunks ready for a quick cover-up. He grabbed for them and pulled. Unfortunately, that was the very motion he needed to trigger his orgasm.

Helplessly, in front of those total strangers, he shot his wad into the air. An uncontrolled groan accompanied it. As if observing from afar, he heard himself announcing, unnecessarily, 'I'm coming! I'm coming!'

A spatter of semen landed in his hair. As he felt it splat and realised what it was, he told himself that this was the final humiliation, that nothing else could go wrong.

He was mistaken. Another jet hit his hair. Then he saw the nightmare.

Two uniformed cops, one male and one female, had parked their bicycles and were coming towards them. Now he was in bad trouble, for sure.

Tamsin saved him by tossing him a beach towel. He grabbed it gratefully and covered his lap with one end, while attempting to remove the evidence from his hair with the other.

'What's the problem here, folks?' It was the female cop.

'Nothing, officer. My friends are visiting from London, and I wanted to show them the beach. But it seems the natives here have never seen English people. They surrounded our car and stared at us so rudely that I would have called you over if you hadn't already seen the problem.'

'Break it up, folks! Show's over. It's just a couple of British tourists. Stand back and let the car through.'

'Thank you, officers.' Leandra smiled sweetly at both of them and drove into a parking space.

Jamie checked to make sure he was decent. The leopard bikini barely covered his slowly deflating erection, but there was nothing to see that would interest the cops. He kept the towel on his lap, just in case. The crowd had drifted off.

Leandra was the stern Mistress again, no longer smiling and sweet.

'I *ordered* you not to get an erection. But what did you do? You not only got one, you encouraged it. Don't tell me you weren't thinking about sex all the way down the highway. You must have been, or this wouldn't have happened.

'I don't have time to punish you now; it's time for my film shoot. You almost made me late for it. Tamsin will deal with the first part of your punishment. And remember, there will be a lot more when we get home.'

'Yes, Mistress. I'm sorry, Mistress Leandra.'

Ignoring his attempt at an apology, she turned to Tamsin.

'I want you to do me a favour and supervise him while I'm working. First, take him into the ocean and clean him up, especially his hair. I want him to wear this collar and leash until I'm finished for the day. Don't let go of the leash. He is to follow you at three paces. Are you willing to do this for me?'

'Sure, Leandra. But what if he runs away?'

'He won't. I know he won't. He's too afraid of displeasing me again.'

Jamie listened while they discussed him as if he were a disobedient pet. At first it made him a little angry. Then, when he thought about it, he understood that he'd brought this upon himself. Mistress Leandra had ordered him not to get hard. He had disobeyed. She had told him last night that he must never touch himself in a sexual way without her permission. He had disobeyed that order, too. He was a bad, bad boy. He thoroughly deserved any punishment she might see fit to give him.

'Isn't that true, Jamie? You're afraid to disobey me now?'

'Yes, Mistress Leandra.'

'And you'll stay with Tamsin and do what she says?'

'Yes, Mistress.'

'Very well, then. I'll see you back here in a couple of hours, if you don't find me at the shoot. She fastened the dog collar around Jamie's neck and handed the leash to Tamsin. After telling them where her shoot was, in case they wanted to watch, she was off.

Tamsin and Jamie looked at each other. 'What do you think, Jamie?'

'We'd better do what she said.'

'You mean *you'd* better. I'm just doing her a favour.' Tamsin paused for a few seconds, then began to laugh. 'If you'd *seen* yourself, Jamie. The expression on your face –' Tamsin succumbed to a fit of giggles.

Jamie's frown slowly turned into a smile. Tamsin's giggles were infectious. Soon Jamie, too, was giggling helplessly. They both roared and guffawed until their legs would no longer hold them up. Then they collapsed on the sand in gales of laughter.

After they had recovered somewhat, Tamsin stood up. 'I'm supposed to dunk you in the ocean, but now I need it myself. Look at all this sand that's stuck to me.' She pulled at her thong in front, releasing a flood of sand. Jamie laughed even harder.

Tamsin tugged at the leash. 'Come on, Jamie. Get up. Let's jump in the ocean and get clean.'

The water was surprisingly cold. Tamsin started to swim out from shore in order to get warm. She felt a tug at the leash. Jamie had dug in his heels.

'Don't go out too far. I can't swim.'

Tamsin turned around, trying not to let her disappointment show. She'd been looking forward to a good long swim. Now that wasn't to be. She'd promised Leandra she'd look after Jamie.

She ducked Jamie's head under water and scrubbed at the gobs of semen. When she could feel no more of it, she dived and grabbed him below the waist. He resisted.

'No! No! Mistress Leandra said –' Jamie struggled to free himself.

'Relax. I'm not being sexual with you. I'm just trying

to get you cleaned up.' This was merely a half truth. Her intent had been to give him another erection and then laugh while he tried to get out of the water inconspicuously. 'And what's with all this "Mistress Leandra" stuff? You only met her yesterday.'

'You wouldn't understand, Tamsin.'

There it was again. She was so tired of being told she wouldn't understand. What was there to understand? She had been intimate with Leandra too, but she wasn't expected to address her as 'Mistress'. Jamie was right. She certainly didn't understand. Jamie seemed so happy being treated this way. She wouldn't have put up with it for a second. At least, she didn't think she would. Still . . .

'Hurry up, Jamie! I want to get out of the water. I'm cold.' Without waiting to see if he was finished, she tugged on the leash and ran to the shore. She wanted to play in the surf, but it was just too cold for her. She hoped Jamie had had enough of being in the ocean for one day, too.

Jamie ran up beside her.

'Three paces back, Jamie.'

'Blast. Do I have to?'

'Yes. I promised Leandra. I'm sure she'll want a full report.'

The threat of a negative report seemed to subdue Jamie. He trotted meekly behind Tamsin, gawking at the sights. One sight that captivated them both was the throng of young girls on in-line skates, weaving in and out among the horde of beachgoers. Most of them were dressed in thong bikinis that were even skimpier than Tamsin's. Jamie's cock started to react.

'Down, boy,' he admonished it. 'Mistress Leandra would be angry.'

'What?' Tamsin had heard him muttering behind her.

'Oh, nothing,' mumbled Jamie, blushing.

'What do you mean, nothing? I distinctly heard you say "down, boy".'

'I said "nothing". Leave me alone.' Jamie's face flushed a deeper pink.

'You were talking to your dick, weren't you?' Tamsin began to snicker.

'No!' shouted Jamie, the pink deepening to a fiery red. 'Of course I wasn't talking to my dick!'

Several passers-by regarded them with interest.

Tamsin could not stop staring at the beach gods on skateboards: buff young men who were clearly no strangers to workouts. Her gaze alternated between them and the girls. It was a feast for anybody who appreciated the human body.

At the edge of the boardwalk were fortune-tellers of all types, musicians, crafts vendors, even several masseurs with portable tables. The proprietor of one of the latter was one of the most gorgeous men Tamsin had ever seen: a blond Adonis with hair curling down to his shoulders, obvious but not excessive musculature, a trim waist, a flat stomach, and a most interesting bulge in his tiny black bikini trunks.

'We're stopping here, Jamie. I want to get a massage.'

'With what? Mistress Leandra has our money.' He tugged on his leash, urging her away from the temptation.

'Of course. You're right. Silly me. I don't know what I was thinking of.'

'*I* do! Come along, then.'

They passed food stalls of every description. After their dip in the ocean, hunger was setting in. But, as Jamie had pointed out, they had no money. They'd just have to wait for Leandra.

The clothing stalls caught Tamsin's eye. Vendors were selling everything from heavy jackets and boots to beach wear.

'Look, Jamie! We'll have to come back here. I need a couple more swimsuits, and Leandra said you could buy one here too.'

Tamsin stared with more than her usual interest at the men's trunks on display. She thought of the masseur she'd just seen, and how he would look in the various styles. Meanwhile, Jamie was still staring at the swimsuits filled with live female bodies.

The beach scene was having an erotic effect on both of them. Tamsin began to feel a moisture that wasn't merely a result of her swim.

'Let's go for another dip,' Jamie surprised her by saying.

'Why? The water's too cold.'

'That's why I want to go.'

Tamsin turned away from the swimming trunks display and looked at Jamie as if seeing him for the first time. Her eyes zeroed in on his crotch, which was beginning to expand.

'Oh. I guess we'd better, then.' She led him back across the sand to the water's edge.

After about three minutes in the chilly ocean water, Jamie pronounced himself decent enough for human company again. They wandered further down the beach, looking for Leandra's film crew.

'There they are! But why are they all wearing swimsuits? I thought this was an adult movie.'

'If you hadn't been so busy playing with yourself in the car –'

Jamie blushed.

'– you'd have heard Leandra explain all that. They shoot all the outdoor scenes here, to make it realistic. They do the nude scenes in the studio, later.'

'May we go watch, do you think?'

'Perhaps. It depends largely on *your* behaviour, Jamie.'

'Mine? Why?'

'You see what happened today. You misbehaved, so I get to lead you around on a leash. In public, of all things. Leandra and I are business colleagues, and she treats me as such. We're equals, one adult to another.'

'You sure didn't look very equal last night, when she made you help her.'

'Never mind. That's different. That's something *you* wouldn't understand, Jamie. And she didn't *make* me do anything, just for the record. Anyhow, we're two equal adults. If I asked her to take me to the nude shoot, I'm sure she would. She's a civilised woman who knows how to be polite to her guests. She'd show you the same courtesy if you didn't insist on –'

'You don't get it, do you, Tamsin? You just don't get it.'

'All right. Tell me. What is it that I don't get?'

'I'm her slave, Tamsin. She has the right to treat me any way she wants to.'

'Oh.' Tamsin couldn't think of a single intelligent reply. A *slave*? How could he? He barely knew Leandra. Not that being a slave would be any better if he knew her well.

'What you don't understand is that I'm happy. This is what I've been wanting, only I didn't know it.'

'If you say so. It still seems weird to me. Anyhow, to get back to what I was saying. I could ask her to let you go to the shoot, as a favour to me. But if you behave badly, I'll be stuck with walking you around on a leash again. So I wouldn't get to go to the shoot, either. And it would be your fault. Please, just do what she tells you, all right?'

'All right. But –'

'I'm a photographer, Jamie. I want to see how the cinematographers work. It's a professional development thing for me.'

'Yeah, right. You are forced to stare at naked men only for professional reasons. Poor Tamsin. How you must suffer.'

'I enjoy it, too, all right? Of course I enjoy it. But I'll enjoy it more if I don't have to haul you around on a leash.'

'You enjoy that too, Tamsin. I can tell.'

'No way. I'm just doing Leandra a favour.'

'Have it your way, then.'

'In the meantime, shall we watch the shoot they're doing here on the beach?' She tugged on his leash and led him to where the actors were taking a break. She wasn't totally comfortable with the leash situation. It made her feel conspicuous. But surely Leandra knew what was acceptable and what wasn't.

Jamie, on the other hand, was behaving as if this were the most natural thing in the world. Sensing his ease, Tamsin relaxed. They joined the crowd of spectators. Tamsin pushed her way up to the front so she could watch the cinematographers.

Jamie pulled at the leash to get her attention. 'Did you see that, Tamsin? There's a couple like us!'

Tamsin turned just in time to glimpse the other couple. Much more obvious than Tamsin and Jamie, they had on matching black T-shirts. The woman's said 'Mistress'; the man's said 'Slave'. Nobody was paying them the slightest attention. Tamsin couldn't help feeling relieved.

When the filming resumed, Tamsin forgot about Jamie. While other onlookers were staring at the skimpy swimsuits, Tamsin had eyes only for the filming itself. She'd never seen a professional film crew work before, and she was fascinated. Jamie curled up at her feet and dozed off like an exhausted puppy.

All too soon, from Tamsin's perspective, the shoot was over. Leandra ran over to them.

'It took longer than I expected. I hope you weren't bored.' Her eyes lit on Jamie, still asleep. She nudged him with a toe. 'Stand up and greet your Mistress!'

Jamie came instantly awake and leaped to his feet.

'I'm sorry, Mistress Leandra.'

Again Tamsin marvelled at how easy this was for him.

On the long drive home, the women talked about the shoot, while Jamie napped in the back seat. Tamsin looked back to check on him, and giggled.

'At least he's not embarrassing himself this trip.'

'Let's let him rest. He's going to have a very busy night.'

'Oh? What do you have in mind, Leandra?'

Leandra smiled but didn't answer. They drove the rest of the way in companionable silence, occasionally discussing Mapplethorpe and his influence on erotic photography.

Late that evening Tamsin retired to her room to read and relax before going to bed. Jamie had been sent to his room right after dinner. Leandra was in her studio working on plans for her next day's shoot. No further reference had been made to Jamie's impending 'busy night'. Tamsin began to think she had imagined the whole thing. She browsed through an L.A. guidebook until she was drowsy enough to sleep. The next day they'd be going out to scout places for her to photograph and she wanted to be prepared.

She got sleepy sooner than she'd expected to. The ocean air was having a soothing effect on her; she was much more relaxed than she ever was at home. She lay in bed reviewing the events of the day. Now she was able to admit to herself that she *had* enjoyed walking Jamie on a leash. This confused her. Jamie was her friend and her equal. She'd waited patiently for years for him to make a sexual advance. Some deep corner of her brain persisted in telling her that the man should make the first move. She didn't believe this on an intellectual level, of course. In fact, she'd have scoffed at anybody who had dared to suggest such a thing. But in the privacy of her own bed, with the lights out so she didn't have to see herself in a mirror, she had to admit it was true. Emotionally, she *did* believe it.

That's why she was so confused about Jamie's behaviour and her own reactions to it. Jamie was a man: he wasn't supposed to sit back and let a woman tie him up. Somehow the fact that he liked it made it even more incomprehensible to her.

And she herself? She had *liked* having him on that leash. Yes, she had. Furthermore, she wanted to do it again. Leandra seemed comfortable with all this, but of course she was an American. That explained it. Americans were a different breed. Tamsin was a well brought up British girl who had learned – and then laughed at the idea – that young ladies let the man make the decisions. Not professionally, of course. In the workplace it was a matter of who did the best job, not the gender of the doer. Or so Tamsin liked to think. But in bed, her brain told her, it was still a man's world.

Yet everything she'd seen in the two days she'd been in L.A. showed her that it wasn't true. Leandra ruled in her own bedroom, for sure. And Jamie liked it. Did all men like to be whipped? What about Leandra's partner, Nigel? That was his name, she remembered. What about him? Did Leandra whip him, too? And would she, Tamsin, ever get to meet him?

She started exploring her feelings about leading Jamie on a leash, then found herself becoming excited. She thought about how meek, how abject, he'd been. It was all a game, she told herself. He was physically stronger than she was. She didn't have any real power over him, only the power he chose to give her.

She didn't like this train of thought. Resolutely, she changed the film that was playing in her head. Instead of Jamie, it was the gardener. He was wearing a collar and she was holding the leash, preceding him to the spa.

Her fingers were flying on her clit. Before her fantasy developed into an orgasm, though, a shriek interrupted it.

'No, Mistress! No!' The second 'no' became a drawn-out howl. '*Please*, Mistress!'

Tamsin jumped out of bed. Not bothering with her robe, she ran naked down the hall to Jamie's room. On her way she heard the crack of a whip and another howl. She stopped at Jamie's open door, stunned by what she saw.

Jamie was face down on the bed. All four of his limbs were spread-eagled, chained to the bedposts with hand-cuffs. His cock was visible below the vee of his crotch, stiffening and trying to crawl up his belly. Its path was impeded by the pressing of his groin against the sheet. He couldn't raise up enough to allow for his cock's natural ascent.

Leandra was dressed in crotchless leather pants and a long-sleeved leather jacket that was moulded tightly to her figure. Her ample breasts jutted out where she had undone two of the jacket buttons. She was holding a whip, one that Tamsin hadn't seen before. It was made of several thongs, each one knotted at one end and plaited together at the other. As Tamsin watched, Leandra lifted her arm and applied a blow to Jamie's bare bum. He screamed again.

'Do you want me to stop?' Leandra asked.

'No, Mistress, no,' he sobbed.

'"No", what?'

'No, don't stop, Mistress. Please don't stop.'

'This is what you want?'

'Yes, Mistress.'

'Very well.' She turned to Tamsin, whose hand had resumed the activity that Jamie's scream had interrupted. 'I always make sure it's consensual, you see.' She laid another stroke on Jamie's bum. 'Tamsin, quit playing with yourself. I don't want you to come yet.'

Automatically Tamsin obeyed. It was as if Leandra had taken charge of her hand, and that she couldn't do anything unless Leandra willed it. Mesmerised, she watched as Leandra dealt Jamie two more blows in rapid succession.

This time Jamie didn't scream. Leandra checked and found that his eyes were closed.

'Damn. He passed out. Tamsin, get me some ice from the bucket over there.'

When Leandra put the ice on the back of his neck, Jamie shuddered and opened his eyes. He moaned.

'I'm going to let him rest for a while.' Leandra addressed Tamsin, as if Jamie couldn't hear a word. 'He can be thinking about how it will feel when I start whipping him again. While he's resting, I have something to show you.'

She took Tamsin's hand, ignoring the stickiness of her fingers, and led her to the other side of the king-sized bed. 'Look.' She held up a slender plastic tube that was slightly curved at one end. 'This is a special vibrator. It will get your G-spot. Want to try it?'

When Tamsin nodded, Leandra continued. 'Lie down so your cunt is at the head of the bed and your head is at the foot. That way Jamie can watch, too.' She slathered the vibrator with lube and also lubed Tamsin before she could protest that she didn't need it. Then she positioned the vibrator at Tamsin's opening and slid it in.

It went in easily. Tamsin had been wet for a long time. She accepted it eagerly. It felt different from the vibrator Marcus had used on her, which was the only experience with one that she'd had. This one pressed upward at an angle, as if trying to thrust through her vaginal wall. She felt herself lubricating more heavily in response.

Leandra switched the vibrator on. As Tamsin felt it pulsate all the way up her tunnel, she became more and more aroused. Leandra was moving the vibrator inside her, gently massaging her with it.

It hit a spot deep inside her that she didn't know she had. She began spasming uncontrollably, sobbing with ecstasy at the same time. Then she felt a tremendous gush of fluid soak her thighs and leak down under her to flood her bum. She spread her legs to expel another gush while she frantically fingered her clit.

The spasms continued longer than any orgasm she'd ever had. When they finally died down she was exhausted. She just wanted to lie there on the soggy sheet and go to sleep. She was too tired to think that this wasn't her usual reaction to a good come. She could barely make sense out of Leandra's words.

'– an ejaculator, Tamsin! That's wonderful! Many of us women never get a chance to know that about ourselves, since it never occurs to us to touch our own G-spots. But you ... that was the most beautiful come I've ever seen.'

She bent over and cradled Tamsin in her arms. Tamsin snuggled against her, inhaling the heady scent of her leather jacket as well as the distinct smell of sex – Leandra's, not her own. So Leandra had got all hot just watching her come. Now Tamsin was reviving enough to help her friend, the way her friend had helped her.

'Do you want me to ...?'

'Not now. I've got unfinished business with Jamie.'

Oh, yes. Jamie. Tamsin had – understandably – forgotten about him. Now she became aware that he was struggling and moaning on the bed a scant few inches from her. He had turned his head so he was facing her. He must have seen the whole thing, including her ejaculations and spasms. No wonder he was clamouring for attention now.

She rose up on one elbow and smiled at him. Leandra had picked up her whip and was ready to go again. Tamsin looked at Jamie's bright red bum. She could tell that he would have a hard time sitting down for a few days. However, he looked happy in spite of his obvious pain. His tool was even harder than it had been before. It was still stretched out below his crotch, trying to raise itself up. She hoped Leandra would let him have his release.

Leandra's hand lowered for the first blow. Jamie groaned. His dick bobbed and twitched. Then Tamsin had an idea. She went around the bed and whispered in Leandra's ear. Leandra nodded and brought the whip down for a second blow.

It didn't look as if Jamie would last much longer. He looked as if he was ready to explode. It was time for Tamsin to make her move.

Leandra hit him a third time. Tamsin climbed up on the foot of the bed and crawled between his legs. She lowered her face to his penis then gently took it into her mouth. While she ran her tongue up it and licked his balls, Leandra lay down the fourth and final blow.

Jamie cried out in joy while his balls exploded. Semen shot into Tamsin's mouth. She tried to swallow it as fast as it came, but some escaped and ran down her chin. When it was over, she helped Leandra free Jamie. He started to get up but Leandra stopped him.

'I haven't had my pleasure yet, you selfish boy,' she said. She jumped up on the bed and positioned her pussy where he could reach it by turning his face to the side.

He needed no instruction. He ate her out through her crotchless leathers while Tamsin watched and played with herself.

Leandra came within a few seconds. She had been on the verge of coming anyhow, without any help from them. Now sated, all three of them went to their separate beds.

9

The next couple of days were more work than play. Leandra drove Tamsin all over L.A. and the surrounding area, while Tamsin made notes of the places she wanted to return to and photograph. The second afternoon she did finally get started. Leandra took her to the Echo Park area, at her request. She also helped Tamsin carry her equipment and set it up. Then she got out of the way while Tamsin lost herself in her photography. While Leandra sat on a bench and read, Tamsin got some passers-by to volunteer for portraits: anyone who looked interesting, and as if they'd lived a little. She was looking for style and irony, like a modern-day Diane Arbus, always with an eye for the curious among the everyday.

Finally she checked with Leandra. 'You aren't expecting all architecture, are you? I hope not. This area is wonderful for characters.'

'No, of course not. People, places, ducks, buildings, nature – whatever interests you. That's what's so much fun about this project. Everybody has a different idea.'

'It's too bad Jamie is incapacitated, Leandra. I hated to ask you to help me carry all this equipment. But poor Jamie can't even sit in a car right now, much less carry things.'

'Yes, I know,' Leandra said ruefully. 'Helping you is the least I can do, since I inadvertently deprived you of your assistant.'

'Are you ready to go back? The light is getting too dim for any more work.'

'Sure. Let's go.'

* * *

'I got a little carried away,' Leandra had confessed to Nigel. 'I didn't intend him to have to eat his meals standing up. But he was so good. He took it all and didn't want me to stop. That boy is a real find.'

'Yes, but be careful, love,' Nigel had said. 'Sometimes novices don't know their limitations. I know you'd hate to see him seriously injured.'

'Yes, I would. But I'm getting punished right along with him. Since he can't sit or lie on his back, the only thing he's capable of is missionary position. And you know how I hate that.'

Nigel's raucous laughter drowned out her final words.

'Be quiet, you beast!'

'I can't help it,' Nigel managed to say between snorts of mirth. 'I well remember being rash enough to suggest that to you once, back in our early days. That time it was me who couldn't sit down for a week afterwards. I learned not to come up with foolish ideas.'

The next day Leandra and Tamsin returned early from their L.A. exploration. Jamie was seated gingerly on a pile of soft cushions watching one of Leandra's adult movies. He was naked except for a T-shirt and a dog collar around his neck. The T-shirt was cut off short so it wouldn't brush against his fiery bum. Thus it was obvious that his penis was rising to greet them.

'What a polite cock you have,' Leandra said. 'It stands up when ladies enter the room. It has more manners than its owner.'

'I'm sorry, Mistress Leandra. I'd rise to greet you, of course. But I move so slowly that I can't behave like a gentleman.'

'You're forgiven this time. Just remember, though, that when you're healed from your beating I'll expect you to show the proper respect.'

'Yes, Mistress.'

'I have an idea,' Leandra continued as if he hadn't spoken. 'Why don't we get hold of the woman you met on the plane – Vanessa, isn't it? Since our games are severely limited until Jamie recovers, maybe Vanessa could come over and offer us some diversion.'

She turned to Jamie, who blushed with pleasure at being the focus of his beloved Mistress's attention.

'Go to your room and get the phone number. Then come back here instantly.'

'Yes, Mistress.' He was gone.

'I'm curious, Leandra,' Tamsin said. 'The first day we were here you told Jamie he couldn't leave his room unless he was decently dressed. Today he's going about the house naked from the waist down, and you haven't reprimanded him. Why is that?'

'It's because I don't want to be cruel. He can't wear clothes right now; it would be agony for him. And I don't want to confine him to his room. So I'm letting him run around like that until he heals. I've applied some soothing unguent to his little butt so it shouldn't take too long.' She smiled to herself.

Jamie returned with the phone number. He hadn't dared to tell Leandra that it was unnecessary, that he'd memorised it the minute Vanessa had given it to him. Now he made a pretence of reading the slip of paper as he punched in the number.

When the phone rang, Vanessa was involved in an unplanned dalliance with a repairman. Her air conditioning didn't work, and she had called the front desk to report it. The motel had immediately sent up an engineer right out of her California wet dreams. He looked as if he spent all his spare time on a surfboard – which he probably did. His hair was bleached almost white by the sun, and his blue eyes sparkled at her above his wide grin. Unfortunately his baggy trousers refused to reveal what Vanessa most wanted to know. He left the door of the room open, to her chagrin.

'Why don't you close the door? It will be cooler in here.'

'But, ma'am, you reported that your air conditioner wasn't working. Closing the door would make the room hotter.'

'So it would. Silly me. Close it, anyway. I don't want people in the corridor looking in here.' Vanessa wanted to bite her tongue off. That wasn't how she'd meant it at all. She didn't want to give him the idea that she had any other agenda besides the air conditioner. To distract him, she said, 'You're British! What a surprise. What on earth are you doing here, working in this motel?'

His grin spread even wider. He seemed to have understood her meaning all too well. He closed the door and turned to face her.

'First the air conditioning, I think, ma'am. We want the room to be comfortable. Besides, I have a work order here that I need to fill. I don't want you calling back later to say it wasn't done properly. As for your question, I'm just here for the summer, helping my friend who owns this place. It gives me a great opportunity to surf as well as keep up with my dancing.'

His voice was so sexy that Vanessa felt herself getting moist. She wondered what was the matter with her. The man was simply talking about the job, but just listening to him made her want to tear his clothes off and throw him on the bed.

He busied himself doing mysterious manoeuvres with his tools, while Vanessa watched, enchanted. Competence in anybody, male or female, turned her on. She tried not to breathe faster.

After a minute or so, she heard the welcome roar of the air conditioner. The engineer packed up his toolbox.

'That's it. It was only a fuse.' He picked up the box and moved towards the door.

'Wait! I –' Vanessa stumbled over her words, a most unusual situation for her. Usually she radiated self-confidence. She *had* to keep this man in her room, even for only a few more minutes. If she didn't have him, she'd die. She tried again.

'Please, come over to the bed.'

The man looked puzzled.

'I mean, the lamp by the bed needs checking. It . . . uh . . . flickers when I turn it on.' Flustered, she gestured towards the light.

'All right. I'll have a look.'

It was all Vanessa could do to restrain herself from tripping him so he'd fall on the bed where she could devour him. That might be too aggressive, though, even for her.

'I don't see anything wrong with the lamp, ma'am. However, I'll take it with me and come right back with a new one.'

This was better than Vanessa had dared to hope for. When he had left, she had an idea. She quickly changed into a tight, sleeveless black minidress. She made sure the back zipper was undone before she opened the door to him again.

'I'm so glad you're back. I really need a favour. My zipper seems to be stuck. Could you possibly . . .?'

'Sure, ma'am. No problem.' He reached for her, just as she bent to retrieve a lip gloss she'd had the foresight to drop. She twisted around as she bent, giving him a carefully planned view of her gold thong. She heard him gasp. Prolonging the effect, she slowly rose to her full height and tugged her minidress back down to cover her crotch. She smiled at him.

'The zipper, please?'

'Oh . . . sure.' He placed one hand on the curve of her

bum and pulled at the zipper with the other. It didn't budge, which surprised Vanessa. This wasn't part of the plan. She recovered quickly.

'Don't keep jerking it. You'll tear the material. Here, help me off with it. I'll have to wear something else.'

The man blushed but did as he was told. He wrestled the tight skirt up as far as her waist, while she wriggled to make it easier for him. From the waist on up it was easy going. He pulled the dress over her head and let it drop to the floor. Vanessa stood tall and proud, clad only in the gold thong. The man blushed again and averted his gaze.

'Come on, don't be shy. I'm a model. I'm used to being like this in front of men. Look at me. Do you like what you see?'

Speechless, the man nodded.

Vanessa had never been a model. But she'd discovered that when she told new acquaintances that she was a professional dominatrix it tended to be a conversation stopper. This seemed to be a harmless adventure; why complicate things? She was merely making it easier for a rather shy young man who was obviously attracted to her.

Vanessa moved closer and wrapped her arms around him. 'Hold me. I'm cold. The air conditioner is working too well now.'

As if in a trance, the man put his arms around her and pressed her to him. Now Vanessa could feel what his baggy work pants hid from her sight. He was at half mast but rising. She knew her instinct had been right.

She ground her thong into his crotch, feeling him stiffen as she did so. Now she couldn't wait to see what he had to offer her. She reached for his belt and fumbled with the buckle. He didn't protest.

His hardness was making her wild. The belt buckle finally yielded to her frantic hands. Unwilling to wait another second, she put a hand into his trousers pocket and felt for his engorged cock. By now it was sticking straight up, peeking out of the top of his waistband.

She pulled his zipper down and put her hand inside his flies. Changing her mind, she unbuttoned the waistband button and let his trousers drop. She tugged his boxer shorts down after them.

She was greeted by a stunning erection. This man had plenty of what she wanted. She moved closer to him and mashed her thong-clad crotch into his erection, teasing her clit through the flimsy material. On impulse she sprang up and wrapped her legs around his waist, letting his cock rub against her whole sex.

He had had enough teasing. He ripped at her thong, tearing it in his haste. She didn't notice. The waistband fell away, leaving the thong clinging to her. He jerked it away and threw it on the floor. He spoke for the first time.

'The bed. Let's get on the bed.' He started to carry her the few steps to the bed but tripped on his trousers and nearly fell headlong. Though stumbling, he prevented himself from falling on top of her. He made it to the bed before losing his balance entirely. Vanessa landed on the bed, legs splayed, while he landed on his knees in front of her.

His face was just a short distance from her pussy. Seizing the opportunity, she wriggled towards him so that her feet were on the floor and her sex was in his face.

He didn't have much choice. Instinctively he began nibbling and sucking between her legs. She was lubricating copiously by this time. He took her clit between his lips and circled it with his tongue. She ground herself as hard as she could into his face. Within seconds she was exploding into an orgasm.

The man pushed her back on the bed and climbed up,

straddling her. He fitted his cock into her opening and entered her while she was still coming. Pushing in until his balls met her soaked pubic hair, he met her thrusts with his own. Very quickly he too was crying out in ecstasy.

'More!' she yelled as he let loose another load of jizz. 'Give me more!'

He obligingly pumped another load into her. She continued to orgasm, while her juices puddled on the bed beneath them. She moaned and sobbed and clawed at his back.

Finally she was spent. The whole process, from the moment she had started unbuckling his belt until now, had taken less than ten minutes. She smiled up at him.

'Thanks. I needed that. I hadn't had a man in three days.'

'My pleasure,' the man replied with mock formality. 'I'm always delighted to help a lady in distress.'

'You're just what I needed. Sometimes I need to have it hard and fast. You're *good*, stranger. I'll write a letter of appreciation to the motel.'

'No, *don't*!' He looked alarmed. 'My friend would sack me, and then how would I ever get back to London?'

'I mean about your abilities as an air-conditioner repairman. Maybe they'll give you a bonus.'

Just then the phone rang. It was Jamie.

'Would you like to come over and visit us?' he said. 'I can guarantee that you won't be bored.'

'I'd love to. Give me the address and I'm on my way.'

She took a quick shower while the hotel engineer dressed and left the room. In just a few minutes she was in a taxi on her way to Leandra's house.

'Good grief, Jamie! Where are your trousers?' Vanessa hadn't expected him to greet her naked from the waist down. This shy boy was learning fast, it seemed. Then she noticed his blush.

'I ... I can't wear clothes right now. Mistress Leandra punished me, and I can't stand anything touching my bum right now.'

'I see.' Vanessa was carefully noncommittal. He had said she wouldn't be bored. He had been right. But ... *Mistress* Leandra? This situation promised to be very interesting indeed.

They adjourned to the patio, where Leandra brought tea and biscuits for Vanessa, Tamsin and herself. The women sat at the table. Jamie squatted at Leandra's feet, occasionally accepting a morsel of biscuit that she condescended to feed to him. Leandra poured some tea into an antique china bowl, which she placed on the floor in front of Jamie.

'Be careful, Jamie. You know what will happen if you break that bowl. It belonged to my great-grandmother, and it's irreplaceable.'

Jamie carefully lapped his tea from the bowl while the women chatted. Vanessa sought to bring Jamie into the conversation.

'And you, Jamie, are you enjoying L.A.?'

Jamie looked up at Leandra but didn't speak.

'Our guest asked you a question, Jamie. You have my permission to answer her.'

Jamie muttered a reply. Vanessa was impressed at seeing how well Leandra had trained him in such a short time. Vanessa had sensed his possibilities on the plane, but she had had no time to develop them. Something about him attracted her strongly. Even though she made her living providing services for submissive men, she knew that a man like Jamie would never call her for that purpose. He was simply too passive to do so. Fascinating.

It was obvious to Vanessa that Tamsin had told

Leandra all about what had happened on the plane, for Leandra was openly caressing Tamsin in front of her. Perhaps Leandra behaved like that with everybody, but Vanessa didn't think so. She noticed that Tamsin didn't initiate any of the caresses herself. Yet she didn't have slave status, as Jamie did. Perhaps she was just inexperienced. Yes, that was the explanation. She remembered how Tamsin had been when they all made love on the plane: inexperienced but willing to learn.

Thinking about this was making her damp. Watching Leandra caress Tamsin wasn't helping, either. She decided to join the party.

'That beautiful pool of yours is calling to me. Any chance I could take a dip? The pool at the motel is three-quarters chlorine. Most unappetising. I've been dying for a real swim ever since I got here.'

'Sure. I've got some extra swimsuits you can try on.'

'Thanks. But why bother? I became well acquainted with both Tamsin and Jamie on the flight over here. I doubt if they'll be embarrassed if they see me starkers.'

'Then we'll strip down and join you. OK, Tamsin?'

Tamsin nodded. Jamie maintained his expression of blank innocence. He hadn't been asked his opinion. The women all stood up and shucked off their clothes. Jamie didn't move.

'Come on, Jamie. You too,' Leandra said.

Jamie hastened to obey. He tugged his T-shirt off and followed the women to the pool.

Vanessa ran up to the high diving board and executed a perfect jackknife. Leandra and Tamsin dived in from the side of the pool. Jamie climbed down the steps at the shallow end.

'That was most impressive, Vanessa. Where did you learn to dive like that?' Leandra asked.

'I was in the Olympic trials when I was at university. I didn't make the final cut, though.'

'You could have fooled me.' Leandra took off in a fast crawl down the length of the pool. She swam well, but Vanessa quickly caught up with her. Tamsin lagged far behind. After they had swum a few laps Vanessa noticed that Jamie wasn't with them. She looked around and saw him still crouched in the shallow end. She called to him to join them.

'I can't swim!' he yelled back.

'Oh yes you can! Or rather, you will. We're going to teach you right now.'

All three women converged on him. He cowered as they approached. Vanessa reached out her hand. He shrank back even further.

'No! Please. I'm afraid.'

'Nothing is going to happen to you,' Leandra said. 'Vanessa is an expert swimmer. She won't let you drown. Come with us now.'

'Yes, Mistress Leandra.' He stood up and walked towards them.

Vanessa was amazed at how quickly he obeyed. Leandra was able to get him to do things that frightened him. Yet with her, Vanessa, and presumably with Tamsin, he showed that he had a mind of his own. This would have to stop. She must train him to obey her, too.

When the water was up to his neck, Jamie balked. Leandra ordered him to continue, but still he didn't budge. Leandra flushed with anger.

'Go into deeper water this instant, Jamie. You're being so silly. I won't tolerate it.'

'I'm sorry, Mistress Leandra, but I just can't.'

'You're ruining our swim. Do as I say. Now.'

'Mistress, I want to obey you. Ask me anything but this, and I'll do it.'

Leandra turned away, frowning. Vanessa seized her opportunity. She grabbed a floating cushion from the side of the pool, threw it in the water, and climbed up on it.

'See, Jamie, this floats. There's no way you can sink while you're holding onto it. You and I will go back to the shallow water so you can try it out. Then, when you feel better about it, we'll join Leandra and Tamsin back here.' She took his hand and led him back to where the water was waist high.

Jamie was a different person in shallow water. Vanessa marvelled at how eagerly he accepted direction from her. Within minutes she had him floating on the cushion, propelling it with his arms. She noticed that it didn't cover him below the waist. This would be useful information when they returned to the deep end of the pool.

When he seemed confident of his ability to stay on the cushion, she towed him to the side of the pool, where he could grab on if he panicked. Then they headed for deeper water.

Leandra's face registered both anger and astonishment. Vanessa knew she needed to smooth this over and let her save face. After all, Leandra's slave had defied her and obeyed Vanessa instead.

'He wouldn't obey you because he's terrified of the water,' Vanessa explained. 'I've been a swimming teacher. I know how to deal with fear.'

Leandra's face relaxed. Vanessa knew she had hit exactly the right note.

'I'm sure he'll be a good boy now, if you let him keep the cushion. Won't you, Jamie?'

'Yes, Mistress. I'm sorry, Mistress Leandra. Please let me keep the cushion.'

'Very well,' Leandra agreed. 'I'll still have to punish you for disobeying me, though.'

'Yes, Mistress Leandra.'

Vanessa towed Jamie around the deeper end of the pool until she could see that he felt comfortable. Then she motioned for the others to join her. She had Jamie straighten up in the water, still holding the cushion. Leandra and Tamsin each supported one of his arms.

'Now, your reward for being such a brave boy.' Vanessa dived in the direction of his crotch where he was sprouting a beautiful erection. She aimed her mouth right at it, but he pulled away. Vanessa popped her head out of the water.

'What's wrong, Jamie?'

'I can't do anything with another woman, unless Mistress Leandra gives me permission.'

Of course. Vanessa had forgotten how much of a slave he had become. She looked questioningly at Leandra.

'Sure. Go ahead. Play with him for a while, if you like.'

This time Jamie didn't pull away when Vanessa took his cock into her mouth. She lapped at him gently, swirling the pool water around in her mouth and over his cock. She felt it growing bigger as she teased him. After a minute she had to come up for air.

'I'm out of shape. I used to be able to hold my breath for two minutes.' She took a big gulp of air and submerged again. Leandra and Tamsin began to get into the spirit of what was going on. Tamsin trailed her fingers into the cleavage of his buttocks, causing him to thrust further into Vanessa's mouth. Leandra ignored Jamie and headed straight for Vanessa's breasts.

By the time Vanessa and Leandra came up for air, Tamsin had wrapped her arms around Jamie's chest and was rubbing herself against his bum. Vanessa towed them over to the side and placed Jamie's feet on the steps. She took the cushion away from him and guided his hands to the edge of the pool.

'See, you're all right. You won't go under if you hold on. Just relax.' She dived for his cock again, but was distracted by the pool mechanism that was pulsating water against her pussy. Leandra distracted her further by taking a nipple in her mouth. Vanessa hooked an arm over the edge of the pool and gave herself up to these most pleasant sensations. The circulating water was stimulating her in a way similar to – yet different from – how it felt when somebody was going down on her.

For the moment Tamsin had Jamie to herself. Still hugging his bum with her sex, she reached down and found him ready to explode.

'I forgot about your sore bum, Jamie. I'm sorry. Does it hurt a lot?'

'Terribly.' His cock leaped in her hand. 'But please don't stop.'

Vanessa had heard their conversation. The thought of Jamie's discomfort, plus what Leandra was doing to her nipple, made both of her nipples stiffen almost painfully. She tried to push her nipple further into Leandra's mouth. Leandra bit down on it. Vanessa jumped at the sudden shock, which pushed her pussy directly over the water jet.

Leandra seemed to have discovered the water jet, too. She shifted position, pressing her sex and breasts against Vanessa's. The two women ground themselves against each other, clit against clit. Vanessa felt Leandra's much larger breasts mashing into hers, their stiff nipples brushing against each other.

Vanessa's sex flooded with more than the jet of water. She thrust her tongue into Leandra's mouth and Leandra met it with her own. They wrapped their arms around each other, treading water the whole time, while they frantically sought their orgasms.

Vanessa was dimly aware of what Tamsin and Jamie

were doing. While Leandra's clit rubbed up and down hers, she listened to Tamsin talking to Jamie.

'Come on, Jamie. Come in my hand. It feels so good, rubbing my hand up and down your cock while I rub my clit against your bum. Let it spurt, Jamie. Let's come together. I'm ready. I'm waiting for you.'

'I can't, Tamsin. I don't have permission.'

'Then I shall have to force you, because I can't wait much longer. If you don't come now, I'm going to spank your bum. You know how much that would hurt.'

'But Mistress Leandra would – oh!' Jamie began to flood the pool with his come. 'I can't help it! Mistress will be so angry. But I'm coming. Now!'

With a final thrust of her clit, Tamsin cried out. Hearing this, Vanessa felt her own orgasm overcome her. Her gasps mingled with Tamsin's and Jamie's, and were joined almost immediately by Leandra's.

The fourfold orgasm lasted for quite a while. Jamie finished almost immediately, but the women went on and on.

Finally all of them were spent. Vanessa towed Jamie to the shallow end so he could climb out of the pool. They all flopped on mats by the side of the pool and collapsed, exhausted. Jamie summoned up enough energy to say, 'I like swimming lessons! When is my next one?'

Nobody responded.

Nigel found them there an hour later.

10

Tamsin blinked awake when she heard the gardener's voice.

'Wake up, sleepyheads! It's time to party!' Nigel patted Leandra's bum and smiled at Tamsin and Vanessa. 'I've already had the pleasure of meeting Tamsin. But who's your friend?'

Tamsin stared. The gardener! What on earth was he doing here? And why was he behaving so familiarly to Leandra? Unless –

She didn't have much time to ponder. Leandra was making perfunctory introductions.

'. . . and this is my partner, Nigel.'

So he wasn't the gardener after all! What must he and Leandra think of her? She'd had sex with him so eagerly. Her hostess's partner! How could she have done such a thing? On the other hand, this was a household like none she'd ever known.

Meeting his cheerful grin with one of her own, she decided to relax and take things as they were. 'I'm glad to officially meet you, Nigel. We were too busy to introduce ourselves when we met before. I didn't realise who you were, you know.'

'Yes, I remember. You seemed to think I was some sort of employee.'

'The gardener, actually.'

'You were right. I *am* the gardener. You'll never see Leandra out here pulling weeds. She's afraid of dirtying her salon-prettified nails.'

Laughing, Leandra splashed water on him.

'Beast! You know perfectly well you *love* my long nails. You love how they feel when I drag them across your back. Especially when they leave welts.'

'Hush. You'll give away all our secrets. Anyhow, what I came out here for was to remind you that George's party starts in an hour. You're all invited, of course.' Nigel turned and headed for the house.

'Come on, Vanessa. Let's go get ready,' Leandra said. She and Vanessa ran off, leaving Tamsin alone with Jamie.

'Can you stand to wear trousers, do you think? I doubt if Leandra will take you to this party with your bum hanging out,' Tamsin said. 'Apparently it's rather posh. Leandra said it may be a tad boring but one has to make the effort to socialise, especially if one is trying to make it in the art world.'

'Trousers, possibly. Underpants, unthinkable. Help me find something I can tolerate, will you? Mistress Leandra will be very angry with me if I don't go.'

Tamsin felt relieved as she helped Jamie to his feet. She'd been on the verge of feeling hurt because Leandra seemed to have abandoned them. But Jamie needed her now. How awful it would have been if she'd unthinkingly gone with Leandra and Vanessa, leaving Jamie with nobody to help him.

They went to Jamie's room. Tamsin helped him choose a pair of baggy black trousers that didn't hurt his bum too much. Still, he was uncomfortable. Tamsin had an idea.

'Wait here, Jamie. I have the perfect solution for you.' She ran to her room and returned with a black silk teddy. 'Try this on. I think it will feel softer against your skin.'

Jamie did as he was told. Tamsin was right. She could tell that the silk felt cool and comforting on his tortured flesh. Jamie strutted around the room, showing off his borrowed finery. His penis began to rise.

'Stop that, Jamie. Are we going to have a repetition of what happened on Venice Beach?'

'I can't help it. I feel so much better now. I've never felt silk against my dick. You can't imagine how stimulating it is.'

'I can *see* how stimulating it is. And you're wrong when you say I'd have no idea. It's my teddy, remember. I know what it feels like against my clit.'

Jamie's cock strained for the sky.

'Oh, Jamie, not again. You couldn't take another beating right now. If Leandra comes in here and sees you . . .'

Tamsin whacked the offending body part. It didn't help. Jamie's cock got even stiffer. Tamsin gave up.

'Here, Jamie. Put your trousers back on. Maybe your erection won't be so noticeable.' She helped him with the trousers. It was still obvious that his dick was sticking straight out. She grabbed his jacket and helped him shrug into it.

'You look all right now. But for heaven's sake keep that jacket buttoned.'

For the first time she remembered that she was naked. She had to hurry or she'd make everybody late.

Back in her room, throwing her clothes around in search of the perfect outfit, she reflected in amazement on the fact that she hadn't been embarrassed when Nigel appeared. She wondered at herself. For a woman who had always been embarrassed about sex and nudity, she was making remarkable progress. Now she could sit in the nude, chat casually with another woman's partner – one she had had sex with, outdoors at that – without even a hint of a blush.

In addition, look at how far along she and Jamie had come. Less than a month ago he'd come in his pants while dancing with her, and both of them had pretended it hadn't happened. Yet here she was, naked, having just finished dressing Jamie in one of her sexy undergarments. She certainly hadn't been brought up this way. Yet she felt no guilt; she had hurt nobody, and her life had suddenly become a lot more fun.

Tamsin was surprised to find Vanessa in Jamie's room when she stopped by to pick him up. She'd thought Vanessa was still with Leandra. Vanessa and Jamie looked comfortable together. Jamie was kneeling in front of Vanessa, helping her put on her stiletto-heeled sandals. This worried Tamsin a bit. If Jamie kept behaving like this, he was sure to continue getting erections. Leandra would not be happy.

In a flash of insight, Tamsin understood that she had done all that she could. She had warned Jamie several times. It was up to him now. If his behaviour earned him another flogging, it was his own fault. It was none of her business. She resolved to quit trying to protect him and to concentrate instead on enjoying her own evening.

The party was in full swing when they arrived. Leandra had been right. Maybe 'boring' wasn't quite the word, but 'staid' described it exactly. Dress was formal and semi-formal, for the most part. A string quartet was playing Haydn and conversation was subdued. Some people were listening to the music instead of socialising. Uniformed waiters circulated, serving champagne and bite-sized hors d'oeuvres.

Tamsin recognised a few people she had met during her stay in L.A. Relieved, since she was shy in large groups of people, she hurried over to join them. Caught up in the excitement of the evening, she didn't notice that the friends she'd arrived with were no longer there.

Then she saw him.

The first thing she noticed was his eyes. That in itself was unusual for her. His eyes were expressionless. They seemed to her to be cold, forbiddingly cold, like a melting glacier.

He lifted his hand in a discreetly beckoning gesture. No smile, no sign of welcome or recognition. He might as well have thrown a net over her, as powerless as she felt. His eyes reeled her in; she had no choice but to follow him to the door.

The elegant carpeting in the hallway muffled their footsteps. The tinkling party laughter and polite party chatter receded into the distance. She could still faintly hear the string quartet as they moved down the corridor.

He motioned her into a room. It was huge, with a canopied bed and a cheerfully crackling fire. Real wood, not gas logs. A hod full of aged, white birch logs stood at one side of the fireplace. On the other side was a black leather umbrella stand, which held several whips.

She knew this was going to be special. When the man closed and locked the door, he didn't lunge for her as other men did. Instead, he stared without speaking. She saw his eyes move from her face, downward, ever so slowly, and stop at her breasts. Her nipples hardened under his gaze. She wondered if he could tell through her silk blouse. Her nipples pushed against the lacy confines of her bra in a way that hurt but was, at the same time, oddly pleasurable. He continued his eye feast. It felt as if his laser eyes would set her blouse afire.

After what seemed an eternity to Tamsin, the man began to move. He took a step in her direction. Then another. She felt exposed and totally vulnerable, even though she was fully clothed. She couldn't move. She felt like a wild animal transfixed by light – immobile, frozen. Not frightened, though, no way, even though some of the physical signs were the same. Her heartbeat became more rapid and she had to force herself to breathe naturally. She didn't want him to see how much power she gave him. Perhaps he already knew.

Slowly he reached for her upper arms and gently touched them. Even more slowly, his hands caressed the silk of her blouse, moving to join in the centre where the buttons were. She watched the dark hairs on the back of his hands leap and dance with a life of their own.

She expected him to fumble with the buttons. Most men do. He didn't. His fingers were sure as he eased the top silk-covered button from its imprisoning buttonhole. How could he do that, be that sensitive, with those calluses on his fingertips?

Calluses? What were the calluses from? Did he work with his hands? Maybe he was some kind of artist. Perhaps a musician.

Tamsin closed her hand over his and gently felt a callus. It was rough and strangely sensual. She shivered at the thought of it brushing across her nipple.

He moved to the second button, oh so slowly. How long could this take? There were three more after this one. If he maintained this pace, she was afraid she'd come before he reached the last one. Her panties were already damp, even though nothing had happened yet. She willed him to hurry.

The third button lay in the hollow between her breasts. She shuddered as he touched it. He pulled back the upper part of the blouse, exposing her wispy black lace bra.

She thought that up to now he'd seemed in control of himself, and of her. Now a sharp hiss of breath escaped him when he saw her deeply tanned mounds peeking through her elegant bra. He reached inside her blouse and softly traced a circle around each nipple.

The effect was exquisitely painful: the calluses rubbing the lace, rubbing her nipples, which were already stiff with lust. She needed him to hurry.

He returned to her buttons. He freed the last two a little more quickly, while Tamsin barely contained her impatience.

Slowly he bent down and kissed her just below the band of her bra. His tongue gently lapped up under the bra band, roaming over the smooth, tanned flesh. Tamsin shuddered again.

He lifted his head and covered her mouth with his. He slipped the blouse off her shoulders. She strained towards him, pushing her engorged nipples into his white Egyptian-cotton evening shirt. She was wild with her urgency. Her nipples were going to explode if they didn't get some attention. She rubbed them across the exquisite material, mentally urging him to hurry.

Without abandoning the kiss, he reached behind her and unhooked her bra clasp. Her breasts sprang forth at full attention. Ah, relief! Tamsin shrugged the straps off her shoulders and her bra slid to the floor.

Her nipples were stiffer than they'd ever been. She wanted him to look. She wanted him to admire. She wanted him to worship.

Finally he lifted his head and looked. He looked again. Tamsin disengaged herself from his chest so he could see better, thrusting her nipples up as far as she could, almost into his face.

His hands came up slowly. He cupped both breasts, gazing at them intensely. He continued his exploration. His hands traced the soft mounds on top and on the sides. He circled both breasts, not touching the nipples. Tamsin felt the little bumps on her areolas becoming stiff, like miniature nipples. She knew they would be getting very dark, forming a lovely contrast to the tan on the rest of the surface.

His hands hovered over her areolas, close but not

touching. She wanted him to touch. She wanted to feel the calluses on the little joy bumps. She wanted those calluses to tweak her nipples. She wanted him to *hurry*! Everything he did was so slow, too slow. In her limited experience Tamsin had never encountered a man with such control.

He had more of it than she did. She was squirming, trying to mash her sex into his erection. Her panties were sopping by now and she wondered if the dampness could be felt through her miniskirt.

She was not to find out, though. The man's whole attention was focused on her breasts. Gently he tweaked a nipple between two of his calluses. Too gentle. Harder, please! Harder!

As if reading her mind, he grasped both nipples and pulled. Ah, that was better. He rolled his callused fingertips around her nipples. His palms brushed her areolas. A *frisson* of pleasure shot from her nipples to her clit. Her pelvis thrust forward, again seeking his erection.

While he continued to play with her right nipple, his other hand reached for the umbrella stand. His eyes didn't leave her as he chose his instrument. Tamsin didn't know what kind it was or if it had an exact name. She'd never done this before. Part of her wanted to run. Most of her was too aroused to do so.

He hefted the crop and smacked the handle into his palm. It made an ominous sound. *Thwack*. Tamsin heard it swish through the air as he tested it. There was a knot on the end of it. She smelled the leather.

His head tilted, the glacial eyes asking. She nodded almost imperceptibly.

He grabbed the waistband of her miniskirt. Tamsin wriggled and squirmed to help him ease it over her hips. It slid to her ankles and she stepped out of it. Now she was clad only in her leopard-print thong panties and black spike heels.

He pushed the crotch of her panties aside, then stuffed the end of the whip into her sex, and dragged it from her sex up to her breasts. The little knot tickled her clit. She felt the damp trail of her own love juice as he traced this path. He flicked the end of the whip against her nipple. She barely felt it, it was so light. He did it again.

This time she felt it. Her nipples instantly stiffened even more. He hit her with the whip again. She heard the swish before it landed. This time it was no gentle tap. It didn't hurt much, but it gave her a taste of what might be about to happen. Another slash. She stifled a moan, whether of pain or desire she wasn't sure.

Another. This one was right across her nipples.

Pain seared her sensitive flesh. She was aware of the knot and the way it was bruising her. Her clit swelled in response. Her nipples and her clit were on fire. She wanted him to do it again.

As if reading her mind, he brought the crop down again across both nipples. Then again. Tamsin closed her eyes against the pain. She was afraid that if she showed him she was in pain, he would stop. She thought she'd die if he stopped.

She lost track of how many times the whip landed. She was aware that he was dancing back and forth with it from her nipples to her crotch.

At first Tamsin wasn't aware that he was flogging her crotch. The pain in her nipples engulfed her. She was acutely aware of every sensation and yet could pinpoint the location of none of them.

All at once she could feel the knot of the whip as it slammed into her clit through her panties. She realised that this had been happening for some time. He was alternating strokes: one across her nipples, then one across her mound.

Tamsin willed herself to stand still, welcoming the

pain, embracing it. The more he whipped her, the more she wanted him to continue.

Nothing in the world existed outside of her pain. And her desire. Her clit was on fire. She bit her lip to keep from crying out.

She became aware that she had been moaning for some time. Her sense of urgency became more intense. She knew she was going to come before they ever made it to the bed but she no longer cared. Her orgasm was building. Soon she would have to let it happen. Very soon.

Tamsin was almost at breaking point. She wanted to feel his hardness, feel him inside her, but there was no time.

She was starting to come. She couldn't hold it back, nor did she want to. The wave began, a tsunami overwhelming her clit.

Then she peaked. Wave after wave of spasms shook her. She shuddered and sobbed.

He continued to whip her. She found herself wetting her panties a little bit.

The whipping continued. Finally Tamsin was drained.

As if the man understood this, he lowered his whip hand.

He smiled for the first time.

He led her to the bed.

11

Tamsin heard Leandra's voice berating Jamie as if from a distance. 'What's the meaning of this, Jamie? What on earth is that garment? If I didn't know better, I could swear it was a teddy.'

'It is, Mistress Leandra.'

'But . . . why?'

'I hurt too much to wear underpants, Mistress. Tamsin very kindly lent me this.'

'Very well. But next time you must tell me. I was so embarrassed when we were in the dun –' She glanced at Tamsin. '– I mean, basement, when I commanded you to strip. Imagine my surprise when you stripped down to this flimsy feminine garment. Worse yet, you were hard again. I've told you about that.'

'I'm sorry, Mistress. But I can't help it. The silk rubbing on my dick makes me very hot.'

At this point Tamsin tuned the conversation out entirely. What had Leandra started to say? Where had they all been while she was in the bedroom with the mysterious stranger? Never mind. Where they were was none of her business. She had enough to think about without worrying about them. Her experience with the stranger had done more than shake her up. She was totally confused now about who she was. She'd seen herself as more like Leandra than like Jamie. The idea of dominating a man made her wet every time she thought about it, which was often. She'd been wet almost constantly ever since she first witnessed Leandra punishing Jamie.

Yet tonight she had allowed herself to be whipped by a stranger. What's more, she had liked it. She hoped it would happen again. Although having no desire to take it to the lengths that Jamie had, she had to admit that the experience turned her on very much indeed. She thought she was beginning to understand Jamie a little bit.

It was different when she had let Marcus tie her up. Marcus and Gina were close friends; Tamsin knew that she was never in any danger. Part of the excitement tonight had come from the fact that she didn't know the man who was whipping her and had no idea what he'd do to her next. This situation had caused an orgasm so intense that she'd actually wet herself.

Just thinking about it now made her start to get damp. She hoped nobody was paying attention to her. She was sure they weren't. Everybody was gathered around Jamie's bed, staring at him and the unfortunate teddy. As she watched, Jamie's cock began to rise inside the flimsy material. His erection cast a shadow as it climbed up his belly. That was even more arousing to her than seeing it naked. She was more than damp now; she was downright wet.

She realised that the attention of the others was focused on Jamie. She'd just die if they saw her, but there seemed to be no danger. Thinking about her evening and watching the shadow of Jamie's cock at the same time made her want to play with herself right here, right now. She had to have relief. She couldn't help it. She pulled up her miniskirt with a tentative finger, knowing that her soggy thong was exposed if anybody should look. Sliding her finger under the thong, she rubbed her finger along her stiff clit, squeezing her legs together. Her breathing became more rapid.

Gradually she became aware that a hand was roving down her bum. She heard Nigel's voice.

'Want some help?' Without waiting for an answer he insinuated his hand between her thighs. Her moisture made it easy for him to slip in. His fingers massaged the back of her sex. She felt herself ooze all over his hand. At first she was embarrassed. Then, as the gentle massage continued, she didn't care.

'What's got you so turned on?' Nigel whispered. 'I don't think it's Jamie's teddy.'

'At the party there was a man.' Tamsin decided to tell him the whole story. Maybe he could help her sort out her feelings.

While she talked, Nigel's massaging fingers became more insistent. Moisture was creeping down her thighs. She found she was so aroused that she couldn't finish her story. About halfway through it she gave up on trying to talk, and took Nigel's free hand and placed it on her crotch on top of her own. He pressed down on top of her hand and began a slow, circular motion. Tamsin's clit throbbed and stiffened even more. She squirmed, leaning back into his rigidity.

While she was masturbating against both of Nigel's hands, she listened to Leandra and Vanessa berating Jamie about his teddy. The shadow under the material was growing bigger, which made Tamsin hotter. She wished someone would take her as the stranger had at the party. Reliving that, she felt close to the edge.

All of a sudden Jamie exploded. His cock leaped forward, thrusting into the flimsy material of the teddy. With a loud groan he spewed his come into the teddy, again and again. Some of it stuck to the silk; some leaked out of the loose legs of the garment and dribbled down his thigh. Tamsin stared at the sopping material. Her favourite fantasy had just come to life. Although Jamie hadn't technically come in his pants, this was close enough for her.

It was also the final straw. With a loud gasp she

convulsed in orgasm. She shoved a finger into her opening as far as it would go, sobbing as she felt the contractions gripping her finger. Nigel slipped a finger in beside hers. He pulled her thong aside at the back and lubricated her with the juice from her sex. When she was thoroughly wet, he aimed his cock at her back opening. It slid right in. The tight sphincter ring gave, allowing him full access.

Tamsin's orgasm intensified as she felt the pressure of his cock and realised what he was doing. She looked at Jamie again as he stood there in his wilted teddy, oozing all over the bed. Leandra got out her whip, and Tamsin moaned in ecstasy. She pulled her finger out of her sex and grabbed Nigel's bum with both hands. She pushed him further into her while grinding herself back into his crotch, trying to capture his cock.

Her efforts made Nigel cry out. He flooded her with a jet of semen. Then he let loose another blast.

Tamsin was dimly aware that Leandra and Vanessa were staring at her. Normally this would embarrass her half to death. Right now she didn't care. She knew that they could see the juice glistening on her thighs. This, too, didn't bother her. In fact she was rather proud of the way she was turning them on.

She spread her legs further apart so Nigel could play with the entire area. She hoped he would understand what she wanted without her having to spell it out. She'd never been able to talk to a man about sex. It didn't seem ladylike. In the past she'd experienced a lot of frustration because she'd left everything up to the man. Most of the time the man couldn't – or wouldn't – read her mind.

This time, though, she got lucky. As she exposed more of herself, Nigel spread his hand, cupping her whole crotch. His thumb circled her clit. Then he pinched it between his thumb and forefinger, initiating another orgasm.

Tamsin cried out again. She moaned and sobbed while the contractions built up and exploded. She felt Nigel still hard inside her, even though he'd just come. He began to thrust again and his fingers moved faster on her clit.

Tamsin continued to watch the drama being played out around Jamie. He was now kneeling on the floor in front of Leandra.

'Suck them! Every one of them!' Leandra indicated her bare toes.

Jamie lowered his head and began his task. His cock began to rise. Leandra didn't miss it.

'Look at you! You're getting hard again.'

Jamie didn't answer. In vain he tried to cover his offending cock with the hand that wasn't supporting Leandra's foot. The harder he tried, the stiffer his cock got.

Tamsin saw what Leandra apparently didn't: Vanessa was crawling under Leandra's thigh towards her exposed pussy. Leandra gave a startled jerk when Vanessa's mouth clamped onto her clit. Tamsin felt hot again as she watched the scene in front of her. The visual effect, plus the stimulus of Nigel's manipulations, pushed her close to the edge once again. A male voice mingled with hers as Jamie cried out. Then came Leandra's voice. Then Vanessa's. Finally Nigel made it a vocal quintet. Tamsin was no longer thinking. She could only smell the sex that permeated the room and listen to the ecstatic voices. Finally she collapsed back against Nigel and knew no more.

When she came to, she was lying on her back on a bed. Someone – perhaps everyone – had stripped her clothes off. She was totally naked. She stretched luxuriously, enjoying the feel of the satin sheets on her bare skin. As she became more aware, she felt an itch on her thigh. Moving to scratch it, she discovered that her hands were tied to the bedpost.

The itch turned into a tickle. She tried to see the spot, but the swell of her breasts blocked her view. All she could see was a hand holding the quill end of a feather. Turning her head, she saw that she was on the other bed in Jamie's room.

She opened her mouth to speak and found that she couldn't. Her mouth was gagged with what felt like a silk scarf. Experimentally, she tried to move her legs. It was no use. For the first time she realised that she was helpless.

Leandra appeared in her field of vision, holding a large piece of black leather. 'We wanted to wait until you were awake before putting on the hood. We didn't want you to be frightened. If you indicate "no", we won't use it. If you accept the hood, nod. I assure you you'll be able to breathe inside it, but you won't hear much. And of course, you won't be able to see.'

Tamsin was nodding vigorously long before Leandra finished her speech. She'd be helpless, at the mercy of four other people. Perhaps even more. She couldn't tell how many people were at the foot of the bed. She wanted to experience this, but she hoped they wouldn't whip her.

As if reading her mind, Leandra said, 'Don't worry, We aren't going to hurt you. I promise that everything we do will feel good.'

Tamsin could only nod in response. She'd seen some of the whippings, and she wanted no part of it. Unless, of course, she could be the one wielding the whip.

Leandra slipped the hood over Tamsin's head. While

Tamsin was revelling in the scent of fine leather, Leandra tightened the various straps on the hood. If Leandra said anything else, Tamsin didn't know it. Her hearing was effectively cut off. 'Won't hear much', indeed. She couldn't hear anything at all. Now she was completely at the mercy of the others.

She didn't understand why she was afraid of being whipped. After all, she had experienced the lash this very evening, and it had given her intense orgasms. Maybe it was the fact that there were at least four people here, three of whom were known to be experienced floggers. She'd watched Leandra in action. It scared her. It intrigued her. It made her sex wet. The one thing it hadn't done was to leave her with a desire to be at the business end of Leandra's whip.

If Leandra, Nigel and Vanessa took it into their heads to whip her, there was nothing she could do about it. She couldn't hear them, she couldn't see them, and she couldn't talk to them. She probably couldn't smell them, either, since the aroma of the leather hood obliterated all other smells. However, Leandra had assured her that they wouldn't hurt her. And she knew that the violence between Leandra and Jamie – violence that frightened her in its rawness, yet excited her so much that she had to masturbate – happened only because Jamie wanted it. Begged for it, in fact. So she felt quite safe and only a little apprehensive. How would she let them know if what they were doing wasn't all right for her? She wouldn't. She couldn't. She would just have to trust.

Although she didn't know what they were doing or saying, she was very aware of her own sensations. She could feel that the situation was making her wet. She wondered how she knew she was wet. She couldn't put her legs together to feel the slickness ooze between her thighs. No finger was sliding up and down her clit. She felt no damp clothing rubbing against her sex. Most of all, she couldn't measure her wetness against another person's sex pressing into hers.

Ah! There it was. She felt moisture trickling down to her bum. It oozed into her crack like oil lubricating a machine. Or like a soothing massage oil. But this wasn't exactly soothing. In fact she felt extremely aroused.

Nobody had touched her yet. She felt more fluid ooze down to her bum. Was it fluid that her sex was producing, or was it massage oil or some other lube? She had no way of telling. She thought about how helpless she was, how completely at the mercy of others. These thoughts made her sex tingle. She wished one of the others would do something. Anything.

Somebody put a mouth to one nipple, while some satin/silk was rubbing on the other. She felt a tongue begin to lick her rigid nipple, circling the areola, faster and faster. Then the satin/silk was replaced by a mouth. Somebody else's. Another tongue lapped at her navel. Down further, please go down further, she silently urged.

The tongue stayed at her navel. Somebody else's mouth clamped onto her sex. This person was gently licking her clit, licking up all the moisture that she had produced. Tamsin tried to thrust her clit into the person's mouth. She found that she couldn't move at all, so short were her bonds.

Four people were accounted for, she thought. Two at her nipples, one at her navel, one at –

For a moment she felt nothing at her breasts. Then came the unmistakable feel of nipple clamps. Two of them. She knew what they were from watching Leandra and Jamie. She cried out with the pain, even though she knew she couldn't be heard. The lovers at her navel and her clit licked faster.

She felt another area of pleasure being explored. Her toes. Nobody had ever done this to her before.

The pain in her nipples dissolved into ecstasy. She forgot that she was helpless. She no longer felt isolated. She gave herself over to sensation.

Whoever was working on her toes moved up her legs to her inner thighs, nibbling all the way to her sex. Now Tamsin could tell that her thighs were soaked, from the way her lover's cheeks felt sliding up them.

There were now three people making love to her crotch. She couldn't tell where one ended and another began. She was aware, however, that somebody was masturbating. There was rapid finger movement against her thigh. Masturbation was the only thing it could be. Male or female? She pondered that for a moment, then realised it must be one of the women. A man would be moving up and down on himself; this was a circular motion all in one place. The thought that she was making someone masturbate, no matter how passive her part in it, aroused her even further.

She felt something brush across her pubes, so lightly that at first she thought she had imagined it. It happened again. She knew it wasn't her imagination this time. She strained upward, seeking contact with whatever it was. She couldn't move, couldn't get purchase with her feet. Thinking that nobody would hear her moan, she moaned nevertheless.

It happened again. This time it moved more slowly and made better contact with her skin. Could it be velvet? Its texture was different than what she had felt before. She couldn't describe the difference. All she knew was that it was indeed different.

She felt the same texture down lower, very close to her opening. Yes, velvet. It must be. Somebody was covering her whole sex with it. Somebody's (the same person's?) fingers started playing with her through the velvety material. She knew she was oozing again because she felt another trickle go between her cheeks.

The velvet was removed, to be replaced by silk. A silk scarf, she thought. Silk moved all over her: around her clit, around her opening, up into her opening. She felt the velvet again, on her thighs this time. Somebody pinched her clit, hard, through the silk. The silk felt like a vice.

Now there was more silk, brushing across her nipples. Just when Tamsin thought she couldn't stand the delicious torment another second, a mouth came down on top of the silk and began nibbling at her nipples, which had now attained a ferocious state of rigidity. She sensed, rather than felt, facial hair on the other side of the silk. This must be Jamie or Nigel.

Someone climbed on top of her body and stretched to full length. She felt silk again. A teddy. Jamie? Must be. Then something stiff began probing her sex. Jamie again? Not very likely. They certainly wouldn't let him be the first to enter her. Nigel, then.

The bonds on her ankles loosened and someone placed a pillow under her bum. The stiff object slid down to her bum opening. Tamsin felt it probe, slick with her juices, and then she felt a buzzing sensation that she couldn't hear. Definitely not a penis, then. A dildo maybe?

The dildo probed past the tight guardian ring and filled her. The nipple clamps seemed tighter. But no, it was because her nipples were stiffer. Again she tried to thrust upward. Again she failed.

She distinctly felt the buzz of the dildo deep inside her. Her sex was flowing now along the crack and between her cheeks. Her juices oozed further under her bum and onto the pillow. Tamsin visualised soaking the fingers of whoever was holding the dildo. That made her lubricate even more. She wished she could hear, so she could experience the sucking sound of the dildo as it was guided in and out.

She felt another penis-like object at the top of her cleft. This was definitely a penis. She was surprised that she had failed to discern the difference before.

The penis slid along her clit toward her sex opening. It had no trouble attaining entrance, as she was wet and very slippery. Again she wished she could hear what was going on. She knew it couldn't last long. Her orgasm was starting to build, with an almost frightening intensity. She hoped the others would know when she came. She was going to any second now, no doubt about it.

She felt a flood inside her as the penis let loose with a gush of semen. That started her own orgasm. She thrust her sex up as best she could, her crotch grinding into that of the penis's owner as the first waves of climax engulfed her. She heard herself moaning inside the hood. When the second wave hit, there was an incredible rush of pain in her engorged nipples. Someone had removed the clamps. The pain was almost unendurable as sensation returned all at once. Then, once again, the pain turned to pleasure. It intensified her orgasm, magnifying it to the hundredth power. She cried out as the vibrator buzzed faster.

Everything was speeding up, it seemed. The dildo was vibrating at top speed. Whoever was sucking on her clit was moving faster. And there was a mouth on each nipple again.

The penis exploded again. The masturbator had given up fingering herself and was bringing herself off on Tamsin's thigh. Tamsin felt a stiff penis somewhere near her other thigh. A hand pushed it away.

Tamsin breathed in the scent of leather and once again wished she could hear and smell. But the deprivation of her other senses made her sense of touch all the more acute. Her skin was exquisitely sensitive. She was in tune with everything that was happening on the surface as well as inside her.

She felt a sudden sensation of liquid on her thigh. The other penis had shot its load. At the same time she was aware of pressure from the woman on her other thigh. The other woman was coming too. A viscous fluid trickled down Tamsin's thigh as the pressure relaxed.

She realised that there was no longer a penis inside her. She didn't know when it had disappeared. It was replaced by a new sensation; a crotch brushed against hers. Female, this time. The woman's mound rubbed against Tamsin's, lazily at first, then faster. The woman spread her legs in order to grind herself as close to Tamsin's crotch as she possibly could. Tamsin felt more fluid, but she had no idea whether it was hers or the other woman's. Perhaps it was both. She felt the other woman's sex throbbing against hers. As she cried out one more time, Tamsin knew the other woman must be moaning too.

Someone turned the vibrator off and eased it out of her. The other woman was no longer grinding on her clit. Everything seemed to have stopped. Yet Tamsin knew that nobody had left the room. With the heightened awareness brought about by sensory deprivation, she knew that the others were close to her, on or near the bed. She waited. That was her only option.

After several moments of relaxed silence, Tamsin felt a hand outside the hood, working at the straps. At the same time she felt the hand and foot bonds loosen. When one hand was free she groped for the hood, seeking to help with the straps. Before she could do so, however, the hood was pulled free. Tamsin opened her eyes and took great gulping breaths. It felt wonderful to be liberated. She enjoyed savouring the odours of sex rather than the scent of fresh leather. But she was exhausted. All she wanted was a shower and then bed – alone.

Leandra seemed to understand her mood. She said, 'Jamie, go turn on the shower. Hot, but not too hot. Come back and tell us when you're done, so Tamsin can go in.'

'Yes, Mistress.'

Tamsin gave Leandra a grateful look.

'Tamsin, you may have realised that we're testing you. So far you're doing very well indeed.'

Tamsin didn't feel much closer to understanding the things she was curious about. But she said nothing. She finally had a sense that all would be revealed in its own good time. In the meantime she was having some incredibly interesting experiences.

Right now a shower sounded like heaven. She climbed off the bed and left the room.

12

Tamsin was dozing off when she was jolted awake by the sound of Vanessa's voice. 'What I don't understand is, how did you get to the advanced age of twenty-two and remain such an innocent?'

Tamsin and Vanessa were stretched out on air mattresses by the pool, clad in the briefest of bikinis. Vanessa unhooked her bra and freed her perky breasts to enjoy the sun. 'Rub some sunscreen on my breasts while you answer me, will you?'

Tamsin picked up the lotion and began to smooth it on as Vanessa requested. Touching another woman's breasts in what was supposedly a non-sexual manner was another new experience for Tamsin. She wondered why Vanessa didn't do it for herself. After all, the bottle of lotion was closer to her. There was something ... intimate ... about what she was doing. Perversely, she found herself enjoying it.

Vanessa wriggled under Tamsin's hands. Her nipples were standing straight up.

'Well?' she asked.

'Well, what?'

'Quit gawking at my boobs and tell me how you managed to remain so innocent.'

'Oh. That.' Tamsin realised with a jolt that Vanessa was right. She *was* gawking.

'My dad died when I was a child, and he left us no money. Mum had a bit of money, which Dad frittered away. So Mum went to work, and I was left with nannies who went everywhere with me when I was young, and there were always people checking up on me, even when I was in my teens. As soon as I got my A-levels and Mum's permission I took a photography degree. I had a small bursary, but I had to work part time, too. So I didn't have much time for boys. My main focus was on learning my art and becoming self-supporting as soon as possible. Fortunately I had a talent for it.'

'But what about sex?'

'Oh, there were a couple of chaps. They were about as experienced as I was. Missionary position or nothing. Then there was Jamie, who has been my best friend for years. But we never had sex. I used to wish we would. I daydreamed about him all the time. But he was so shy.'

'He doesn't seem so now. Nor was he on the plane.'

Thinking about Jamie, combined with massaging Vanessa's breasts, made Tamsin tingle all over. She thought about how Jamie had looked when he was coming in her underwear, how he looked when he was trying to control his erections. Then she thought about Vanessa sneaking up on Leandra to lick her pussy. She felt a flood of juice in response.

Vanessa noticed. She pointedly stared at Tamsin's crotch. 'That's an interesting response to my comment.'

'What is?' Tamsin followed her friend's eyes and regarded herself with horror. 'You mean you can *see*?'

'Absolutely. Your crotch is so wet that one might think you'd peed on yourself. It looks so pretty, open and pouting and straining to escape through the material of your bikini.'

'Stop it, Vanessa!' Tamsin's face was scarlet.

'Don't tell me you're embarrassed! How could you be, after what we did to you the other night?'

'That was different. The other night I was...' She paused, groping for the right word.

Vanessa waited for a few seconds. When the completion of Tamsin's thought wasn't forthcoming, she asked, 'You mean because you were tied up? Helpless?'

Tamsin brightened. 'That's it, exactly.'

'And today you're embarrassed because you think that since you're not tied up and helpless, you should be able to control your reactions?'

'Something like that, yes.'

'My innocent friend, you have so much to learn.'

'Everybody keeps telling me that. I'm tired of it. When are you all going to start teaching me?'

'We are, Tamsin. We are already; you just don't realise it yet. But back to our present situation. You're embarrassed because this isn't a sex scene? Just two girlfriends sunning themselves by the pool? And your pussy got wet all by itself?'

'Yes. I think so.'

'Then here's your lesson for today. Never leave a wet pussy unattended.' Vanessa swooped down and buried her face between Tamsin's legs. Tamsin felt her nuzzling and licking through the soaked material of her bikini. Her pussy produced another gush.

'Ooh! That one got me right in the face! Made mine do the same thing. See?' Vanessa spread her legs, displaying her crotch to Tamsin.

It was soaked. Now Tamsin understood what Vanessa had meant when she'd described her pussy in the way she had. It did look as if Vanessa's labia were trying to escape from their cotton prison. Fascinated, she continued to stare.

'And . . .?' prompted Vanessa.

'And, what?'

'And what's your lesson for today? Never –'

'– leave a wet pussy unattended!' Tamsin finished for her. She dived for Vanessa's sex, then raised up and yanked Vanessa's bikini bottom down in one fluid motion. Diving again, she connected with Vanessa's clit and began to suck. While she sucked, Vanessa moaned.

Tamsin sucked faster. She wanted to make Vanessa come – instantly. She was suddenly fed up with all this slow sex. She wanted to come now, and she wanted Vanessa to come with her. Without moving her mouth from Vanessa's clit, she swivelled around so they were in sixty-nine position, with her on top. Spreading her legs, she placed her sex over Vanessa's mouth.

'Eat me! Now!'

As she returned to Vanessa's clit, she couldn't believe she had made that demand. She also couldn't believe that Vanessa was obeying her so meekly. But she was. Tamsin felt Vanessa's tongue moving from one crevice to another as she licked up her juices. When she was finished she returned her tongue to Tamsin's clit.

Tamsin felt her clit stiffening. She pressed her pubes down on Vanessa's mouth, trying to convey her sense of urgency. She squirmed on Vanessa's face as Vanessa continued lapping.

Groping in her backpack, which she had conveniently left by the side of her mattress, Tamsin found her small emergency vibrator. After lubricating it with Vanessa's love juice, of which she had a copious supply, Tamsin popped it into Vanessa's rear opening and pushed. Vanessa's sphincter opened to receive it. Tamsin felt a second of resistance; then it was all the way in. She turned it on.

Vanessa's pussy responded instantly. She gushed fluid all over Tamsin's mouth and chin. Tamsin lapped it up as fast as she could.

Her own clit was on fire. She writhed with lust on Vanessa's face, needing desperately to come. Her orgasm built up and then hung there. Try as she might, Tamsin couldn't come. The telltale throbbing would start; then, just as she was about to scream, it stopped. She was frantic to make it happen.

Vanessa seemed to sense what Tamsin wanted. The pace of her lapping increased. She swirled her tongue around Tamsin's clit while her hands played with her friend's nipples.

Tamsin wanted Vanessa's tongue on her bum. Perhaps even more than that. Perhaps inside, with her tongue lapping around the rim. She knew that would make her come instantly. But how could she make such a request? What if Vanessa refused? It seemed a lot to ask of a person. But the clit work wasn't doing it and Vanessa obviously wasn't reading her mind. Clearly she would have to help this situation along.

She raised her sex up off Vanessa's mouth. Squirming around a bit, she managed to position herself so that her bum was over Vanessa's face. Vanessa raised her head to resume contact with Tamsin's clit. She just wasn't getting it.

There was no way around it; Tamsin would have to tell her what she needed.

'Tongue me – back there,' she blurted. She waited for Vanessa to call her every kind of pervert. Instead, Vanessa obediently began licking further back.

Tamsin went wild when she felt a soft, slippery tongue at her back opening. She pushed down hard, hoping that Vanessa would get the message without her having to say it. The whole situation was strange to her. She'd never made demands, or even many requests, of her lovers. She passively accepted what they gave and was grateful. Now, however, she wanted Vanessa to do exactly what she, Tamsin, ordered her to do.

Fortunately she didn't have to verbalise all her needs. Vanessa began worming her way inside. Tamsin, for some perverse reason, didn't want Vanessa to know how good that made her feel. Yet she couldn't stifle a moan of bliss.

As she thought about how Vanessa had done exactly what she wanted, her orgasm exploded. Vanessa reached a finger up to rub Tamsin's clit but it wasn't necessary. Tamsin cried out with the intensity of her orgasm. She spread her legs and pushed her clit against Vanessa's chin while Vanessa continued her internal tongue massage.

The tongue faltered when Vanessa gasped. Then it resumed at a faster pace.

They had come together! Tamsin was ecstatic. Still – there was something missing. She thought she knew what it was.

'Put your tongue up further, and be quick about it!' Tamsin couldn't believe she was talking to Vanessa in this manner. She was ordering her around like a servant. It felt wonderful.

'I said faster! Hurry up, girl. Make me keep on coming.' With great satisfaction she felt Vanessa do her bidding. Giving orders was a real turn-on. And Vanessa had obviously got off on servicing her. At least, if an orgasm was any indication, she had. Tamsin had neglected Vanessa while she got her own needs met. Part of her didn't care. The other part, the major part, got busy again on Vanessa's clit.

She felt Vanessa's bud stiffen. Then a gush, followed by an explosion. Vanessa's whole sex was throbbing, right in Tamsin's mouth. Tamsin flicked the vibrator switch to high speed and was rewarded with another flood and a gasp. The throbbing intensified. Soon Vanessa sighed and collapsed. Her tongue continued to work on Tamsin as if it had a life of its own.

Tamsin felt finished, but Vanessa had a final surprise for her. Still tonguing, she produced a vibrator (where it had come from, Tamsin had no idea) and slid it into Tamsin's cunt. She pushed as far as she could and then pressed the vibrator towards the front. She hit the spot exactly right. Suddenly Tamsin was pouring juice, flooding Vanessa's face and breasts. Tamsin cried out and fell on top of Vanessa, bathing both of them in the flood.

After they had rested for a few minutes, there was nothing for them to do but get into the pool.

13

Vanessa smiled with satisfaction as she opened the door and greeted the engineer. Blushing, he avoided her gaze and went directly to the air conditioner. 'I don't understand how that fuse came loose so fast. I just fixed it a few days ago.' The engineer shook his head as he stared at the offending air conditioner. 'But not to worry, ma'am. It's not a serious problem.'

Vanessa knew perfectly well that it wasn't serious. She'd loosened the fuse herself in the hope of seeing this gorgeous man again.

'I knew you'd be able to fix it. I requested you, in fact.'

'How did you know my name?'

This man definitely wasn't very bright.

'Your shirt, of course. Marcus.' Vanessa pointed to the name tag that was prominently displayed.

'Oh.' Marcus looked down at his name tag as if he'd never seen it before. He paused for a beat, as if trying to think of something to say. 'Well, I guess that's it. It shouldn't give you any more trouble.'

He turned to go, and stopped dead in his tracks.

Vanessa stood before him, resplendent in a deep purple micromini dress that barely reached her crotch. As he stared, Vanessa hooked a finger under her skirt hem and pulled it up just far enough for him to see the white vee of her panties.

'Do you like it? I bought it especially for you.'

Marcus was speechless. He stared, mouth agape.

'I see that you do like it.' Vanessa lowered her eyes

meaningfully to his crotch. 'Here's another treat for you.'

She spread her legs and thrust her pelvis forward. She hoped that the dampness she felt in her panties would be visible. Judging from the look on his face, it was.

'See? I'm so wet for you. I want to see what it is that's trying to break through your flies.' She stepped forward and reached for his crotch. Grasping him through the material of his trousers, she moaned when she felt his hardness.

'Oh, you're so big and hard! I want you inside me. I want you to make me come!'

Marcus was still speechless, though his breathing was growing more audible.

Vanessa took his hand and led him to the bed, which she had prepared by tying cotton restraints to the bed-posts. She pushed him down on his back and quickly fastened his wrists to the cuffs. Now that his arms were immobilised, she had to deal with his trousers herself.

Fumbling with the buckle in her haste, she managed to unbuckle his belt and slide it out of the belt loops. She pulled on the tab of his zipper, but he was too stiff underneath it. She couldn't pull the zipper down until she'd unbuttoned the top button. This she did, slipping her hand inside his trousers to feel his iron-hard cock.

Marcus thrust his pelvis forward. Playfully, Vanessa slapped it with the belt.

'Hold still. I'll never get your trousers off if you keep wriggling.' She swatted him again, a little harder. Her efforts with the belt didn't have the desired effect. His cock swelled to a dangerous size. He continued to move, although more slowly. Instinct had taken over and he couldn't stop thrusting. Vanessa grappled with the zip-per, hoping he wouldn't come before she got it undone. She had enough of that kind of thing in her professional life. Now she was on holiday, and she wanted a few cocks to explode in her rather than at her.

The zipper finally gave way to her tugging, eliciting a yelp from Marcus as it slid over the most sensitive part of his anatomy.

'Sorry, Marcus. That couldn't be helped.'

Marcus found his voice enough to choke out, 'That's all right.' His cock sprang out from between his flies, pushing a mound of boxer shorts in front of it. He raised his hips so that Vanessa could slide his trousers down. With one hand inside his underpants, Vanessa used her other hand to pull his trousers all the way off. She used both hands to attack his boxers. When they, too, were off, Vanessa fastened his feet to the ankle cuffs. Then she stepped back to admire the sight on her bed.

Marcus lay spread-eagled with his cock in the air and his balls full to bursting. He clearly was no stranger to a gym or some other kind of conditioning activity. Every inch of him below the waist was firm and well toned. Vanessa wished she had taken his shirt off too, so she could admire what the shirt was covering. But a woman couldn't have everything. She'd done very well, considering she'd taken him by surprise.

She climbed up on the bed and straddled a thigh, making sure Marcus had a good view of her sopping crotch. She pressed herself into his thigh and moved back and forth. Her clit stiffened at the contact.

Marcus evidently was enjoying the view. A drop of clear fluid oozed out of the tip of his cock and made its way down the side, followed by another.

Vanessa slowly made her way up Marcus's thigh, her eyes never leaving his cock. She bent over and took one of his balls in her mouth, gently licking it all over. Marcus moaned and struggled to free himself.

Oh-oh. If she didn't speed things up, he was going to

come all over her hair. That wasn't quite what she had in mind. She raised up off his thigh and, with practised fingers, quickly slid her damp panties off. She kicked them to the floor, then pressed herself against his thrusting cock, forcing it back down against his washboard abs. She wanted him in her, now.

She wriggled until her opening was poised at the top of his cock. By now she was ready to come herself. She had speeded it up so he wouldn't come in her face; now she was in danger of coming before he had a chance to enter her.

She lifted herself up again. With one quick motion she was straddling his hips. Reaching between her legs, she found his cock and pointed it in the right direction. It slid in so easily that she hardly felt it at first. Then she did feel it as he started to pump. She realised that their joining had been so easy because of the excessive lubrication they both provided.

His pubic hair massaged her clit as he thrust in and out. She lubricated even more and her clit was so stiff that she thought she'd explode.

Just as she was beginning to feel the telltale sensations that signalled impending orgasm, Marcus pulled all the way out.

'What are you doing?' Vanessa complained, feeling her orgasm slip beyond her reach. She was tingling all over inside, hovering on the edge. What was worse, she felt out of control. Marcus suddenly had charge of the situation.

'I'm making it better,' Marcus said, 'for both of us.'

Vanessa grabbed his hard cock and fitted it once again to her pussy hole. But no matter what she did, she couldn't get it back in.

She needed it now. She knew that if she pressed her legs together she would explode. She could also get herself off with her finger. That was not, however, what she wanted. She wanted Marcus's cock, and apparently she'd have to get it on Marcus's terms.

After a few minutes, during which Vanessa cursed and muttered under her breath, Marcus told her to put it back in. She obeyed without thinking. Then she swore at herself. What was she doing, obeying this man? She'd tied *him* up, not the other way around. She wished she'd tied his mouth up, too. Now she was in the humiliating position of knowing that he knew she'd done something just because he told her to. She could never regain any semblance of power after this. And to think that just a few minutes ago she'd decided he wasn't very bright. Now he'd manoeuvred her into a position where if she wanted sex it would have to be his way.

The one thing that was clear to her was that she wanted him more than ever. She made up her mind to play by his rules, whatever they turned out to be.

While all this was going through her mind, she was bouncing up and down on his cock. She leaned forward so her clit made contact with his pubes and rubbed herself on him just as she had done earlier on his thigh. The warm glow came back. She revelled in the slap of his balls on her as she lowered herself onto his cock. The orgasmic sensation was starting again deep inside her. This time it would take off like a rocket, after the frustration of the first time, and then she –

'Stop!' Marcus jolted her out of her mood. Again. What was wrong with this chap?

'Get up,' Marcus said. 'Get off my cock!' Once again he managed to pull himself out from under her.

Vanessa was furious. Never in her life had a man treated her like this. He didn't even seem to understand that his purpose was to please her, to seek actively to give her pleasure. But it was beginning to be an interesting experiment, and she decided to free him from the cuffs to see what he'd do. He wasn't doing her any good right now anyhow.

Perhaps he couldn't keep it hard. Perhaps that was why he kept calling for rest periods.

She looked at his cock. It was still waving in the air, and looked harder than it had before, if such a thing were possible. No, that wasn't his problem. Not that it mattered. He wasn't going to enter her again until he wanted to. And there was nothing she could do about it.

She unfastened one cuff; he used the freed hand to undo the other. Then he raised up on the bed to free his ankles. He just lay there, making no move to use any of his freed limbs. His cock remained rigid.

'All aboard!' he said after a few minutes. Vanessa wondered what sort of nut case she'd hooked herself up with. Then she realised that he wanted her to climb back on his cock. Immediately she was on the edge of orgasm again. Maybe this time . . .

But it was not to be. After a few thrusts he used his hands to push her off his rigid organ.

'Thanks for untying me,' he said. 'It's a lot easier this way.'

Strangely, she found his matter-of-factness to be wildly erotic. She was used to men who would promise her anything, if only she would deign to let them touch her. Marcus was acting as if he didn't care whether they had sex or not. This made her want to hurl herself at him and beg for it. Not that she ever would, of course.

Just when she was ready to give up, he put his hands around her waist and lifted her up over his raging cock. He held her so that just the tip of it touched her. She struggled and wriggled, to no avail.

At this point he started toying with her in earnest. He lifted her so far above his cock that she couldn't sense where it was at all. Then he put her back down so that she felt the bare tip. Up and down, up and down she went, almost as if he were using her for a set of weights. When she looked down at his arms all she could see was rippling muscles – the man was clearly exceptionally strong. Of course he would be, slinging air conditioners around all day. Vanessa wasn't used to sexual interludes with men who worked with their hands. She was fascinated.

She was ready to give up all thoughts of an orgasm and just enjoy this unusual experience, when he suddenly set her down hard on his engorged penis. She slid effortlessly all the way down until she could feel his balls slapping her bum again. After feeling so empty she relished the fullness of him expanding within her. Her orgasm began to build again.

Not that she'd tell him. Every time she'd indicated that she was ready to come, he'd pushed her away. She was sure he would do the same thing again, momentarily. If he did, she didn't know what she'd do. By now she desperately needed to come.

Her orgasm continued to grow, taking on a life of its own. There was no way he could stop it for her now. No way.

She tried to free herself so she could lean forward and rub herself against him. He held her back, not allowing it to happen. All of a sudden, without warning, he placed his thumb on her clit and rubbed in a circular motion. At the same time his cock began to pump, moving her whole body up and down.

It no longer mattered to her that he knew she was about to come. Instinctively she knew that this was it, that she'd come no matter what he did. She felt his thumb moving faster and she pressed into it, frantic for release. His thrusts heightened. Unwillingly, she began to moan. Then she no longer cared what he thought or did. She cried out. She sobbed. She clawed at his chest.

Then it hit: a veritable tsunami of an orgasm. Lost in it, she cried and bucked, impaled on his rigid cock. She hardly noticed when he came. The first instant she was aware of it was when his cock began to shrink and she was able to fall forward onto his chest. He held her and stroked her hair, still spurting into the cleavage of her bum.

The phone rang.

14

'Blast!' Vanessa muttered as she groped for the phone. 'Good timing, whoever you are.' She had to answer it or she might miss a party invitation.

'Oh, hello, Harry. I was going to call you tonight.'

'I got the report you faxed to me, and I wanted to talk to you in person.'

'I'm glad to hear from you, Harry, but frankly it's a tad inconvenient right now. Could I call you back?'

'What's going on that can't wait for a few minutes? I'm just going out for the evening. Have you forgotten there's a time difference?'

'Oh. Right. I did forget. Truth is, I'm just finishing a fuck with the hotel's air-conditioning engineer.'

'Sure, Vanessa. Don't tell me. He's on his back under you, and he's still shooting off.'

'How did you –? Never mind, Harry. What did you want to tell me?'

'I want to know the instant there's the slightest change in Tamsin's behaviour.'

'That's why I was going to call you. Since I reported on how she seems to passively accept everything that comes her way, she's starting to do an about-face. The last couple of times I've seen her, she's taken the initiative in a lot of what we do. She and I had a scene the other day, just the two of us. She actually ordered me around. I think she may not be as much of a submissive as we thought. Stop it, Marcus.'

'What?'

'Sorry, Harry. I was talking to Marcus, who is scrambling to get out from under me. Just a minute.'

After dealing with Marcus, who simply wanted to get dressed and get on with his work, Vanessa returned to the phone.

'He's gone now. We can talk.'

'You've told me what I wanted to know. There's nothing more to talk about.'

'Yes, there is. Have you ever had phone sex, Harry?'

'No. Never.'

'Would you like to? It can be a lot of fun. But you have to use your imagination.'

'I don't know. Perhaps it's not such a good idea.'

'You're not contradicting me, are you, Harry? I'd hate to think you were. You know what I do when you contradict me.'

'Yes, Mistress.'

'Tell me, Harry. What do I do when you displease me?'

'You pull down my trousers and you paddle my bare bum.'

'What else do I pull down?'

'My underpants.'

'Very good. Do that now, Harry. Pull down your trousers and your underpants. Lie across my lap on the chair.'

'But –'

'But nothing. Do as I say. Imagine I'm there. Imagine you feel my thighs under you as you lie across the chair. While you do that, think about how bad you are and how much you need to be punished. Can you do that?'

'Yes, Mistress. I feel your thighs under my naked penis. I'm waiting for you to spank me.'

'Are you hard yet?'

'I'm getting hard, yes, Mistress. Just thinking about

what you're going to do to me is making me hard. I'm a bad boy.'

'Yes, you are, Harry. You're a very bad boy. I'm going to punish you now.' Vanessa held the phone close to her thigh and slapped herself so Harry could hear. 'How did that feel, Harry? Did it hurt?'

'Yes, Mistress. It hurt a lot. It made my penis stiffer.'

'Talking like that is bad, Harry. It's disgusting. I'm going to hit you harder now.'

'Oh, please, Mistress, don't hit me. It hurts.'

'I have to punish you. You're a very bad boy. You have dirty thoughts. Not only that, but you're daring to say nasty things to your Mistress. I'm punishing you for your own good. I'm helping you to become a better person.' She slapped her thigh into the phone again. Harry howled.

'Don't be silly, Harry. I'm not hurting you that much.'

Harry's breathing became more audible.

'Harry, are you playing with yourself?'

'No, Mistress.'

'It sounds like it. I hear heavy breathing. Are you telling me the truth, Harry?'

'Yes, Mistress.'

'Very well. Of course you're not playing with yourself. You wouldn't do such a thing while talking to me on the phone. It would be so rude.'

'Yes, Mistress.'

'Since you're being such a good boy and not touching yourself, I'll tell you what I'm wearing. I have on a black leather thong. Since it's so hot in L.A. I'm not wearing any trousers. On the top part of my body I'm wearing a black leather bustier. It's so tight that my tits are pushing out like melons. The bottom of it comes to the top of the thong. It covers the waistband but reveals the vee of the leather that covers my mound. On my feet I have a pair of extra-high-heeled black stiletto sandals. Other than that, I'm wearing nothing. Since I wasn't planning to work while I'm here, I didn't bring my hairbrushes and whips, but I borrowed some from my friend Leandra to use while I punish you. Like this.' Vanessa slapped her thigh again.

'Ow!'

'Harry, I'm not sure I trust you. Are you sure you're not playing with yourself?'

'Of course I'm not playing with myself! I wouldn't touch my nasty pee-pee. That's dirty!'

'But you're bad in other ways, Harry. I know about all the bad things you do. And you always come when I correct you. I'm going to hit you again now, harder than before.' Vanessa's thigh was getting sore from the repeated slapping. This time she slammed a book on the table, making a satisfactory *thwack*. 'I forbid you to come yet. If you do, I'll be very angry with you.'

'Yes, Mistress. I'm a good boy. I won't come.'

Vanessa noticed that the telltale noises had stopped. Perhaps he really was controlling his hands after all. If he had come, she was sure she'd know. Not that it mattered. She was getting involved in her fantasy now; she wanted him to come when she decided he would, just as he did when they were in the same room.

'Harry, I can tell you're getting harder. I feel it on my thigh. Your nasty man-thing is making a disgusting, rigid lump. I'm going to have to spank you harder.'

'Please don't, Mistress. It hurts when you spank me.'

'Stop being a bad boy, then.'

'I can't help it. I have no control. The nasty thing gets all hard, even when I try to be good.'

'How hard is it, Harry? Is it as hard as it was the last time I punished you?'

'Oh, yes, Mistress. It might even be harder.'

'Can you feel my strong thigh muscles as you press your dick into them?'

'Yes I can, Mistress. I'm afraid something bad is going to happen if I don't stop thinking about it.'

'Get your mind off it. Instead, picture me in my tight bustier and thong. See how long my legs are, how perfectly my stiletto heels set them off. See how my breasts rise as I lift my arm to spank you with the hairbrush.' She lowered the phone and slapped her hand on her thigh again. It had to sound loud to Harry.

Harry's response was unmistakable. With a loud groan he came copiously, not bothering to muffle the sound. Vanessa waited until he had finished spurting. When his breathing returned to normal she said innocently, 'Why, Harry, I hardly touched you!'

'Bloody hell, Vanessa! I got it all over the upholstery. Now I have to clean it up before my housekeeper sees it.'

Vanessa had an almost irrepressible urge to laugh. But she didn't dare. Harry was, after all, a client. Besides, the bit of play-acting had got her all heated up as well. She slipped a finger into herself, surprised to find how wet she was. No leather thong impeded the progress of her finger, nor was there a bustier encasing her upper body. She was naked, of course, having just got up from her romp with Marcus, but the fantasy she had created for Harry was so real to her that it had turned her on in a most unprofessional way. She blamed the climate of Los Angeles. It had been bloody hot ever since she arrived. That must be why her libido was running away with her.

Somehow she got through the rest of the conversation with Harry. Letting her brain run on automatic, she made the appropriate responses while fiercely fingering herself with her free hand. Or rather, she *thought* her responses were appropriate.

'Are you all right, Vanessa?'

'Of course. Why do you ask?'

'It sounds as if you're breathing hard.'

Blast! 'No, I'm fine. I think I may be allergic to something in the air here. That's what you're hearing, probably.'

'All right. Take care. For a minute I thought you were getting excited.'

Finally he rang off. Vanessa fell back on the bed and devoted herself to her demanding clit. Face down, she thrust herself onto the sheet while continuing the finger motion up and down.

That wasn't enough. She inserted her other hand into her soaking bush and frantically worked her clit with both hands.

Suddenly she felt something at her back opening. She looked over her shoulder and saw Marcus aiming his condom-covered penis between her cheeks. She raised up to allow him entrance. He plunged in with no pre-liminaries. She was wide open and ready for him. As he filled her she came, a great explosive come that made her cry out so loudly that everybody in the hotel probably could hear her. Her orgasm continued for a long time while she lay there moaning. As it started to subside, Marcus exploded inside her, spurting great jets of come into the rubber.

Cradling her in his arms, he fell asleep. After a few minutes of wondering at the strangeness of it all, so did she.

15

The next week was a busy time for everybody. Tamsin, with Jamie's help, completed a series of photographs for the book. One day they set out before dawn for a shoot on Carroll Street.

'What's that? And why so early?' Jamie grumbled.

'I want to get there at first light. It's a street of perfectly restored houses from the turn of the twentieth century. Wait until you see it. You'll love it. The street looks like a museum, but people are living in all of the houses.'

After two more cups of tea, Jamie pronounced himself awake enough to go. They left the house as quietly as they could, forgetting that the silence wasn't necessary because Leandra was up before they were.

Jamie was properly impressed by Carroll Street. 'You're not doing this in black and white, are you, Tamsin?' he asked.

'No, of course not. That would miss the whole point. It's the delightful pastel paint jobs with contrasting trim that I want to get on film. Now be quiet for a while. I need to concentrate.'

Tamsin went up and down the short street, setting up her tripod and photographing everything that caught her eye as translating well to the camera. The light was amazing. A little later, some of the homeowners came out to watch, unused to seeing photographers working with large, non-digital formats. Tamsin told them briefly about the project, and they said they'd be watching for the book when it came out.

By midmorning they were ravenous. 'Let's go home and eat,' Tamsin said. 'I think I've done all I can here.'

When they got home they had the house to themselves. Jamie went to take a nap while Tamsin busied herself in her darkroom.

Leandra had been gone for hours. She left at first light every morning in a rush to finish her film as soon as possible. Nigel was off on another business trip. Vanessa spent most of her time in bed with Marcus. Nobody, except Vanessa, had any time for play.

A little later Tamsin came out of Leandra's well-equipped darkroom beaming with satisfaction. Her photographs were perfect, just what she wanted: large-format prints shot on large-format cameras. She knew she had entered into a new phase of her art: a new maturity, a growth phase. Looking for someone to share this news with, she ran into Leandra. Literally.

'What are you doing home this early?' she asked as she got up and brushed herself off.

'The film is done! A week early!' Leandra did a little dance. 'I'm sorry. I didn't mean to knock you down. But I'm so excited!'

'I've got good news too, Leandra. I finished that series I was telling you about. I'm really pleased with it; I can't wait to hear what you think.'

'Wonderful! We'll have a celebration for both of us. Our wrap party is tomorrow night. It'll be great fun.'

Tamsin had been looking forward to the wrap party ever since she'd first heard about it; it was going to be a totally new experience for her. Rumour had it that there would be a dungeon. She couldn't imagine what it would be like, and she was eager to find out.

That Thursday night she and Jamie waited impatiently for Leandra and Nigel to return from the airport. Nigel would just have time for a quick change before they left for the party. Vanessa and her new friend Marcus were meeting them at the party, Vanessa finally having managed to get out of bed and accept her phone invitation. Tamsin was a little anxious about seeing Vanessa. She wondered how things would be between them after their scene at the pool. She tugged at the hem of her red silk minidress.

'Am I decent, Jamie? This feels too short.'

'If you're careful how you walk, you should be all right. One can see your panties, though, if you're not paying attention.'

'I was afraid of that, but Leandra said I'm just right.' She stretched her arms over her head, noticing that her skirt now rode on her hips. 'Can you really see, Jamie? I feel naked.'

Jamie's tight black shorts were beginning to bulge. 'Yes, I can see. Your skirt is up so high I can see the crotch of your panties. Don't do this to me, Tamsin. You know what happens to me, and then Mistress gets angry.'

Tamsin lowered her arms. 'Sorry, Jamie. I forgot. If my panties are going to show anyhow, perhaps I should wear a different colour than white. What do you think? Black lace or red silk?'

'Tamsin, please!' Jamie's bulge was obvious now.

'Oops! Sorry again. I'll go to my room and change, so I won't bother you.'

'No, don't do that. I'd like to watch. Just don't talk about it, all right?'

'You've got it.' Tamsin ran to her room and returned with the two pairs of panties she'd mentioned. She wriggled out of her white ones and stepped into the black lace pair. Remembering her promise to Jamie, she twirled silently before the mirror. This wasn't good, she decided. The black was too visible under the red of her dress. She hooked her thumbs under the waistband and slowly pulled them down. Jamie moaned when her pubic hair became visible. Tamsin turned to him and pulled the panties the rest of the way down. She raised her arms, exposing most of her bush.

'Come on, Jamie, don't torture yourself like this. Take your shorts off and have a good come. Leandra and Nigel won't be here for at least another half hour. You have plenty of time, and she'll never know.'

'Yes, she will. Mistress knows everything about me.'

'All right. I was just trying to make it easier for you.'

She slipped on the red panties and pulled them up so that the silk hugged her crotch. 'There's still time to change your mind, Jamie.'

'Tamsin, what's got into you? In all the time we've known each other you've never pushed me like this. You used to respect my decisions. I'll tell you one more time. I made a free choice to be Mistress Leandra's slave. That means doing what she tells me to and not sneaking behind her back. I'm surprised at you for encouraging me to disobey. What's going on with you, anyhow?'

'I'm sorry, Jamie. I don't know what got into me, either. I'm very horny, and I was hoping that you –'

'I'm flattered. But the answer still has to be no. I won't touch you, or myself, unless Mistress Leandra gives me permission. That's just the way it is.'

'All right. I understand. I won't ask you again. But let me just ask you this: do you find me unattractive?'

'No, of course I don't! You've seen what happens to me every time I look at you. Actually, I think you're gorgeous. But you're off limits. Besides, I need a dominant woman. That's what's been missing from my life, and I didn't even know it. That's why I've never had a real relationship with a woman. I never found one who would meet these needs until I met Mistress Leandra.'

Tamsin had no response to this. She contented herself with pulling up on her skirt to make sure her red panties covered her entire bush. She could see that this made

Jamie wild. She didn't really intend to tease him, but she couldn't help herself. She was beginning to wish she had a regular partner like everybody else. Leandra had two partners and she didn't have even one. That seemed hardly fair.

Perhaps she wasn't ready for a regular partner, though. She was enjoying herself so much playing with everybody who came along. What she really wanted was a relationship like Leandra had with Nigel – a secure relationship that wasn't threatened by the multiple sexual adventures of either partner.

Her musing was cut short by the arrival of her hosts. Quickly she smoothed her skirt and returned the other two pairs of panties to her own room.

Twenty minutes later everybody was ready to go. Leandra and Nigel, both in full leathers, carried a selection of whips. Jamie, in his tight black shorts and black T-shirt, with 'Slave' in large white letters across it, trotted on a leash behind Leandra, carrying her toy bag. Only Tamsin looked as if she were going to a conventional party.

She wasn't sure how she felt about that.

The drive to Leandra's friends' house wasn't very long. Tamsin had most of the back seat to herself, since Leandra had ordered Jamie to lie face down on the floor. Tamsin was having trouble controlling herself. Anticipating what might happen at the party was making her panties wet and she hoped they wouldn't get too soaked before it even started. How she wished she'd thought to bring a fresh pair, or even both pairs. She might need all three if she continued this way.

When they entered the house Tamsin gasped. This certainly wasn't what she'd imagined when she thought of a dungeon. She found herself in a brightly lit room full of chattering, laughing people. Most of them were in some kind of leather outfit. Only a few, like Tamsin, wore regular clothing. Many wore masks. Tamsin wished she had a leather miniskirt, at least, but nothing could be done about that now. She'd ask Leandra to take her to West Hollywood and help her shop before the next party.

What made Tamsin gasp was the view through a wide doorway into another brightly lit room. She saw all kinds of strange devices. Some of the equipment reminded her of what she'd seen in gyms: vaulting horses and weight benches. There was also a tall cross, similar to what one might see in a Protestant chapel. And that thing that looked like an X – what on earth could that be? She saw some strange harness-like affairs hanging from the ceiling, too.

Was that the dungeon? It couldn't be. It was so bright. She'd expected darkness, barely lit by smoky torches, and rather evil-looking people, all armed with whips, gleefully flogging each other. Here this didn't seem to be the case at all. It was all so ... civilised was the word that entered her mind. There was a background of soft classic rock tunes, punctuated by the swishing of whips and an occasional groan.

Where were all the young people? This was definitely an older crowd.

Curiosity pulled Tamsin into the room.

This part of the party wasn't in full swing yet. Some of the equipment wasn't in use.

'Come with us, Tamsin. The real party is happening in here.' Leandra took her hand and led her across the room to a closed door that she hadn't noticed.

A blast of music nearly knocked Tamsin down when Leandra opened the door. It was the unexpectedness of it more than anything, for it really wasn't that loud. But it was wild, sexual, indescribably erotic. Tamsin felt a tingling in her crotch as her pussy responded to the music. She was getting damp again, too, although she no longer cared.

This room was fitted out with the same kind of equipment as the room they'd just left, although more of it was in use here. A woman, naked except for a series of straps that pushed her abundant breasts straight out, was swinging in a sling suspended from the ceiling. Her partner, in full leathers, was flogging her with a vicious looking knotted whip. A young man wearing nothing but a cock ring was tied to one of the crosses. His female partner was choosing from a collection of riding crops.

A scream caught Tamsin's attention. Turning around, she saw a young woman in black leather bra and panties being tied to a vaulting horse by two large, leather-clad women. One of them had just finished clamping alligator clips to her erect nipples. Directly in front of Tamsin was a kneeling woman performing fellatio on a dildo worn by another woman. The dildo jutted out from the woman's leather flies, looking exactly like a real penis.

The other woman was being forced to a kneeling position by a leather glove on the back of her neck. Both of her bare nipples had been pierced. Silver studs ran through them, connected by a silver chain.

Tamsin saw something else she'd never seen before: the kneeling woman was wearing crotchless panties that revealed pierced labia, laced together by a thin silver chain fastened with a tiny padlock.

A closer look told her that the woman receiving the fellatio was Vanessa. Tamsin's sex dampened as she thought about wanting to be in Vanessa's position, standing there with her pelvis thrust forward, having someone suck on her erect cock. Mindlessly she began to finger herself. She splayed her legs and stood there with her pelvis thrust out in unconscious imitation of Vanessa.

Her panties were destroyed. Not caring who saw her, she tugged them down over her hips. At some point she was aware that she was being helped. Somebody's hands covered hers. She felt a tongue at the top of her bum crack. A woman's, she thought, though she didn't know how she knew. The woman licked her way downward, spreading Tamsin's cheeks with her hands to allow easy access. She stopped at Tamsin's bum, rolling her tongue around her back opening and finally inserting it.

Tamsin felt an orgasm building. She grabbed her sopping pussy and fingered herself again, gasping loudly as her orgasm overwhelmed her.

Vanessa and her partner stopped what they were doing to watch. At a signal from Vanessa, her partner crawled to Tamsin and, pushing Tamsin's hands away, fastened her mouth on her clit. She proceeded to lick Tamsin into a state of constant orgasm. Tamsin's knees began to get wobbly, and she slid to the floor in front of Vanessa's partner. The woman who had been working on Tamsin's bottom cleavage put her arms around her and tweaked her nipples.

Tamsin recognised her by her hands: Leandra. She grabbed the hands, forcing Leandra to pinch harder.

Leandra co-operated. Her nails dug into Tamsin's engorged nipples, making her howl with pain and joy. Tamsin's sex spasmed again, into the mouth of Vanessa's partner.

Vanessa and Leandra lowered Tamsin to the floor, with Vanessa's partner keeping a firm grip on Tamsin's clit. Her panties got lost in the confusion.

Leandra kept on digging into Tamsin's nipples until her orgasm had run its course. Vanessa and her partner were too excited to wait now. Vanessa unlocked the padlock on her partner's sex chain, unthreaded it from the rings, and plunged her dildo in. The other woman came almost instantly. Then Vanessa came with a long, drawn-out moan.

The sound and smell of Vanessa and her partner in orgasm made Tamsin hot all over again. She raised her head to watch but couldn't see them from the position she was in. She squirmed to a sitting position, dislodging Vanessa's partner from her clit. The woman got up on all fours and moaned as Vanessa's dildo found a new hot spot. Watching the two women going at it doggie style, Tamsin touched herself again. Then she collapsed, exhausted.

She regained her energy in time to help Vanessa and her partner bring Leandra to orgasm. Leandra, the only one who hadn't come yet, was groping for a whip to use on Vanessa's partner. She flicked the whip up, lashing at the woman's breasts. The second stroke hit both nipples. The woman cried out, and Leandra exploded.

'That was quite a show,' Nigel said breathlessly, as if he had been running. He and several other men, cocks jutting out, had formed a circle around the women. All of them were masturbating openly, except for Jamie who, as usual, was trying to hide his erection. A couple of the men lost it when they became aware that the women's eyes were upon them. Jets of come sizzled onto the floor to mingle with the spent juices of the women.

Vanessa's partner, the woman with the pierced labia, jumped to her feet and leaped into the arms of a masked man, impaling herself on his erection. He lifted her off his cock, lowered her to her feet, and led her by the hand to one of the waiting crosses.

'Who is she? And the man? He looks familiar, for some reason, but it's hard to tell with a mask.' Tamsin knew it was none of her business, but she couldn't resist asking Vanessa.

'That's Annie. Marcus's girlfriend. The man is Marcus. I forgot you haven't met him. The three of us have been having a glorious time. I've been able to show them a few tricks.'

'I bet you have.' Tamsin was envious. Why did women like Leandra and Vanessa have no trouble finding sex partners who wanted them to be dominant, while she, Tamsin, was automatically assumed to be passive? She'd been quite aggressive with Vanessa at the pool the other day. Yet tonight Vanessa was putting her in her old role.

No, it wasn't Vanessa, she had to admit. It was she, herself. She fell into the submissive role because it was what she was used to. Maybe it was too late for this party but tomorrow she'd have a long talk with Leandra and ask her to help. Tonight, however, she'd forget about it and just enjoy the party.

She followed the men over to watch Annie and Marcus. Most of the men were still fondling their stiff dicks. They formed a semicircle around the cross and stared as Marcus bound Annie to it with old-fashioned metal handcuffs. He put a metal bar between her knees to hold her legs open. Annie squirmed and moaned and begged him not to hurt her. Even Tamsin could tell that this was play-acting: Annie was so aroused that her pussy was glistening before Marcus had even touched her. Still, the sound of her words made it easier to believe that she was there against her will. Listening, Tamsin got excited all over again. That man, Marcus. He couldn't be Gina's friend. Impossible. That Marcus was in London. Then Tamsin remembered; that day at Gina's flat, Marcus had said he'd be in California for the summer. Clearly, however, this wasn't the right moment to renew their acquaintance.

Marcus chose a whip and showed it to Annie.

'No, Marcus. That one will hurt. No!' Marcus lashed her pussy with it. 'Ah!'

He hit her again. More beads of moisture formed on her pussy. Marcus himself was clearly aroused. His dick still jutted almost straight out of his flies. Tamsin saw a drop of clear fluid ooze from the end of it and drop to the floor.

Marcus's whip cracked again. Annie shrieked as it landed on her clit. Since her pussy was shaved, her clit was in full view of everybody as it swelled and stiffened. Tamsin noticed that Annie had an unusually large clit. She wondered how she knew that.

The group continued to watch while Marcus gave Annie several lashes. Annie's pussy belied her screams of pain. The more she howled, the wetter she became. Tamsin wished she could be up there with them, flogging Annie's nipples while Marcus worked on her sex. So strong was this desire that she edged over to the wall and took a whip from Leandra's pile. After testing it in the air a few times, she strode over to the cross and took her place beside Marcus.

She watched Marcus for a few strokes, absorbing his whipping rhythm into her body. When she felt in tune with him she lifted her crop and aimed at Annie's navel. Her first stroke was synchronised perfectly with Marcus's. It missed its mark, though, deflected by Annie's elaborate network of crisscrossed leather straps. Annie's breasts would be an easy target, though. The straps in that area served to push out her abundant breasts in a perpetual thrust, not to cover them. Tamsin waited until she felt Marcus's rhythm again. Then she aimed her instrument at Annie's nipples.

Bull's-eye. The whip lashed across both erect nipples at the same time, leaving a faint pink welt. Tamsin didn't want to whip too hard, as she was afraid she'd really hurt her. But Annie's eyes begged for more. More, and harder.

Tamsin obliged. She lashed out again, putting more force behind it. This time when she connected, Annie emitted a most gratifying scream. Tamsin felt fresh moisture oozing down her thighs.

She lashed Annie a few more times, still landing on Marcus's beat. Gradually she got bolder. Since Marcus's strokes were as steady as a bass drum beat, she began to improvise within the spaces: hitting exactly between the beats then just before the beat, like a jazz riff. Before long her whip was dancing to all manner of eighth-note and sixteenth-note combinations that ran through her head.

Throughout it all Annie was crying out and coming. Tamsin paid little attention to her, fascinated as she was with the rhythmic patterns she was creating with her crop. Annie's breasts were glowing bright red now, and still Tamsin kept on lashing.

A strong pair of arms pinned Tamsin's to her side. 'Enough, Tamsin! Stop it! You'll injure her!' Nigel said, giving her a little shake.

Dazed, Tamsin lowered her arm and shook her head. Her pussy was slippery and for a moment she didn't know why. As her mind returned to her surroundings and took in the scene, she was horrified.

'What happened? How's Annie? I didn't really hurt her, did I?'

'No, you didn't. You might have if I hadn't stepped in. Normally I wouldn't do that. But I know you have no experience, and things were starting to get out of control.'

'I'm sorry. I don't know what came over me. I just had this urge.'

'I know. Something like that has happened to many of us, those of us who are natural dominants. Look, this is a party. We'll talk about it at home, all right? Promise me you won't use a whip again for the rest of this evening. Instead, watch the other dominants. Learn from them. If you want to play tonight, do so as a submissive.'

Tamsin nodded her assent. She felt overwhelmed. There was so much to learn. Now she'd almost done serious harm through her ignorance.

'I'm sorry. I'm so ashamed,' she said.

'Don't be. No harm was done. Now go and enjoy yourself.'

Noticing that nobody was paying the slightest attention to them, Tamsin allowed herself to think that maybe it wasn't such a disaster after all. Marcus had released Annie, who was again on her knees giving a blow job – to a real penis this time, Marcus's. She seemed none the worse for her experience with Tamsin. In fact she looked happy.

Tamsin strolled as casually as she could around the room, trying not to gawk – after all, she'd never seen a dungeon before. Even though this wasn't quite what she'd expected (it had bright lights and music instead of darkness, primitive fires and dank smells), it was still a real dungeon. In spite of her recent *faux pas* she was excited. She wandered among couples and small groups, most of whom were involved in activities that involved whips, until she came upon Jamie and her other friends.

Nobody greeted her. Everybody was intent on Jamie, whose wrists were shackled to metal rings suspended from the ceiling. Since his toes barely touched the floor, he swung gently, swaying with each whiplash. His erection was gigantic.

For once nobody was complaining about it, not even Leandra. She, Nigel and Vanessa were taking turns lashing him. He had several painful-looking welts across his belly and his penis, but he made no sound.

Tamsin watched for a while. Finally Leandra came up to her and handed her a whip.

'Nigel tells me you like to use a whip. Here, join us.'

'I – I can't. I get too carried away.'

'One lash, then,' Leandra said. 'Just one. Hit him once, then give the whip back.'

Tamsin thought this was reasonable. One lash couldn't do that much damage. And she really wanted to. She'd been fantasising about whipping Jamie, though she hadn't told him. He was Leandra's slave, after all, not hers.

She hefted the whip and cracked it twice to get the feel of it. Then she approached Jamie. She stood a little closer than the others had. She wanted to be sure he saw who she was. Raising her arm, she swung back in preparation for the blow.

Jamie recognised her, all right. He lifted his head and looked directly into her eyes. He attempted to smile in spite of the pain he was obviously feeling.

Before her whip landed on its target, Jamie exploded. His cock erupted all over Tamsin's whip. With a yell he came again, then a third time.

Tamsin watched, fascinated. Leandra took the whip out of her hand, though it hadn't occurred to Tamsin to use it again.

When Jamie had finished coming he hung slumped in his chains. Tamsin waited for Leandra to berate him, but she didn't. Tamsin was intensely aroused by the situation in spite of the orgasms she'd already had. The others, however, betrayed no sign of sexual excitement.

An older man in a tuxedo entered the room. He saw Leandra and his face lit up.

'Ah, my most delectable Mistress from George's house! I'm so glad to see you!'

Leandra looked puzzled for a moment. Then her face lit up too. 'Oh, yes. The gentleman who studies sumi-e.'

This conversation seemed surreal to Tamsin in these circumstances. Leandra and the man were behaving as if they'd just run into each other at a gallery opening or a similar event. Both seemed oblivious to the fact that they were in a dungeon, and that people were running about naked or dressed entirely in leather.

Then the man shocked Tamsin even more.

'Vanessa! What are you doing here?' he said.

'Harry! I'll ask you the same question. I thought you were in London.'

'No, I came back to visit my friend George again. He brought me to this marvellous party. A wrap party, is it?' He turned to Tamsin. 'Will one of you introduce me to this delightful young lady? I was watching you wield that whip, my dear, on that young woman over there. You were formidable.'

Tamsin thought this gentleman was wonderfully old-fashioned, even though he seemed rather young for such mannerisms. Introduce her, indeed. She stepped forward, holding her hand out to shake. 'My name is Tamsin.'

Tamsin couldn't read his expression. Could it be shock? Why? Had she committed another *faux pas*?

He hesitated for a moment, then took her hand in his. 'My name is Harry.' He bent over her hand and gravely kissed it.

Vanessa seemed tense too. Leandra and Nigel were the only ones acting normally.

'Would you like to play with me again?' Leandra asked.

'I'd be honoured. But could we go into the other room, please? There's a cross in there for which I've developed a particular fondness.'

'Of course. Come on, then.' Leandra strode towards the door. Harry nodded a farewell to the others and followed her.

'What's his problem? He seemed in a hurry to get away from us,' Tamsin said.

'Oh, he's a good chap, but he has his strange moments. Don't worry about it,' Vanessa answered.

Tamsin still wondered, but she decided Vanessa's friends were not her business. Still, it surprised her that Leandra had run off so quickly with him. She turned to Jamie.

'Come on. Let's go find something to watch.' She helped him down from the chains and sat down on the floor with his head in her lap. When he'd recovered a bit, she snapped his leash back on him and led him to where she had last seen Annie and Marcus.

They caught them scrambling back into their clothes, preparing to leave. Marcus did a double take when he saw Tamsin.

'Tamsin? Is it really you? You look so different from the last time I saw you.'

'Do I? The last time you saw me I was helping you whip Annie.'

'I don't mean then, silly. I mean in London. At Gina's. Remember?'

'Of course I remember! How could I forget? You taught me so much,' Tamsin said.

'You seem to have learned a lot more since then,' Marcus said. 'Tell me, do you know Vanessa?'

'Oh yes. We've become quite good friends.'

'Ask her about me. Perhaps we can all get together sometime,' Marcus said.

'Good idea. I'd like that.'

Annie tugged on Marcus's arm. He smiled at her. 'Annie is telling me we have to leave. I'm working the early shift at the motel tomorrow, before my ballet class. So we've got to get our beauty sleep. See you later, then.'

Tamsin said her goodbyes and led Jamie off on another tour of the party.

16

'Are we still going shopping today?' Tamsin asked, as she scooped up another bite of yoghurt and papaya. It was the morning after the party, and she and Leandra were starting their day early.

'Sure, but I don't think we'll buy you any whips today. You may use my whips until you decide what kinds you're most comfortable with. I have other plans for us today.'

'I can't wait to get started!' Tamsin said. She had slept very little, entertaining herself instead with fantasies about her new life as a dominant. 'Who am I going to practise on?'

'Nigel, for starters, though he usually doesn't take the submissive role. He likes you, though, so he's agreed to help out. After you show us that you can use the whip responsibly, I'll turn you loose on Jamie.'

'Jamie? But he's your slave!'

'Precisely. That's why you're going to practise on Nigel first. He'll speak up and tell you when you're out of line. Jamie wouldn't, he's too passive. He'll do anything I tell him to – he'd allow you to flay the skin right off his body if he thought that would make me happy. Of course that might be appropriate in certain circumstances, but it's not the way to train a novice. You need to learn how to inflict pain without inflicting real injury. That's what we want to teach you.'

'You're so good to me, Leandra.'

'Don't kid yourself. We're not being altruistic. It'll be as much fun for us as it will be for you. Now let me tell you what I have in mind. I'm proposing a day off from the fun and games we've been enjoying so much. Let's do something different. To begin with, a whole day without sex of any kind, just you and me. We can go shopping. I'll show you some really great places that you probably would never get to with Jamie along. Maybe we'll talk a little business. I have some ideas I want to run by you about another project I have in mind. Maybe we won't. Maybe we'll just have fun today. Let's go with the flow.'

'But what about Jamie and Nigel? What will they do without us?'

Leandra laughed. 'I think they can deal with it for one day, don't you? They aren't helpless. They'll do whatever males do when they don't have females around to distract them. Besides, it will be good for Jamie to have a day's respite from being a slave.'

'This sounds like fun. But will we look at leathers too?'

'Of course. We'll just do the other things first. Come on. Let's get out of here.'

'Did you tell Jamie and Nigel?'

'Nigel, yes. I don't discuss my plans with Jamie.'

'No, I guess you wouldn't. I wasn't thinking,' Tamsin said. 'I keep forgetting that he's a slave.'

Very shortly they were on the freeway. Tamsin still hadn't figured out which road went where; she was content to let Leandra make the driving decisions. But she was curious. 'Where are we going first?'

'Beverly Hills. Rodeo Drive. It's a famous shopping street.'

'I've heard of it,' Tamsin said. 'Isn't that where that actress was caught shoplifting, with drugs on her?'

'Allegations, Tamsin, mere allegations. In this town the media love to make a fuss about everything, particularly when it involves a celebrity. I think she was acquitted, but I'm not sure. I didn't follow the case that carefully.'

'What are we going to buy on Rodeo Drive?' Tamsin asked.

'Absolutely nothing. It's too expensive for the likes of us. It is where the rich and famous go to see and be seen. Keep your eyes open and you might see someone you recognise. And it will be fun to go browsing in the shops. Too bad we didn't wear shades – we could pretend we're celebrities going incognito.'

They parked in a valet parking lot. Tamsin couldn't help noticing how cute the attendant was. 'Is it illegal to be ugly in this town, Leandra? All the men I see are absolutely gorgeous. Do the plain ones only come out after dark, or what?'

'You'd think so, wouldn't you? But the way it works is that all these cute guys you see aren't really parking lot attendants or waiters or whatever else they seem to be. They're actors looking for parts. So they try to get day jobs where the famous people are, hoping to be discovered. The industry doesn't really work that way, of course. But try telling that to the kids from Middle America who flock out here. Old legends die hard.'

'Well, they really are beautiful people, whoever they are. I like looking at them.'

'Don't get any ideas, girlfriend. This is our day of abstinence, remember?'

They strolled down the famous street, window shopping and looking for celebrities. Tamsin saw an actor she recognised from a television drama, and Leandra almost had to hold her back bodily from following him and getting his autograph. 'I didn't know you were such a fan, Tamsin. I'll have to keep a close eye on you, I see.'

'I'm not usually like this. I'm just playing. But I'll stop if it makes you uncomfortable.'

'Just kidding. I'm playing, too. Let's just pretend we're tourists and do whatever we feel like.'

Venturing into a jewellery store, they were greeted by a rather plain-looking young man, the first one Tamsin had seen. He was neat and clean and impeccably dressed, but he didn't have the stunning looks that Tamsin had grown used to.

Leandra told him that they were looking for a brooch for their grandmother's eightieth birthday. He showed them the most expensive pieces in the store, and they were impressive. Massive diamonds, rubies like rocks, scintillating emeralds. Tamsin was speechless, looking at all the gems.

Without warning Leandra flashed the man a dazzling smile and asked, 'How's your script coming along?'

The serious young man brightened at the question. 'It's almost finished. And a man I met in a bar hinted at an option on it.'

'That's wonderful!' Leandra replied. 'Good luck with it.'

They thanked him for showing the jewellery and, after a little more chat about the script, left the store without buying any diamonds for their grandmother. The man didn't seem to mind.

'How did you know he's writing a script?' Tamsin asked. 'Is he a friend of yours?'

'If he were, I wouldn't have had to make up a story in order to get to see the jewellery. I could tell he was a scriptwriter because he has a New England accent, so he's not a local boy. And he isn't handsome enough to be a wannabe actor. The plainer ones are all writing scripts. And meeting a man in a bar, that's the oldest line in the book. "Come up to my place and read me your script. I'll get you an agent – if you're nice to me." It'd be funny if it weren't so sad. Someone ought to write a guidebook for people moving to L.A. to work in movies or TV.'

'Let's go in there,' Tamsin said, pointing across the street to a store that had grabbed her interest.

'OK. We can go in and look, I guess.'

They hurried across the street and entered a large boutique. 'Look, Leandra. No price tags. How can we tell what we can afford?'

'I told you, we can't afford *anything*. The philosophy of these places is, if you have to ask how much something costs then you can't afford it. But here we are. Let's pretend to be customers.'

A young personal shopper rushed up to help them. 'Would you ladies like to see the new fall collections?'

Leandra fell right into the role, while Tamsin only gaped. 'Yes, please. We're particularly interested in the New York lines.'

'Very well. Please have a glass of champagne while I arrange a viewing for you.'

A few minutes later came the first of a long procession of models, all impossibly thin. 'I couldn't squeeze any of those dresses past my left tit,' Leandra whispered to Tamsin.

'Why are they showing these styles, then? It's obvious that neither of us has anorexia.'

'These clothes aren't sold in conventional sizes.' Leandra explained. 'You make your choice, and they fit it to you.'

'More champagne, ladies?' A waiter in a uniform that revealed buns of steel was hovering over them, teeth gleaming. This one obviously isn't a scriptwriter, Tamsin thought, stifling a giggle.

She shared this thought with Leandra when they left the store, a little giddy from the unaccustomed champagne. They both giggled all the way back to the car.

'How's your script coming along?' Tamsin asked the valet parking attendant, the same one they'd left the car with when they arrived.

'I ain't no writer, miss.' He pulled himself up to his full height. 'I'm an actor,' he announced with an unmistakable note of pride. 'A good one, too. I had the lead in all my high school plays back home. Everyone said I should go to Hollywood, so I did. And the other night I met this guy in a bar who said he'll help me get an agent.'

'If you're nice to him?' Tamsin couldn't resist.

'Huh?' The man scratched his head. 'Uh, I'll get your car.'

'Too bad,' Leandra said after he left. 'What a waste. All looks, no brains. Actors in this town do need a few smarts.'

Tamsin was laughing too hard to comment.

From there they headed for Melrose. 'These boutiques are more our speed,' Leandra said. 'I wanted you to see Rodeo Drive, but here we can do some serious shopping. In fact I've got just the store for you. You'll love it. It's a little pricey, but all the clothes are imported. Ah, there it is.'

She slammed on her brakes and screeched into a parking place, ignoring the angry honks behind her. 'Isn't it cute?' She pointed to a storefront that bore the legend LONDON WAVE.

'Wait, Leandra. Are you taking me to a shop where the clothes are imported from *England*?'

'Of course. From London, to be specific. The clothes are so cutting edge – oh.' She noticed the look on Tamsin's face. 'London imports. Not a good idea. I wasn't thinking. My other tourist friends love this place.'

Tamsin giggled. 'May I assume your other tourist friends aren't from the UK? If you want to go in here I'll go with you. But don't expect me to buy anything that I can buy at home for half as much.'

'No, we can skip this one. I don't need anything from here today. Since we were lucky enough to find a parking place, let's walk for a while. That's the best way to see Melrose, anyway.'

They'd only gone half a block when Tamsin stopped in her tracks. 'That one. Let's check it out.' She led the way into a store called OUT RAGE. Something about the shop seemed off-centre. For one thing, all the clothes were impossibly large. It wasn't the kind of large one would find by wandering by mistake into an outsize women's store. These clothes were large, but the proportions weren't those of outsize people. It seemed more a store for giants.

And the shoes! Tamsin didn't know American sizes, so she had no basis for comparison. But she had eyes, and these told her the shoes were enormous. Even the heels were higher than the outrageously high heels that were the current fashion norm.

'What is this?' she whispered to Leandra.

'It's a drag queen store,' Leandra answered in a normal tone of voice. 'Where did you think they get all their lovely outfits? In a women's boutique? The smaller ones, yes. But the big girls come to stores like this one. And the smaller ones come here at least for their shoes. Most men do have bigger feet than we do, you know.'

Tamsin had never wondered where drag queens bought their clothes, but she found the shop fascinating. The larger proportions of everything intrigued her. She thought she might want to return to photograph the interior.

They continued to wander down the street, stopping in every shop that took their fancy. An hour later they could scarcely see above the bags and boxes they were carrying. 'Are you hungry? We haven't had lunch, and now it's almost dinner time,' Leandra said. 'I know just the place. Chicken and waffles.'

'What?' Tamsin didn't believe she'd heard correctly.

'Chicken and waffles. And maybe a plate of collards. If we're hungry enough, sweet potato pie. I feel like being wicked. We've been so good ever since you got here, eating healthy food all the time. But once in a while I've just got to indulge myself. And chicken and waffles are calling to me. OK with you?'

'Excellent.' Tamsin could have eaten an entire chicken by that time. She hadn't realised how hungry she was until Leandra mentioned lunch. 'Is it far from here?'

'No, just around the corner. Let's go.' Leandra stepped up the pace, walking briskly back to the car.

Two hours later they pulled into the parking lot of a large building that was set back from the street. 'Wonderful lunch,' Tamsin said, patting her stomach. 'I'm so full I could just go to sleep.'

'Chicken and waffles will do that to you,' Leandra agreed. 'That's why I don't do it very often. I'd never get anything productive done. But our day out together is sufficient excuse, I think.'

The shop assistants greeted Leandra like an old friend. Tamsin commented on this. 'They *are* old friends,' Leandra said. 'I've partied with most of them. They work in a sex department store, after all. It figures that they'd enjoy a few kinks.'

Leandra led the way to the clothing department, followed by several of the assistants. In the back of the store the heady smell of leather was overpowering. Tamsin tried her best to take in all the sights and smells as Leandra strode purposefully towards a rack of leather trousers.

'Since you're a novice, Tamsin, let's start you off with something basic. In black leather trousers and jacket, with a whip in your hand, you will look exactly like what you are – a dominatrix.' She chose two pairs of trousers and handed them to one of the assistants while she went to look at jackets.

'Those look awfully small.' Tamsin, though intimidated by the atmosphere, found her voice to object.

'Leather stretches. Those will be fine. You'll see. And how about this jacket?' She held up a long-sleeved leather jacket with epaulettes on the shoulders. 'We can get some heavy silver neck chains too, if you like. And biker's gloves? I think so, yes. Most definitely, you need leather gloves.' Leandra was picking up items as she spoke. 'Boots, too. You need real stompin' boots. You want to look as if you're going to grind your heel into your victims and crush them.'

Tamsin picked up a boot with a wickedly high heel. 'How about this one?'

'Perfect. Now let's go try everything on.'

One of the shop assistants parted a curtain, revealing a large communal dressing room. Several men and women in various stages of undress looked at them curiously.

Tamsin didn't wait to be told what to do. She wriggled out of her miniskirt and kicked off her sandals. Standing in only her T-shirt and a wisp of a high-cut brief, she looked at Leandra with a puzzled expression.

'Leave your panties on while you're trying them on,' Leandra directed. 'But when you wear them for real, you won't wear panties. You can't have a panty-line with leather trousers.'

Tamsin picked up a pair of trousers, and, stepping into them, started to pull them up. She couldn't budge them past her knees. Frustrated, she tugged harder.

'I told you they're too small!' she protested.

'No, they aren't. Here, let us help you. Lie down.' Leandra pointed to a mat on the floor.

Tamsin lay down and submitted herself to the ministrations of Leandra and the shop assistants. It took two people to pull the trousers up over her thighs as far as her crotch. They continued to pull and tug until the trousers were up over her hips. The leather did give, Tamsin had to admit, but how would she manage if she needed two or three people to help her every time she wore them?

'Get up and look in the mirror,' Leandra ordered. 'Now, don't you agree they're a perfect fit?'

They were, indeed. Tamsin was delighted with what she saw. She shrugged into the leather jacket and slowly turned around, admiring herself from all angles. If it took a few friends to help her get dressed, she thought, it was well worth it.

'Now the boots,' said one of the assistants. She bent over to help Tamsin tug them on.

'Wonderful! You look fantastic!' Leandra enthused. 'Put on the gloves and neck chains, too. And Katie, would you please go and grab a whip? I want to see what she looks like with all her equipment.'

One of the assistants scurried away. When she returned she put the whip into Tamsin's gloved hand. 'Now you look like a Mistress, for sure.'

'We'll buy it all. Everything but the whip. We'll save whips for another trip,' Leandra said. 'Come on, Tamsin, let's go home and show the boys.'

When they arrived at the house they could hear the television blaring as soon as they got out of the car. 'What on earth . . .?' Tamsin said.

'That's American football. Lucky you, not recognising it. I think Nigel must be corrupting Jamie.'

Inside the house they were greeted by the smell of

beer and pizza. Then apparently somebody scored, and Nigel and Jamie roared their approval.

Jamie skittered off the couch when he saw Leandra. 'I'm sorry, Mistress,' he apologised from his usual position on the floor.

'It's all right, Jamie. I told you to enjoy yourself today. Obviously you're doing so. Good.' She turned to Tamsin. 'Do you want to stay with these animals and learn the mysteries of American football? Or shall we go upstairs and try on what we bought?'

'Oh, yes, I'd rather do that. I'm not fond of spectator sports – except the coeducational kind.'

Collecting all their parcels, they ran up the stairs to Leandra's room.

17

That afternoon Tamsin wriggled into her new leathers and presented herself to Leandra.

'What do you think?'

'Perfect! I told you those trousers weren't too small. You wouldn't want them any bigger.'

Indeed she wouldn't, Tamsin decided. They felt like a second skin. She knew that people could see her sex outlined by the soft doeskin that hugged her body. She picked up a whip and struck a pose.

'You look ferocious, Tamsin. But you're not going to tempt me. This is a work session. I want to teach you how to use the whips. We'll play afterwards.'

'Where's Nigel? I want to show him what we bought.'

'You'll see him and practise on him later. First, you're going to practise on inanimate objects. You need to be able to control your whips before you use one on a human being. Now, let's get started.'

Leandra put Tamsin through some rigorous paces, having her practise whipping a mattress until she thought her arm would fall off. Then they went to the basement, where Leandra had attached a full-sized outline of a human male to a tackle dummy. Tamsin practised hitting the spots that Leandra indicated. At first she was way off mark, but gradually her skill improved. When she hit the penis ten times out of ten and the right and left nipples eight times out of ten each, Leandra pronounced her ready for a human target. They went outdoors to find Nigel, who was relaxing in the pool after a day of gardening and bouts of watching the football.

'Get out of that pool. Now!'

Nigel looked startled at Tamsin's tone. He stared at her as she stood with her legs apart and her sex outlined through the leather. Slowly he climbed out of the pool, naked and dripping.

'Time for me to get whipped, eh, Tamsin?'

'*Mistress* Tamsin, to you!'

'I see. Very well. *Mistress* Tamsin. Leandra, I think you've taught her too well.'

Tamsin ignored this. 'Over there.' She pointed her whip in the direction she wanted him to go.

They made their way across the garden to a large oak tree that had chains hanging from one of its lower branches. At the end of the chains hung a pair of wrist cuffs. Nigel obligingly held his arms over his head so that Tamsin could fasten the cuffs.

'I can't reach them.' Tamsin was embarrassed. She had done so well up to now, and now she thought she looked ridiculous due to a problem she could have foreseen.

'No problem,' said Leandra. 'Unlock those small padlocks and pull the chains down. Hook him up and then pull the chains back up to where they were.'

'Oh.' Tamsin's voice was tiny.

'It's that kind of thing that makes us lose our credibility. I did that deliberately, to teach you. Next time you'll know to check out your equipment before you start to play.'

Tamsin lowered the chains and fastened the cuffs to Nigel's wrists. She pulled the chains back up higher than they had been, leaving Nigel hanging with his arms over his head and his feet barely touching the ground.

'Tamsin, this is merely another practice session. You're to use the whip I select and hit him where I tell you to and with the degree of force I specify. Your purpose is not to get him aroused, but if that happens

209

it's OK. He's not Jamie, after all. Part of Jamie's discipline is to learn to control his cock, but Nigel is different. Another thing: if Nigel says his safe word, you stop instantly. If he merely tells you to stop, ignore him. When he does that, he's just playing his part.'

They determined a safe word for Nigel, and Tamsin began. Every so often she stopped and Leandra asked Nigel for feedback. Tamsin was a quick learner. Before long she could control the force of her lashes so that occasionally she was able to merely brush or tickle the area that Leandra indicated. Nigel finally said his safe word because he needed a break.

'I've never been a punching bag before,' he told Tamsin, while Tamsin and Leandra were massaging his shoulders. 'Actually, I rather like it. Be careful, or you'll turn me into a submissive.'

'I very much doubt that!' the women replied, almost in unison. They looked at each other and broke into startled laughter.

'All this is very good for me, Nigel,' Tamsin said. 'But did it turn you on at all?'

'No. But don't be disappointed. I have the wrong mindset, for one thing. Right now I'm a tackle dummy, and you're training for a sport. That idea doesn't get my gonads in an uproar. Besides, I'm by nature a dominant. The submissive role doesn't normally trip my trigger, except occasionally with Leandra. I have to keep her happy, you know, and the woman dearly loves to whip people.'

Leandra pretended to punch him, and they both laughed.

Nigel good-naturedly put his wrists back into the restraints. Tamsin hauled his arms back over his head for another practice session. This one was shorter. Both Tamsin and Nigel tired sooner than before. When Tamsin's accuracy began to falter, Leandra called a halt.

'Leave the man alone now, Tamsin. You can't perfect your technique in just one day. Besides, I want there to be something left of him for tonight.'

'Tonight?'

'He's my partner. I want some fun and games with him later. Now let's go and see what Jamie's up to.'

Jamie wasn't up to much. He was squatting inside the door, dressed in nothing but a dog collar. At Leandra's command he trotted off to the kitchen to set the table and serve the meal the cook had prepared for them, while the others showered and put on fresh clothes. Very shortly they gathered in the dining room. Jamie waited until the others were seated before he squatted on his heels by Leandra's chair. He waited respectfully for Leandra to begin eating. About halfway through the meal Tamsin noticed that Jamie hadn't eaten anything.

'Jamie, aren't you hungry?' she asked.

'Good heavens!' Leandra answered before Jamie had a chance to. She looked guilty. 'I'm so sorry, Jamie. I forgot to give you permission to eat.'

'It's all right, Mistress.'

'No, it isn't. Since you're my slave, it's my responsibility to see that your needs are met. I was remiss, and I apologise. Please eat now, Jamie.'

'Thank you, Mistress.' He bent to the floor and began eating out of the dish he had prepared for himself, punctuating his chewing with slurps from the adjacent water bowl.

After dinner Tamsin questioned Leandra. 'Since you forgot to let Jamie have his dinner, couldn't you do something special to make it up to him, maybe let him have an orgasm when the rest of us do? Just once?'

'No, Tamsin. I'm sorry, but I can't. Jamie would lose respect for me if I did. I apologised to him, and that's enough.'

'That seems so strange to me. When I make a mistake and hurt a friend, I do something special, like take them out for dinner or buy a gift, besides apologising. "I'm sorry" isn't always enough for me.'

'I know. I'm like that with my peers, too. But it's different with a slave. If you lose their respect, you've had it. They won't want to obey you again. And of course they're free to leave any time they want to. You don't want them to do that; you want to be the one who sends them away.'

Arms around each other's waists, they strolled to Leandra's room so Tamsin could try on Leandra's leather clothing. Tamsin had fallen in love with leather in just one day. She wanted to see bustiers, vests, jackets, skirts and shorts, so she could decide what she might like to buy next.

The first garment that caught her eye was a black leather bustier with a double row of metal studs down the front. She stripped off everything but her panties and put it on. It was too big in the bust, as expected. Leandra cinched it tight in the back and tightened the neck strap for her. This left the top half of her breasts exposed, but it did fit better. The tight strap pulled the front up so that the bottom edge exposed the vee of her panties.

'Lacy yellow panties are pretty, but they don't quite go with this outfit, Tamsin. Here. Take them off and try this.' Leandra held up a black leather thong.

Tamsin fumbled with her panties, but the leather garment seemed to hold them prisoner. 'Help me,' she said. 'I don't want to tear them.'

Leandra knelt and slid her hands under the leather. 'You're right. They're stuck. Give me a minute here.'

'Wait. I'll do it.' Nigel strode into the room.

Instead of tugging on the panties, Nigel buried his face in Tamsin's crotch. 'You're wet,' he mumbled into her panties. 'Why am I not surprised?' He licked at the panties. 'Yum. I love the taste of you. And the smell.' He continued licking, his tongue pressing the panties against Tamsin's clit.

Tamsin was already moaning and thrusting herself against Nigel's mouth, trying to get him to engulf the whole thing. The heat of his mouth was setting her on fire. Entwining her fingers in his hair, she pulled his head closer.

'Do me, Nigel. I need to come.'

'Let me get your panties off.'

'No. There isn't time. Do me through the silk. I want to come against your mouth.'

Nigel gripped the back of Tamsin's thighs and pulled her closer. After only a few seconds Tamsin felt the tingling that was the precursor to orgasm. Warmth rushed through her body. Then the build-up began. When she couldn't stand it another second, she exploded. Crying out, she thrust and bucked, nearly knocking Nigel over with the force of her need.

Tamsin sank to the soft fake fur rug, with Nigel still tonguing her crotch. She stretched out full length and spread her legs to allow him access.

'Panties. Get panties.' Tamsin knew she couldn't get what she wanted now with her panties as a barrier. Yet she couldn't form a coherent sentence for Nigel. 'Off. Panties. Off.'

Apparently this was clear enough for Nigel, who pushed Tamsin's legs back together. Tamsin fought him. Wild with lust, she kept trying to push her legs apart, exposing her whole sex to Nigel and Leandra.

'Hold still, Tamsin. He can't get them off if you don't hold your legs closer together,' Leandra said.

Tamsin was beyond listening. Moaning and thrashing her whole body around, she spread her legs and thrust herself at Nigel's face. Nigel resisted the temptation. He forced her legs back together and finally managed to free the panties. He pulled them down and buried his face between her legs again. Tamsin spread them once more.

He tongued lazily, lapping at the juice that was flowing copiously. His tongue moved down, back to the forbidden opening, but the bustier impeded his progress. Tamsin whimpered and wiggled her bum. Nigel couldn't reach where Tamsin wanted him to. He sat up and rolled her over on her stomach. Loosening the bustier, he pushed it aside so that her back and bum were exposed.

She moaned and raised her bum in invitation. Nigel probed the opening with his tongue, gently, then more forcefully. Tamsin shuddered. Nigel started inserting his cock, and Tamsin took it all with no problem.

'More. Please, more,' Tamsin begged. She moaned, urging him on. Wriggling her bum, she tried to suck his whole cock in.

Too slowly for Tamsin, Nigel began to thrust. Tamsin's moaning got louder. Nigel's back-and-forth motion was hitting her magic spot. She felt the flood coming. Before she could warn him, she gushed all over the rug. Nigel pumped faster. His free hand slid under Tamsin's body and found her sex, now soaked with her ejaculation. He groped for her clit, which had swelled to an enormous size. He rubbed it while maintaining his thrusts.

Tamsin managed to get to her knees. Thrusting her bum into Nigel's face, she moved her pubes against his hand. Her orgasm was building slowly. She wanted this phase to last, wanted it not to be over. But it was too late. The orgasm swelled and finally broke. Her sex throbbed and gushed. While her spasms racked her she called Nigel's name over and over.

Nigel flipped Tamsin over on her back, hurled himself on top of her, and entered her. Still orgasming, she was wide open to him. After a few hurried thrusts he exploded in her.

Leandra, who had been watching the whole thing, cried out and came on her own hand. When she recovered, she gave Nigel a quick kiss on the cheek.

'Come on, Tamsin,' she said, jumping to her feet. 'Let's shower and get out of here. Jamie will be waiting for us. As for you, Lover Boy, you'd better get some rest. I have plans for us later.'

18

Tamsin's routine for the next few days was exceedingly demanding. Up early to work on her photos, she spent the afternoons practising on Nigel and her evenings frolicking with her housemates until far into the night. So far the lack of sleep wasn't bothering her. Life was far too exciting to waste a moment more than necessary in sleep.

The work with Nigel was having an unexpected benefit. Her upper arms, which had been getting flabby since Jamie had been carrying all her equipment for her, were firming up most attractively. Whipping definitely agreed with her. She felt more energetic than she had since she was a little girl. For the first time in her life she felt complete. Her photography skills were blossoming, she'd found herself sexually, and she had lots of new friends. The only thing that was missing was a special person to be with, but she told herself she had plenty of time for that later.

One morning while Tamsin and Jamie were packing up their equipment for the day's photo shoot, Leandra came in, flushed from her morning run. Tamsin jumped up, a delighted smile on her face.

'Why don't you come with us, Leandra? Now that your film is finished, you have the time. Besides, I'd like you to show me more of L.A. I'm running out of places to shoot.'

'That's impossible. There's always something to shoot in L.A. I've been remiss. I've neglected to show you enough of the city: we've been too busy most of the time doing other things.' Leandra thrust her pelvis forward suggestively so there could be no doubt as to her meaning. 'I'm glad you asked me. Actually, I came looking for you so I could invite myself along.'

They piled into the car and headed for downtown L.A. Leandra was an excellent tour guide. She knew the area well, and she pointed out many spots that Tamsin wanted to photograph. Many rolls of film later they had lunch in an out-of-the-way rooftop restaurant.

'I've noticed that you like to photograph fountains, Tamsin. There's one you haven't seen yet that I think you'll like best of all. But it's not operative until evening. There's a jazz concert there tonight, too. How does that sound?'

'Wonderful. Let's photograph more of this area this afternoon, then have dinner and go to see your fountain. I want to do a photo study of Jamie in the afternoon sun. You did wear something decent under those jeans, didn't you, Jamie?'

Jamie nodded, since he hadn't been given permission to speak. He'd almost embarrassed the women by automatically squatting in his usual place at Leandra's feet. Leandra ordered him into a chair before anybody noticed.

They spent a delightful and productive afternoon posing Jamie in his black bikini swimming trunks. He proved to be an adaptable model: co-operative, never complaining. Some of the shots were perfect for the current book effort, but Tamsin wanted more.

'The book of nudes we were talking about, Leandra? How about Jamie? We could come down here after dark, he can take off his trunks, and . . .'

'Perfect!' Leandra studied Jamie thoughtfully. 'He's really looking good since I've had him working out in our weight room. He's developed a California tan, too. And Vanessa's swimming lessons have helped. I think he'll do nicely. And we don't have to pay a professional model's fees. Yes! Let's do it! We can start tonight when we go to the concert and photograph the fountain.'

It occurred to Tamsin that Jamie ought to be consulted about this. Being a slave in private was one thing – having one's naked body, however delectable, displayed in a book for the world to see was something entirely different.

'What do you think, Jamie? Would you like to do this?'

Before Jamie could respond, Leandra shot him a warning glance. He closed his already half-opened mouth. Finally he almost whispered, 'Whatever Mistress wants.'

'I don't think he's happy about this, Leandra. Perhaps we should forget about it.'

'It doesn't matter what he thinks. It doesn't matter if he's happy. What's important is that I want him to do it. So he will.'

'Let's at least take some test shots first before we decide. He may not be a photogenic nude at all.'

'You're the expert, Tamsin. If you don't like the results, we'll stop. I'll defer to your judgement. But I want him to try, at least.'

Tamsin still didn't know what Jamie thought about the whole thing. She sternly told herself to quit worrying about it. He'd chosen to be Leandra's slave; he hadn't been forced. It was up to him.

Tamsin still wasn't used to how early it got dark in Los Angeles. Before she knew it, it was time to think about photographing Jamie in the nude.

They returned to the steps across from the library. About halfway up was an alcove that was out of sight of the outdoor diners at the top. Tamsin ordered Jamie to pose there while she adjusted the settings on her camera. Perfect. Jamie appeared as a silhouette, outlined by shadows and city lights.

'Strip off,' Tamsin commanded.

'B–but . . .'

'Do as she says, Jamie.'

'Yes, Mistress.' His face a fiery red, Jamie took off his sandals, jeans, and shirt. He stood there in his swimming trunks, hesitating.

'All of it, Jamie. I want you naked. Now.'

Obediently but slowly, he hooked his fingers in his waistband and tugged the trunks down. When he reached his pubic hair, he stopped. He looked pleadingly at Tamsin.

'Please don't make me.'

'Since when have you been so shy? Do as I say. All the way off.'

'I – I can't.'

'What's wrong with you?' Tired of playing games with him, Tamsin grabbed at his trunks and yanked. She encountered an obvious barrier.

'Blast! You're hard. Is that why you didn't want to take them off?'

Jamie nodded, not meeting her eye. Tamsin reached inside the trunks and closed her hand around his cock. She gently eased it out of the confining material and shoved the trunks to the ground.

'I'm going to shoot you anyway. If we wait for it to come down, the lighting will be all wrong.' Tamsin turned him away from her so his erection wouldn't be obvious. 'I'll shoot your bum first, just to get you used to the idea of being photographed starkers.' She quickly set up her equipment and adjusted her settings.

'Look at me over your shoulder, Jamie. Wink. Give me a half smile. Perfect.' She snapped the picture. 'Hold still for another one. Good. Now spread your legs wide and bend over so I can see your balls. That's great. Now hold it.'

Instead of standing still, Jamie moved. He shuddered and lurched and nearly fell over. He groaned.

'No, Jamie. Don't come. Not now. Stop it!'

Jamie, of course, couldn't stop it. He shuddered and gasped while his body spewed the semen that had been building up all day in his tight jeans. Tamsin watched in amazement while it spurted, sizzling, all over the hot rocks of the alcove. Fortunately she kept her wits enough to snap two photos before it was over.

'At least in a few minutes I'll be able to get some good frontal views. Go wash in the fountain, Jamie. You're a mess.'

Jamie did as he was told and returned to his post. The cold water had done the trick and only the slightest trace of an erection remained.

Working quickly before darkness descended, Tamsin shot a series of photos. Jamie's cock was beginning to rise again when she finished.

'Why can't I be hard for the photo shoot?'

'Not for a *book*, silly goose. This is a book of artistic nudes. We can take some pictures of you hard just for ourselves. But not until your Mistress gives you permission.'

'I think that can probably be arranged,' said Leandra. 'I have some ideas of my own of pictures I'd like to have of him.'

When Jamie was dressed again, the three of them walked to the top of the steps. Faint sounds of jazz beckoned from nearby. They followed the sound, which led them to the water court. Constantly changing coloured lights played on the fountain at the back of the band. Tamsin was entranced.

'I must photograph this! All of it!' She set up her equipment and began to shoot. The others stayed out of her way while she photographed the fountain and the band, separately and together. Then she turned her attention to the audience, revelling in the display of multicultural splendour. She photographed people in the bright dress of various African countries, people in the robes of the Middle East, and people from Asia, South America and Mexico. The people she photographed were good-natured about it, smiling and laughing into her camera. All too soon the set was over and the lights came up.

'Come with me. I have something more to show you.' Leandra took Tamsin by the hand and led her to the other side of the performance area. A flight of over a hundred steps led to the street below. About halfway down, Leandra turned away from the steps and led them into a tiny, grassy park.

'Don't worry. Nobody can see us, unless it's somebody else coming down the steps. That's unlikely. Most people are too lazy to climb back to the top again. If anybody does come down here, they're here for the same reason we are.'

'Which is?' Tamsin asked.

'Sex, of course. And we can take some more photos of Jamie here.'

'It's too bad we don't have any toys with us.'

'Oh, but we do.' Leandra gestured to her large handbag. 'I always carry wrist restraints, a vibrator and a small whip wherever I go, just in case.'

Jamie started to peel off his jeans. As usual, his trunks revealed a pronounced bulge.

'Keep that, Jamie. This time it's OK. Just don't let yourself come, or you'll be very sorry,' Leandra warned. 'I have plans for you. Now pull down those trunks.'

While Jamie was obeying, Leandra conferred with Tamsin, who busied herself setting up her camera. She nodded to Leandra when she was ready.

Leandra reached into her bag and pulled out a small dildo. Jamie's eyes gleamed when he saw it.

'Don't get too excited, Jamie. How do you know this is for you? Maybe I'm going to use it on Tamsin.'

Tamsin turned Jamie so he was almost in profile. His growing erection was clearly visible. He reached for it.

'Bad! Don't touch! Put your hands down at your side. And remember what I told you about coming.'

The view in Tamsin's lens looked perfect. She'd never tried what she was about to do now. Yet she felt no pressure, just a growing excitement. If it didn't work out, that was all right. She could try it again. Could, and would. But if it did work out, it could make her reputation.

She looked again, just to be sure. Her photographer's instinct had been right. It was perfect. Now she had to time her shot just right. A split second of error in her timing would ruin it. She closed her eyes for a few seconds to centre herself. When she opened them, Jamie was still there, frozen in time. His jutting penis, in silhouette like the rest of his body, looked ready to erupt. Not for the first time she noticed that Leandra's conditioning regimen had produced an extremely attractive man. There was no trace of flab anywhere on his body. Furthermore, his slightly scrawny adolescent build had filled out into a new maturity. Tamsin felt a twinge of regret that Leandra had seen his potential before she had. She was beginning to understand that her feelings for Jamie were stronger than she'd thought they were.

Never mind that now. There was work to be done. She nodded to Leandra, who was standing behind Jamie, vibrator in hand.

Leandra reacted instantly. With lightning speed she thrust the dildo between Jamie's cheeks and turned it on, then jumped back out of the way of the camera.

Jamie stifled a yell as his penis began to spurt. Jets of semen shot out and landed in the flower bed. The effect was as if he had shot it clear down into the street.

Tamsin got it all on film. She clicked shot after shot as Jamie helplessly came in front of them both. His ejaculation was copious, a photographer's dream. Tamsin had wondered if it would be possible, since he'd come fairly recently, at the fountain. She'd obviously underestimated him. She'd underestimated him in a lot of ways, apparently.

While she was putting her equipment away, Leandra, in an unusual display of tenderness, helped Jamie dress. Tamsin was suddenly aware that the concert had resumed. The music wafted through the air above them.

All that Tamsin wanted to do was go home, develop her film, and see if these photos were indeed as good as she thought they were. But she didn't want to miss the opportunity to get some more good shots for *L.A. From Other Eyes*. That, after all, was the main reason they'd come downtown.

They climbed back up the hill and again mingled with the other concert-goers. Tamsin relaxed and lost herself in the music and the ambiance. A small dance floor off to one side of the fountain caught her eye.

'Come on, Leandra, Jamie. Let's dance!' She grabbed Jamie's hand and tugged him towards the dance floor. Leandra followed close behind.

Dancers squeezed together to make room for them on the crowded floor. Tamsin suddenly recalled the last time she'd danced with Jamie – when he'd come in his pants and run off the floor in embarrassment. She wasn't going to let that happen again. Well, maybe he'd come in his pants this time, but she wouldn't let him run away if he did.

The three of them danced in the tiny space, separately but together, until a slow dance started. Leandra turned and began dancing with a stranger, leaving Tamsin and Jamie staring into each other's eyes.

Tamsin put her arms around Jamie and felt a rush of anticipation when he reciprocated. She snuggled her body into his and nuzzled his earlobe with her lips.

'I'm going to make you come now, all right?' she whispered.

'But Mistress Leandra said –'

'I'm your Mistress too, now. Remember? And I want to make you come.'

The mere thought made her breathless. This felt much different than the sexual games she'd been playing with everybody since her arrival in Los Angeles. This was her friend, her pal, her Jamie. She didn't want to whip him or dominate him in any way at the moment. She wanted him to come because he wanted to, not for any other reason. She had to find out what he really wanted.

'Do you want to come for me?'

'Yes. Yes, I do. Very much.'

She wanted to tell him how happy that made her, but the intense training she'd had from Leandra took over her emotions and stopped her. She couldn't tell him how she felt. If she did, she'd never be able to take a dominant role with him again. And while at the moment being dominant was the last thing in the world she wanted, she was still aware enough to know that that wouldn't always be the case.

Right now she wanted them to be equals. Tomorrow she might want to whip him senseless. She could handle both situations if she was careful and kept her head.

The steady jazz beat was making the floor vibrate. The rhythm went from the floorboards up through her feet and legs, straight to her sex. It was a raw, primitive feeling. Her entire body was responding now.

Jamie inched his hands lower, pressing her pelvis against his. He continued to move until his hands were toying with the hem of her miniskirt. There he stopped, as if trying to decide what to do next.

The sensation left Tamsin breathless. She ground harder into his pelvis, in the process hitching her skirt up a bit. Jamie took advantage of the opportunity and worked his hands under her skirt, cupping her cheeks and pulling her towards him.

Tamsin was glad she'd worn panties. She knew that anyone who happened to be looking could see them. But she was too caught up in the experience to care. She flipped her skirt up in front, pressing against his bulge with the silk of her panties. Now she could feel his erection rubbing her clit as she rocked up and down against him.

Using the material of her skirt as a cover, she reached down and tried to unzip his jeans. She couldn't; his bulge was too big. She undid the waistband and tried again. After a false start the zipper slid down, releasing his full erection encased in a black bikini. It sprang to her clit as if aimed from a gun.

Tamsin wriggled and tried to press even closer. If only they could pull down their underpants and do it right. But they couldn't, not on a dance floor. What they were already doing was wild enough. Tamsin knew she was flooding his bikini as well as her own. She couldn't stop. She didn't want to.

With what little thought she was still capable of, she tried to identify her feelings. Mixed in with her almost overwhelming desire was a hint of something else. Joy, perhaps? Yes, that was it. She felt joy at being almost united with Jamie, even though it was a public place and they couldn't do all that they wanted to. She could tell that Jamie wanted her too, that he wasn't just programmed to perform as a stud.

She wanted him inside her. She wanted to pull him out of his bikini and mash him into her crotch. She thought about how it would feel if she pulled her panties aside and let his naked penis rub against her clit.

This was all happening too fast. She needed to give

herself a little space and give herself some breathing room. She wriggled, trying to push herself back. Jamie splayed his hands over her cheeks, forcing her tight against him. She tried once again to pull free. This time he let her.

She pulled back so there was space between her crotch and his and felt a warm rush of air brush over her soaked panties. She stood silently for a moment, breathing in the mingled scents of their arousal. She felt as if she might collapse if it weren't for the fact that Jamie was holding her up. She leaned forward and rested her head on his shoulder. He nuzzled her ear.

Tamsin wrapped her arms around his neck and rested against him, her breasts pressed close to his chest, her nipples so tender it was almost painful.

The jazz continued to pound out its rhythm. Once again she was aware of it, through the floorboards, through the soles of her feet. She kicked off her sandals in order to feel it more intensely.

Thrusting her thighs tightly against Jamie's, she still avoided crotch-to-crotch contact. She didn't want it to happen too soon. She sensed his cock in its black sheath reaching for her. Her response was to slide her head down to his chest and suck on a nipple through his shirt. He gasped. She felt a sense of wonder at how stiff his nipple was, how sensitive. She nibbled at it and was gratified by his long groan.

Jamie suddenly took the initiative. He pulled her so close that she couldn't avoid contact with his cock even if she wanted to. She didn't resist this time. She clung to his neck and pressed herself into the length of his body, with her pussy almost straddling his bulge. The pressure on the silk of her panties was driving her crazy; she had to feel his naked cock against her. She just had to.

Heedless of the other dancers, she pulled her mini-skirt up further in front in an attempt to achieve more contact with Jamie. She slid the crotch of her panties aside and rubbed her naked clit against Jamie's bikini-clad erection. She heard a loud whimpering and was dimly aware of Jamie trying to shush somebody. When he gently put his hand to her lips, she realised that she herself was the source of the whimpers. She willed herself to be quiet, but the sounds still escaped her.

The music was loud and getting louder. Tamsin's moans got louder too. Between moans she whispered, 'Fuck me! Fuck me, Jamie!' Jamie shushed her again and she understood that she wasn't whispering, that she was too loud. She bit her lip to stop the words. Her whimpers continued. She clung to Jamie while the whimpers turned into sobs.

She was only vaguely aware of what he was doing. He was stroking her hair with one hand, calming her sobs. With his other hand he reached down and pulled her panties back so her clit was exposed again. She hoped he was seeking her opening, since suddenly she needed him inside her, needed him desperately. That's not where he seemed to be going, however, and she was in no state to help him.

She pulled herself up on tiptoes, trying to show him what she wanted. He ignored her and continued playing with the crotch of her panties. She felt his erection bob up and down when he cupped his hand over her mound. After a few moments of fumbling, he again placed his spread hands on her cheeks, lifted her up, and set her down so her clit rubbed against his now-naked penis.

His cock brushed against her clit as he thrust. She came almost instantly: sharp, deep spasms that racked her whole body. She sobbed helplessly as she began to ejaculate a flood that she tried in vain to imprison between her thighs.

She could tell from the intensity of his thrusts that his orgasm was fast approaching. He groaned and shot his first load, drenching her panties. She was still sobbing as her own orgasm continued. Her ejaculation mingled with his, all over her panties, her skirt, and his jeans. He shot his last load and was finished.

She held him tightly, savouring the moment. She and Jamie had actually done it. Never mind that she hadn't had him inside. That would come later. Many times later. What she'd just felt with him was something she'd been seeking for years, ever since she first became aware of her own longings. Jamie was special. She had enough experience now to tell the difference. Playing with Leandra and Nigel and the others was fun. She enjoyed them and would continue to play with them. But they weren't Jamie. She wasn't sure she understood what the difference was. She just knew it was there.

Jamie broke into her reverie. 'Tamsin, come on. The music is about to end.'

Oh yes, the music. They were dancing, and the music would end, and everybody would see.

Yet all she could do was say stupidly, 'How do you know?'

'I know this piece well. It's almost over. Come *on*!' He pulled away from her and tucked himself back into his jeans.

Tamsin was still non-functional. She stood and stared at him, still holding the hem of her skirt at waist level.

'Put your skirt down. Quickly!' Jamie put his hand over hers and pulled the skirt down. Then he put his arms around her and danced her off the stage. It wasn't a second too soon, for the music stopped and the lights went up. They clung together in the shadows until Leandra found them.

'That's fine behaviour for a slave,' Leandra said.

Jamie looked stricken, but Tamsin noticed that Leandra was smiling.

'Let's go home. Unless, of course, you want to take

more photographs.' Leandra linked arms with them and steered them towards the car.

'I think I'll pass on that. I'm finished with photography for the day.'

And she was. She was also exhausted and proud. She'd done it. She'd made Jamie come on the dance floor, just as she'd said she would.

When they got home she didn't even develop the pictures of Jamie that she'd been so eager to see. She went straight to bed and fell asleep the moment she turned out her light.

19

Tamsin woke up the next morning more in the mood for play than for work. She wanted to develop the films she'd taken of Jamie and the fountain, but the sun was calling to her. She found it hard to stay inside in this weather. It was a typical Californian summer day, with clear air and lots of sunshine. She'd be out of her mind to spend the day in the darkroom. Lounging by the pool seemed a much saner choice. But if she did that, she wouldn't get any work done. *L.A. From Other Eyes* still needed another series of photos in addition to the ones she hadn't developed yet, and she was getting impatient to finish so she could work on *Naked in L.A.* Sitting by the pool, however tempting the idea, wouldn't achieve this goal.

She was pondering her dilemma over coffee and a croissant when Leandra wandered into the kitchen. Tamsin grabbed her hand and pulled her into a chair beside her.

'Leandra, what would you do today if you were me? Develop film or sit by the pool?'

'Not fair, making me decide. I have another suggestion, though. Why don't you film your last series at that little beach you discovered? That would keep you outdoors all day and you'd get to be productive at the same time. Fun in the sun without guilt. Sounds good to me. Take Jamie with you if you want to.'

'And I can develop my film this evening after the sun goes down. Excellent idea. I'll do it.'

She woke a reluctant Jamie from a sound sleep and

told him her plan. When he was fully awake he was as enthusiastic as she was. Leandra had him pack a lunch for himself and Tamsin while Tamsin checked her equipment.

'You are to obey Tamsin today, Jamie. I'm not going with you. I have to teach my class,' Leandra said. 'But I know that in my absence you'll make me proud of you.'

Jamie put everything in the car and they set out. At first Tamsin had thought she'd never get used to driving on the right, but now she found it much easier. Still, she needed to concentrate on the road, so they rode in silence up the coast. Just past Malibu, Tamsin parked at the top of a cliff and told Jamie to unload the car.

She sent Jamie ahead of her down the steep hill to the beach. He was carrying most of the equipment, and she wanted to watch him unobserved. She enjoyed the view of his muscles as he hoisted the cameras to his shoulders. Leandra's workouts had done him a lot of good; he looked like a young god in his tight bikini swimming trunks.

This promised to be a good place for a shoot. The beach was secluded, accessible only by a long flight of wooden steps. At each end, the tiny beach was protected by caves that extended to the water's edge. Nobody would be likely to disturb them from the ocean side, and anybody coming down the steps would give plenty of warning of their presence. It would be a perfect beach for nude photography.

Be good, Tamsin, she admonished herself. You're here as a professional. Your job is to shoot the scenery first. Jamie comes later.

She tugged at her new bikini. Perhaps she should have bought a size larger. It was definitely skimpy. She was lost with these American sizes. Nothing was at all the way it seemed. The bikini looked good, though. Leandra had persuaded her to get a bikini wax from

Brenda. That had solved one problem. She was glad she'd done that before buying this bikini. She had noticed that Brenda was a real cutie, too. She never used to notice women much. Was Leandra turning her into a real lesbian?

'Looks like rain,' Jamie said.

'Don't be silly, Jamie. It never rains in California.'

'You want to bet? Look!' he pointed out to sea. Sure enough, an enormous bank of clouds was bearing down on them.

'I don't believe this!' Tamsin wailed. 'My cameras!'

'Don't worry. I brought the rain covers you said we wouldn't need on this trip.'

In a few short minutes the cloud was overhead. The skies opened with a roll of thunder.

'Feel how warm it is, Jamie. This is so much fun!' Tamsin began an impromptu dance in the rain.

Impulsively she untied the top of her swimsuit and tossed it on the sand. Jamie's face turned fiery red.

'Good grief, Jamie, what's wrong with you? We've been totally naked with Leandra and the others, and it doesn't bother you.'

'I know. But when it's just you and me alone, it's different, somehow.'

'Silly boy!' She blew him a kiss and lifted her breasts to the rain. 'This feels so good! I think I'll take the bottoms off, too.' She wiggled and thrust her pelvis at him.

'Don't you dare!' If possible, he was blushing even more fiercely.

'Don't look, then!'

Before Tamsin could make good on her threat, the rain changed to hail. At first the hailstones were tiny. Then they grew to the size of golf balls.

'To the cave!' Jamie had already slung the cameras over his shoulder and was folding the tripod.

A huge hailstone glanced off Tamsin's breast as she raced Jamie to the cave. She was glad to get in out of the weather.

'The equipment is fine,' Jamie said, anticipating her question. 'Are you all right?'

'One breast is a little sore. Otherwise I'm fine.'

'That's what you get for taking off your bra,' Jamie teased. Tamsin noticed that he was no longer blushing.

She playfully bumped into him and got no reaction. Becoming bolder, she enveloped him in a huge hug, keeping her crotch a chaste distance from his. He didn't pull away. Taking charge, she dared a full body hug, pressing her wet bikini bottom against his. He didn't react to this either. She'd have to take more drastic steps.

'Too bad it's so rocky in here. We can't even sit down and be comfortable,' she said.

'We can *lie* down, though.' Jamie whipped out an air mattress and proceeded to blow it up. He threw it down on the rocks. 'There. Now we can be downright cosy.'

The hail showed no sign of abating. Resigned to not getting any work done, Tamsin lay down on the mattress. Jamie was right. It was surprisingly comfortable. She motioned for Jamie to lie down, too. He did, but at some distance from her.

'Come on over here, Jamie. I don't bite. Unless you want me to, of course. I need you to keep me warm.'

Slowly he slid over until their bodies were touching. She wondered why he was so hesitant.

'Jamie, is something wrong? You don't seem to want to be near me. After last night, I thought that . . .'

'No, not really. I mean, yes. Mistress Leandra doesn't want us to do anything unless she's with us.'

'She hasn't tried to put any such restrictions on *me*. I'll do what I please.'

'It's different for you, Tamsin. You're not her slave.'

'That's true. And this is now, and she's not here. You're as free as I am.'

'She'd know, Tamsin. I hate to think what she'd do to me.'

'All right. But what if I attacked you? Then you wouldn't be responsible for whatever happened.' She acted on her words by lunging at him, pinning him down on the air mattress. He didn't resist.

'You're stronger than I am, Jamie. You can stop this any time you choose. The only way I can prevent that is to tie you up. Do you want that?'

He shook his head.

'I don't, either. I want your arms and legs free so you can do unspeakable things to my body. Like this.' She licked a trail down to his right nipple, where she stopped. 'Is this so terrible?'

He shook his head again. His nipple was getting rigid under the ministrations of her tongue. She raised her head.

'Easy, Jamie. Let's not rush this. We've got all day.' She lay down on top of him, turning slightly to the side so their groins wouldn't touch. She began licking at his ear, delicately tracing the inner whorls with her tongue. She mashed her breasts into his nipples and slowly gyrated. At the same time she reached a hand behind his back and massaged the area just above his bum.

Finished with his ear, she blew gently on it and encircled the lobe with her mouth. He gasped when she began to suck on it. She stopped when she felt a stirring in his groin. She moved her mouth to his other ear and repeated the process. Then she nibbled gently on his neck, and stroked his flanks in a soothing motion – more like massage than like lovemaking.

He was finally responding. His penis was starting to rise, and he let loose an occasional moan. Tamsin placed her mouth on his and forced his mouth open with her tongue.

Her nipples were stiffening. She wanted him, but she knew that if she moved too fast she'd scare him off. She moved her body so that her nipples connected more closely with his. He slowly raised a hand and placed it on her breast, tracing the outline of it gently with his fingers. Breaking the kiss, he opened his eyes and gazed at her breasts. Tamsin's arousal increased as she realised what he was doing.

'Do you like my breasts, Jamie?'

'Oh, yes.'

'Wouldn't you like to kiss them? That would feel so good. It would feel even better if you sucked them a little.'

He didn't answer, but she felt him nod. Gently she lifted her breasts and lowered a nipple to his open mouth. He closed his lips and gave the nipple a tender kiss. It was a mere whisper of a kiss. Yet she reacted more strongly than if he'd done it more forcefully.

'That feels wonderful. Please do it again.'

His next kiss was a little less timid. Then he pulled back.

'We shouldn't be doing this.'

'We haven't done anything. All right, if it will make you feel better, I promise that I won't let you put your dick in. We'll pretend we're teenagers and I'm a virgin.'

'All right. I guess that would be all right.'

'Of course it would! Quit worrying and kiss my breast again.'

Jamie needed no more urging. He moved back to Tamsin's breast and covered it with tiny kisses.

'Did you like that?'

'Of course I did! Do it to the other one.'

His passivity both baffled and aroused her. She'd

never met a man who needed so much direction. And she was learning to love giving it. But his behaviour was inexplicable, after what they'd done the night before on the dance floor.

She rolled over on her back and pulled him on top of her. He sought her breast again and resumed kissing it. His tongue licked a circle around her areola while she lay back and enjoyed the slow arousal it was causing. She didn't want anything to happen too quickly. The rain seemed to be with them for a while and she couldn't work, so she might as well relax. Besides, she felt like taking it slowly. She usually preferred fast sex, but today she wasn't in the mood. It was different with Jamie. She loved sex with the others, but it was all just for fun, more like practising a sport. Not that she had anything to complain about. But Jamie was special. With all the sex they'd both had since their arrival in California, they'd not yet had sex with each other. They'd had plenty of orgasms in each other's presence. However, that wasn't the same thing at all.

Tamsin wanted this to end with Jamie inside her. She felt a need for the consummation of their years of friendship. Her feelings for Jamie were definitely much deeper than she'd thought. She'd had a crush on him for years, of course, but she'd long ago decided that the crush persisted because he was unavailable. That phenomenon had plagued her for her whole life: crushes on boys and men who wouldn't – or couldn't – reciprocate. Jamie was her closest friend, and had been so since she was twelve. He'd been a gangly fourteen-year-old, teased by his peers because he was scrawny, wore horn-rimmed glasses, and was hopeless at sports. She'd been hated because she was a little too podgy to suit that year's fashion police. The two lonely adolescents had found each other and remained inseparable into their adulthood.

Now she understood why he'd shied away from her every time she hinted at wanting sex. He hadn't realised his own needs at the time, although he'd known that she couldn't fulfil them, whatever they were. She'd accepted his rejection without question, telling herself that he probably didn't understand what she was hinting at. Unfortunately she was too shy to pursue the matter, so the crush remained just a crush, and she'd obtained her limited sexual experience from other men.

Their relationship had to change now. She wanted a real adult relationship between the two of them. His slave relationship with Leandra wouldn't last after they left the States. For Leandra it was a diversion. Her primary relationship was with Nigel, and Tamsin knew that Jamie wouldn't become a permanent member of the household. She hoped that Jamie understood this, too.

But she didn't need to worry about that today. Her current task was to get Jamie to come inside her. In the meantime his tongue on her breast was driving her wild. Her arousal deepened. Instinctively she spread her legs so she could feel more of Jamie's bulge.

Jamie instantly pulled back. Damn. She'd spooked him. That was what she'd been most worried about doing. She couldn't bear it if he stopped now.

Instead, she was aware of fingers groping in their crotch region. Jamie was pulling off his trunks. Excellent.

She willed herself to lie perfectly still while he scrambled out of the restrictive garment. His erection sprang out and lodged in the crotch of her bikini. This was even more than she'd hoped for at this stage. She forced herself to keep her breathing perfectly even so as not to distract him.

Jamie was breathing hard. Tamsin was suddenly worried that he'd come all over everything before she had a chance to coax him inside her. What should she do? If she went into her Mistress mode, that in itself was likely to push him into orgasm. She knew how turned on he got when he was being a slave. Still, she had to risk something, because he obviously wasn't going to last much longer. Then she remembered a crucial detail.

'Jamie, listen to me. Back off a second.' She felt nothing where his erection had been. He had obeyed instantly. 'Would you like to make love to me if you weren't worried about your Mistress?'

She felt him nod. Good. She'd been worried that her words might provoke an orgasm rather than an answer to her question.

'There's something we both forgot. The last thing that Leandra said before we left the house was that you were to obey me today. Do you remember?'

'Yes, Mistress Tamsin.'

'Very well, slave. I want you to take off my bikini bottom. Do it now.'

'Yes, Mistress Tamsin.' His voice trembled. He tugged at the offending garment, hesitantly at first, then with more confidence. Tamsin raised her hips so he could complete the task.

'Good slave. Now lie on top of me. I'm cold.'

Cold was not what she was feeling, in spite of the hailstorm. But she didn't know how else to get him in position.

Her ploy worked. Jamie lay back down on top of her and reacquainted his mouth with her breast. He moved so his erection found her sex with no difficulty.

They lay there holding each other, not moving. Tamsin felt her arousal building again. She still wanted to prolong the outcome as long as she could.

She thought she felt Jamie's erection softening. Reaching down between them, she found she was right. Blast. What had gone wrong?

Of course. Jamie was incapable of taking the lead. She had to do something before it ended in disaster.

'Jamie, you're hard. You know how Mistresses feel about that. Get up.'

While Jamie was obeying, she grabbed his cock and found that it was gratifyingly hard again. She squeezed it firmly. Jamie winced and grew harder.

'Lie down on your back. Now pretend I've weighted down your hands so you can't move them. You're bad. You got hard without my permission. I have to punish you.'

Jamie's cock sprang to attention. Tamsin squeezed his testicles, eliciting a groan.

'I told you not to get hard! Why don't you obey me?'

Jamie didn't answer. Tamsin straddled him, positioning herself just above his straining erection. Jamie thrust up but couldn't reach her.

Tamsin teased him like this for several minutes, leaping out of his way every time he thrust. Her arousal threatened to overwhelm her. She decided it was time to get down to business. Jamie looked as if he were about to burst, and she was afraid he'd come before he touched her.

The next time he thrust, she met him halfway. She gasped as his stiff cock made contact with her opening. Then she sprang back up out of his reach. On the next thrust she landed solidly on his cock, which slipped inside her as if it had been created especially for her. Jamie groaned. Tamsin slid down until her sex pressed against the root of his cock.

Jamie was finally inside her! She'd waited such a long time for this, waited for years. Emotion overwhelmed her and she felt tears sting her eyes. She blinked them back. This simply wouldn't do. A real Mistress wouldn't behave like this. She glanced at Jamie and was relieved to see that his eyes were closed. He hadn't seen.

She remained there, awash in feelings she couldn't identify, while Jamie thrust in a leisurely manner as if they had all day. Which they did, of course. She had never felt so complete. It was as if a part of her had been missing and had finally been returned to her. Every time Jamie pulled back to begin a new thrust, she pushed against him so he couldn't leave her. She gripped him as hard as she could with her well-conditioned inner muscles, in the demented hope of keeping him inside her forever.

Jamie was the first to succumb. 'Mistress, I . . .'

His flushed face told her everything she needed to know. He was about to come, and nothing was going to stop it. Reluctantly, she gave in. Not that she had a choice. At the moment she formed the thought, she felt a surge within as Jamie released his load.

Her response started building. She'd wanted them to come together, but he hadn't been able to wait. It was up to her to see if she could come before he finished.

His hand on her clit would do it. But no. They were pretending he was tied up. He couldn't use his hands.

He was still spurting when she placed her own hand on her clit and rubbed. She came instantly, which triggered another spurt from Jamie. Her spasms milked the last of the come from him.

She was far from finished. His cock was still hard and pulsating inside her when she pulled away and crawled up to his face. She didn't have to tell him what to do. His tongue was already reaching for her while she was lowering herself on top of him. He lapped at her clit. The first touch intensified her orgasm. She went into orbit. She saw stars that existed in no known galaxy. It was as though she and Jamie were alone together, floating in space. Gone was the rocky cave and the pounding rain. The two of them were together among the stars, engulfed in an endless orgasm.

After an interminable time, Tamsin descended to earth to discover that not so much time had passed after all. It was still raining. Jamie's cock, she ascertained when she reached down to check, was still hard. His hands were stretched out to his sides as if they were bound with something unbreakable.

Shyly, in a manner most inappropriate to a Mistress, Tamsin smiled at him. He smiled back.

'Ready for Round Two?' he asked.

She was surprised to find that she was ready, indeed. They had a vigorous Round Two, followed by a rest, followed by a more subdued Round Three. Finally they were both sated. Tamsin noticed that the sun had come out again.

'Time for work,' she said as she bounced up off his cock.

It was already afternoon. They hauled the cameras and their other gear out of the cave and set up for a shoot. Tamsin got some excellent shots of the waves and of the caves that guarded the beach. When she had finished to her satisfaction, she turned to Jamie.

'Your turn. Off with the trunks.'

'Naked? But why?'

'Are you daring to question your Mistress? Never mind. I'll tell you why. I'm starting work on *Naked in L.A.* You're the model. That's why. Now take them off.'

'Yes, Mistress.' Jamie scrambled to pull them off. Naked, he struck a pose.

'That's beautiful, Jamie. Hold it!' She snapped several photos while Jamie tried out different positions.

'You're a natural model,' Tamsin said. 'You know exactly what to do without being told.' She couldn't wait to see how these would turn out.

The glare from the sun as it slowly fell into the sea put a stop to the photography for the day. Tamsin was delighted with the day's work. If the photos were as good as she thought they'd be, she was finished with *L.A. From Other Eyes* and could concentrate on the new book of nudes. She tried not to get her hopes up about how talented Jamie was. Sometimes models didn't look as good in the finished photographs as they did when they were posing.

Refusing to dwell on her doubts, Tamsin kept up a constant stream of chatter all the way back to L.A.

20

'Leandra, look at this!' Tamsin ran out of her darkroom waving a large, wet photo.

It was the morning after the beach shoot. Tamsin was finally settling down to develop all the photos of the last two days.

Leandra came running. 'Heavens, Tamsin, such screeching! I thought you'd hurt yourself. Give it to me. Let me see.' She grabbed the photo from Tamsin's hand and let out a shriek herself.

'It's perfect! Jamie is perfect! He looks even better in the finished photo than he did when you were shooting it.' She studied the photo, which was one of the ones taken at the jazz concert. 'We can use him for the whole book.'

'I was hoping you'd say that. We'll have this book put together in no time. Just wait until you see the ones from yesterday, too.'

Jamie, wearing his dog collar and nothing else, was crouched in the corner by his water dish. Neither woman thought to include him in the conversation.

'We'll have to get a guardian appointed for him. There will be legal contracts involved, and –'

'Wait a minute, Leandra. Jamie is a competent adult. He's not really your slave. That's a role he chooses to play. He can take care of his own legal needs.'

'You're quite right, of course. Sorry. I do get carried away sometimes.' Leandra offered a tentative smile.

'That's all right. I do it, too. Which reminds me, I need to talk to you.'

'Talk away.'

Tamsin glanced at Jamie. 'In private.'

'Sure. Jamie, go to the pool and practise your swimming. Don't come back in until I call you.'

'Yes, Mistress Leandra.'

When Jamie was out of earshot, Tamsin gave Leandra an account of the last 36 hours, beginning with the episode on the dance floor. Leandra didn't interrupt once.

'So you see,' Tamsin finished, 'my friendship with Jamie is changing. We've been friends for ten years, and now ...'

'I've been wondering when this would happen.' Leandra smiled as she hugged Tamsin. 'It's been obvious to Nigel and me all along. The only people who were unaware were you and Jamie.'

'You're not angry? He's your slave.'

'He's been a wonderful slave. I've enjoyed every minute, and I hope he has, too. But it's time to start moving on. Actually, you've solved a problem for me. I've been wondering how to detach him from me when the time comes for him to go back to London. He's been so devoted to me. I wouldn't hurt him for the world. I've become quite fond of him, actually. He's the most naturally submissive man I've ever met. I'll miss him.'

They talked for a while about how to wean him gradually away from Leandra and towards acceptance of Tamsin as his Mistress. Tamsin had a few doubts.

'This sounds fine as long as I have a whip to crack over him. But I don't want a relationship that's all dominance and submission. I want a friend, an equal partner. Making him squat naked in a corner is all right for parties, but I don't want that every minute of every day.'

'Nor do I,' Leandra said. 'You've never seen Nigel and me when nobody else is around. Obviously. That's our real relationship. What we do with our friends is acting. The acting, the role-playing, enhances our relationship, intensifies how we are with each other in private. If you and Jamie decide to live together, no, you won't be running around the house in leathers all the time, lashing out with your whip. Nor will Jamie eat all the time off the kitchen floor. You'll do those things only when the mood hits you. But you may find that happening more often than you think. Being dominant grows on one.'

A shout from outside brought the conversation to a close.

'Help! Help!'

Remembering that Jamie was a novice swimmer, Tamsin raced with Leandra to the pool, prepared to dive in and save Jamie. Instead, they were greeted by the spectacle of Jamie sitting on his raft in the middle of the shallow end, swatting at a honey-bee and bellowing.

Howling with laughter, the women waded out and splashed the bee with water, driving it away.

Resuming their conversation was out of the question. Besides, nothing more needed to be said.

21

In the meantime, Vanessa and Harry were working on plans of their own. Halfway across the Atlantic, Vanessa turned to Harry and asked, 'Are you sure you want to do this?'

'Of course I'm sure! Have you ever seen me hesitate, once I've made up my mind?'

She had, but only when he was lying across her lap with a hairbrush being applied briskly to his backside. 'You really intend to let her have a flat and studio? Just like that? And furnish it and set up a photography studio in it, all in less than a month?'

'Yes, I do. That's why I asked you to come with me. I need you to help me choose a flat in a suitable neighbourhood full of artists of all stripes. I don't trust my own judgement on this. Not that I'm hesitant. I'm not. But like any good executive, I do know when I'm out of my depth. When that happens I surround myself with experts – in this case you.'

'What makes you think I'm an expert? You're an architect. You know a lot more about houses than I do. I know nothing about this.'

'You know about people, though. You're young. You run with the same kind of crowd that Tamsin does. I want you to pick an area that you yourself would be comfortable in. I have in mind three of my rental properties. One of them is a huge loft that I think might do. Another is a ground floor flat with a big yard and room for a studio. I think either of these would be more suitable than the third one. But I want your opinion on all of them. And I can't stress enough the importance of confidentiality.'

Vanessa was offended. 'You *know* I maintain confidentiality. My professional life depends upon it. Why are you bringing it up? Don't you trust me? And speaking of confidentiality, I'd really like you not to tell Tamsin that you hired me to spy on her. She and I are good friends now. Everything has changed.'

'Sorry, Vanessa. That was clumsy of me. It's just that I'm so concerned. If I didn't trust you, we wouldn't be doing this. And of course I won't tell Tamsin about our arrangement.'

'Apology accepted. But Harry, I must admit I'm curious. Why are you providing her with a flat and studio? Isn't giving her a job enough?'

'I'll try to explain. Now is as good a time as any. After all, you can't pull down my trousers and give me a nice spanking on this plane in front of all these people. Though I wish you could.'

'You'd be surprised what I can do on a plane,' said Vanessa with a grin, remembering the first time she met Tamsin and Jamie. 'But never mind.'

'I'm sure you'd spank me without the slightest twinge of embarrassment. Thing is, *I'd* be embarrassed. Extremely so. But back to my explanation.'

He told Vanessa all about his need for his photographer to be sexually dominant. 'I just can't tolerate submissive women, Vanessa. I can't work with them, even in a purely business arrangement. If Tamsin had turned out to be submissive, I wouldn't be doing this. But since I'll be working with her, I want her to have a large flat with a studio so she can just concentrate on her artistic development. That's for my benefit too, you see. She doesn't know that, of course. For that matter, she doesn't even know about any of this, including the job. Maybe I won't be able to persuade her to accept it. Or the flat and studio. I'm not *giving* them to her, you know. It'll just be while she's working for me.'

'Don't frown like that, Harry. It's not becoming to you. Of course she'll accept it. Why on earth wouldn't she?'

'There are lots of reasons a young woman wouldn't accept a flat from a perfectly strange man, Vanessa. Sometime I'll explain them to you. In the meantime, tomorrow we're going to decide which flat to offer her.'

'But why *are* you doing this, Harry? You barely know her.'

'I'd do it if she were a total stranger, after seeing her with that whip. She whips exquisitely. I love her energy. And she doesn't even really know how yet. She's a mere novice. But she doesn't seem like a stranger. She's as kinky as I am, underneath it all. She just doesn't know it yet. Now, if I can only make her understand why she's *got* to take my job offer . . .'

'Tell her just what you've told me. But leave out the part about how exquisitely she whips. That does sound a little strange. Besides, you're not planning on having her whip you, are you?'

'Indeed not! What do you think I am, some kind of perv?'

'I apologise, Harry. No offence intended. But do let's hurry up and find the right property. I want to return to LA as soon as possible. Now, what do you say we try to catch a snooze? We're landing in two hours.'

Harry was already sound asleep.

22

The next month passed in a blur. All too soon it was time to go back to London. Friday, the day before Tamsin and Jamie's departure, dawned hot and sunny. Tamsin finished her packing and then lazed by the pool, enjoying her last chance to feel the California sun on her entire body. Naked sunbathing had been one of the unexpected pleasures of her stay. Of course she couldn't indulge in it everywhere she went, but between the secluded beach where she and Jamie had gone the day of the hailstorm, and Leandra's vast, totally private back yard, she'd managed to become a golden bronze on every inch of her body.

She spread her legs, inviting the sun to join her. There was a languid sensuality to this, she realised, as she moved her hand to her mound and began to pet it. Instead of drying her off, the sun made her wetter. She was about to confirm this with her finger when she heard Leandra calling her. Then she remembered. Leandra was going to take her to West Hollywood and buy her a farewell present. She jumped to her feet, pussy still tingling, and ran into the house.

Not bothering with underwear, she wriggled into a pair of tight running shorts and a tank top. Her rigid nipples nearly poked through the shirt. She wondered how she was going to make it through the day, for she knew there would be no time for sex until the party that night. She was glad she'd had the foresight to choose black shorts so her wetness would be less noticeable.

She found Leandra in the kitchen. 'Let's go, Leandra. I'm ready.'

Leandra laughed. 'I guess you *are* ready. Look at those nipples, girl. Just the sight of you like that is making me wet. I'm glad Nigel isn't here, or we'd never get to leave. But come on, let's get out of here.'

They drove to the sex shop where they'd had the orgy over a month before. The manager remembered Tamsin. 'You look as if you're ready to play in my dressing room again. Those nipples need breathing room.' She took Tamsin's hand. 'Let's go.'

Tamsin would have followed her willingly if Leandra hadn't laid a hand on her arm, restraining her. 'Not now, girlfriend. Save it for tonight.'

Leandra led her to the display of whips. 'You're ready for your own whips now. They're my present to you. Choose the ones you want. I do want you to have more than one.'

Tamsin was overwhelmed by the sheer number of whips. 'Which ones should I take?'

'It's up to you. You're a full-fledged whip-mistress now. You're perfectly capable of making your own choices.'

Tamsin hefted several of the instruments, then grew more confident. The smell of the leather permeated her senses, making her dampen her shorts again. Her nipples stiffened until they were almost painful.

'Do I get to try them out?' she asked.

'No, not here. The first time you use them will be special. You must save them for tonight.' Leandra held a long whip out to her. 'Here. I think you'll like this one.'

Tamsin chose that one and two others: a cat-o'-nine-tails and a small, elegant riding crop. They left the shop, with Tamsin still on the verge of orgasm.

'I can't wait, Leandra. I've got to come.'

'You can wait, and you will. It will be better if you do.'

Tamsin decided to do it Leandra's way. She tried to put the sexy thoughts out of her head, with limited success. Waiting for Leandra to drive out of the parking lot, she could think about nothing but her swollen clit. The sun seemed to be boring a hole in it. She spread her legs and felt the silk of her shorts brush against her. This didn't help her resolve to think about other things. To distract herself, she forced herself to listen to Leandra's chatter about the caterers and the party decorations. She was even able to make an occasional reasonably intelligent comment.

Back at Leandra's house, Tamsin decided it was a good thing they hadn't lingered longer at the sex shop. The caterers had arrived to set up for the party, and Jamie obviously needed help. He was trying to direct them at the same time he was putting the finishing touches to a photo gallery of blown-up nude pictures of himself. The result was chaos.

Leandra took charge, sending the caterers to the far end of the garden, where she planned to have the midnight buffet. Tamsin went inside to help Jamie with the photo display.

He had done an excellent job. All the walls in the house were covered with large posters of the naked Jamie. Leandra had wanted to do this to give their guests an informal sample of Tamsin and Jamie's talents. This being Hollywood, word would spread, and the showing was certain to garner commissions for both Jamie and Tamsin. Jamie seemed to be enjoying the attention he was getting as a model; Tamsin hoped it wouldn't ruin him as a slave.

Since the day of the hailstorm, Tamsin had been too busy to sit down and talk to Jamie, much less be alone with him in other situations. She and Leandra had been involved with all the details of publishing *L.A. From Other Eyes*, which was receiving rave pre-publication reviews. Their editor was pushing them to finish *Naked in L.A.*; she thought it could be even more successful than their first book. Accordingly, Tamsin had been photographing Jamie day and night in all stages of undress. These were the photos she and Jamie were displaying now.

All the frantic work hadn't interfered with their playtime in any way. If anything, the work had the opposite effect. They were excited and burning with creative energy, all of which required more sexual play rather than less. Nearly every night, and many times during the day as well, they'd come together in twos, threes, or fours, or more if Vanessa and Marcus dropped by.

Tamsin had reached a level of contentment with her life that previously she could have only imagined. Professionally, she was on the verge of becoming recognised and respected in the art world. She and Leandra were planning a *Naked in London* book, though that wouldn't be happening for several months. They wanted to wait and see how *Naked in L.A.* was received by the public. If that flopped, there was no point in doing what they hoped might become a series, *Naked in the Cities of the World*. However, both Tamsin and Leandra had high hopes for their success.

Her relationship with Jamie was more uncertain than her career, but she was still pleased when she considered it. Jamie had agreed to live with her in London as her slave. She felt that she would be a good Mistress for Jamie. She'd been working hard on her whipping techniques, coached by both Leandra and Nigel. Today Leandra had pronounced her a full-fledged whip-mistress. The praise meant a lot to her, for earning it hadn't been easy.

Then there was her new business partnership with Harry, who not only had given her a job but was letting her live in a flat and studio in one of his buildings. She couldn't wait to see it. In a mere three months she'd acquired a career, a slave, and a free flat and studio. She was a happy woman.

Earlier in the week Leandra had hinted to Tamsin about a big surprise that would be revealed at the farewell party. Tamsin had pleaded, but Leandra would say nothing more. Now she was waiting as patiently as she could for the party to start, when presumably she'd find out what it was.

When they finished hanging the pictures in the house, they went out to the garden to set up the remaining posters on easels. Tamsin hardly recognised the familiar outdoor space. A team of party decorators had come earlier, transforming the pool into a tropical lagoon and the garden itself into a jungle. Realistic statues of various jungle animals peered out from artificial foliage. Nigel and Jamie had moved all the dungeon equipment outdoors, where they placed racks, slings, and flogging crosses all over the jungle.

The effect on Tamsin was instantaneous, and she tingled in anticipation of the evening to come. She knew she had to wait, though, this time. She had learned earlier that very day that if she forced herself to wait and let the feelings build up, even for a few hours, it intensified her pleasure.

Jamie interrupted her thoughts, asking her something about the placement of the pictures. Tamsin was grateful for the distraction. While she was helping him, she made herself focus on the task. She even succeeded in keeping her mind off sex until they were finished.

Then the thoughts came flooding back. Her thoughts weren't the only thing flooding, either – her sex dampened to the point of overflow as she looked forward to the evening ahead.

Leandra finished with the caterers and approached Tamsin and Jamie. 'All done? Good. Come on, Tamsin.

Let's go get ready for the party. Jamie, you know what I told you to do.' She linked arms with Tamsin and steered her into the house.

After a leisurely shower, Tamsin returned to her room to find that Leandra had laid out her leathers for her and was waiting to help her dress. Unfortunately they had no time to linger; the doorbell was signalling the arrival of the first guests. Leandra hurried Tamsin into a frothy, blue lace thong with a matching suspender belt and black seamed stockings, followed by her tight new leather trousers. A lacy push-up bra ensured that Tamsin's nipples would push out the front of her tight leather jacket in a most enticing manner. They left the top of the jacket unbuttoned as far as her cleavage. Black leather gloves and high-heeled black sandals completed her ensemble. Leandra handed Tamsin her new whips. 'You'll need these tonight,' she said.

'I will? You mean you'll let me play?'

'More than that. You'll play unsupervised. Nigel and I know that you've learned to control yourself. You're the only one who doesn't know that. You must prove it to yourself before you go back home. Now let's go down and mingle. If we stay here any longer, I'm going to be the one who loses control. Just looking at you and thinking about the sexy underwear you have on under that leather is making me hot.'

Pleased murmurs greeted them as they descended the staircase. But the guests were not looking at them. They were gathered in small clusters admiring the posters of Jamie, asking each other who the unknown model was. They were oblivious to the fact that they'd seen him many times over the summer, crouched in the corner wearing only a dog collar.

Leandra and Tamsin moved through the crowd, greeting the guests and accepting congratulations on the quality of the posters. Tamsin modestly admitted that she was the photographer, but only when asked. She was still not used to the limelight.

After allowing a suitable amount of time for enjoying the pictures, Leandra urged her guests to join her in the garden. As they did so, they voiced more sounds of approval at the sight of the jungle, the pool, the instruments of torture, and the easels with more pictures of Jamie. After admiring the pictures, some peeled out of their leathers or their evening clothes and dived straight into the pool. Others, mostly the ones in evening clothes, headed for the buffet. The guests in elaborate leather outfits lingered in the tropical jungle area, admiring the crosses, flogging posts, vaulting horses and slings. There was something there for every exotic taste. Whips, breast clamps, handcuffs, butt plugs, dildos, miniature branding irons and other toys were arranged in attractive displays on shelves for the pleasure of the guests. Nigel emerged from some obscure corner of the garden, but Jamie was nowhere in sight.

Tamsin was beginning to worry about him. Then she saw him. He strode from the house, resplendent in a studded dog collar, a leather ring that pushed his scrotum up and maintained his cock at full erection, and nothing else. With pumped-up muscles from an obviously recent workout, he looked like a model for one of the local skin magazines.

When he got closer to Tamsin, his stride became a shuffle, his head bent, and he seemed to shrink. He sank to his knees for the final few steps. He lowered his forehead to the ground in front of her and said, so softly that Tamsin could barely hear him, 'Whip me, Mistress Tamsin. Please.'

So this was the surprise. She was to whip him in front of all these people. Not that anybody would be watching them. The guests were already engrossed in their own activities. Leandra and Nigel had disappeared. This was to be between her and Jamie.

Very well. She gestured with her head towards an empty cross and walked towards it without looking to see if he was following – which he was. She cuffed him to it, with his feet raised so he could barely support himself on his toes. She stared at him for what seemed a long time, saying nothing.

His lips moved, though no sound came out. 'Please, Mistress.'

Finally, ever so slowly, Tamsin picked up her long whip.

At first she teased him, flicking her whip lightly across his skin while she warmed up her arm. Then she switched to the cat and laid it on him with stronger strokes. Welts were rising, but Jamie didn't flinch. His cock strained against the restraining ring.

Seeing his reaction, Tamsin felt a surge of excitement. Her sex juices were flowing copiously. She knew her thong was soaked beyond redemption, and she felt the leather crotch of her trousers beginning to get damp. She kept on whipping.

Jamie was finally reduced to moans of pain. He begged her to stop but didn't say his safe word. So she continued. She switched to the small riding crop and etched her initials in welts between his nipples. Then she remembered the branding irons. When she'd helped Leandra display the equipment earlier, she'd noticed that one of the tiny irons was made in the initial 'T'.

She headed for the assortment of branding irons and the small gas burners placed conveniently nearby, leaving Jamie alone to wonder what was about to happen to him. She easily located the 'T' and heated it until it glowed red. Returning to Jamie, she made sure he saw the branding iron and had time to understand its implication. His eyes opened wider, but he made no sound. Tamsin tilted her head, questioning. Jamie nodded.

Tamsin removed the harness from his cock and scrotum. His cock did not need artificial assistance to remain aloft. It waved proudly while its owner finally began to register fear. Tamsin lowered the iron towards Jamie's crotch. She wanted it to be obvious to anybody he was with that he was merely on loan, that he belonged to her. With a swift thrust she touched the iron to his skin. The pungent odour of singed hair and seared flesh mingled with his screams. Tamsin removed the branding iron almost instantly, leaving a bright red 'T' emblazoned in Jamie's nest of hair.

Jamie's screams turned to moans as his cock swelled and exploded. Tamsin watched in amazement. The pain of the branding had been an aphrodisiac for him. Her own clit swelled in response. The sheer audacity of what she had done made her so hot she could barely stand it. She had branded a man. She had taken complete possession of him.

Her face remained that of a stern Mistress as her orgasm surged. Contractions racked her as she stood, branding iron in hand, staring at Jamie while he continued to erupt. She didn't want to let him know how he was affecting her.

She knew that this was a turning point for her. Whatever happened in the future, she would always look back on this and remember it as the night she became a true Mistress.

It was also the night that Jamie became truly her slave.

23

It was a rainy, late-winter day in London. Tamsin sat at her kitchen table watching Jamie remove things from the oven. She sniffed in appreciation.

'You've done a beautiful job on this party, Jamie. Those rumaki smell divine. Leandra and Nigel will love all the hors d'oeuvres you've made. It was a real piece of luck, Harry sending you to that cooking class, even if it was for the wrong reasons.'

'He said he wants to have civilised food when he comes over. I think that's a good enough reason, Mistress Tamsin.'

'You don't have to say Mistress when we're alone, Jamie; I've told you that before.'

'I remember. But Mistress Leandra is coming, and I don't want to slip up. She would think you hadn't trained me well. I want to be a credit to you, Mistress.'

Tamsin stared at his unprovoked bulge. 'You are. You've done especially well with your erections. I didn't think I'd ever get you to hold one indefinitely. But you've improved immensely. It pleases me. I do like to see a hard man.'

'What do I do when Mistress Leandra gets here? She always punished me for being hard.'

'I want you hard, and I'm your Mistress now. Leandra will be proud of me for having retrained you so well. Really, Jamie, you do have amazing endurance. Which reminds me, are you ready for your performance with Gina?'

'Of course, Mistress. She's rehearsed me until I couldn't possibly forget.'

'Very well.' Tamsin watched him arrange his miniature duck tacos on a plate. 'Are you almost finished? It's time to go and pick up Leandra and Nigel. Besides, if I stay here another minute I'm going to start devouring all that food.'

Tamsin had hired a limo, just as Leandra had done for her and Jamie when they arrived in Los Angeles. Besides, she didn't want to drive, she wanted to focus on her conversation with their guests. She was glad she'd made this decision when they'd finished their greetings and were settled in the limousine behind the driver.

Leandra was full of questions about their new life. 'Jamie's hard. Did you notice?'

'Of course. It took me months to train him to keep it that way. I don't allow him to wear underpants because I like to see the way he sticks out. Of course, he gets rewarded for it.'

'But isn't it a problem when he walks down the street? I'd think the law would –'

'It's not a problem so far. He's been wearing a heavy coat, and an erection isn't obvious. When it gets warmer I'll let him wear underpants when we're out in public.'

'Ingenious. You've done wonders with him.'

'Wait until you see what else he can do. He's learned gourmet cooking, and our friend Gina has taught him to dance.'

They spent the rest of the journey discussing their plans for *Naked in London*, which was the excuse for Leandra and Nigel's visit. *Naked in L.A.* was, as they had predicted, a huge success so far.

'Jamie is somewhat of a celebrity in Los Angeles,' Leandra said. 'After your farewell party, people thought he'd just disappeared. Rumour has it that more than a few modelling agents are trying to find him. Of course I haven't given out even a hint of his whereabouts.'

'Thank you, Leandra. He'll be famous in England all too soon, when the UK edition of the book comes out. And then, of course, *Naked in London*. I can't say I'm looking forward to it. I won't be able to let him run about with an erection any more.'

'Only in public,' Leandra reminded her. 'And then only in summer. Most of the time you'll be able to enjoy him as you please.'

The conversation was brought to an abrupt end by their arrival at Tamsin and Jamie's house. Leandra let out a cry of admiration and gazed at it, speechless, while the chauffeur carried their luggage up the winding stone pathway to the house. Then she found her voice.

'It's perfect for the two of you! I was expecting something much smaller. You did refer to it as a "small flat".'

Tamsin smiled as she looked at her building through Leandra's eyes. Leandra was right. It was by no means small, and it delighted the eyes. Elaborate newel posts graced the steep front steps, which ended in a double front door. Further back on the left was a wrought-iron fence, through which peeped the earliest and bravest spring flowers. Huge conifers soared at the side of the house. Wisps of smoke curled from the stone chimney, hinting at a real wood-burning fireplace inside.

'We don't have the whole building, you know,' Tamsin said. 'Just the ground floor flat, though we have the use of the yard and garden as well. Come on in. I can't wait for you to see it.'

Tamsin proudly showed her guests her well-equipped dungeon and living area before showing them to their luxurious bedroom next to her photography studio. After the guests had unpacked, they joined Tamsin and

Jamie in the kitchen. Jamie was putting the finishing touches on his party-cooking marathon.

'The smells are driving me wild!' Leandra said. 'Do we really have to wait for the party before we eat any of this?'

'Of course not. I thought you might be hungry, so I put two plates aside just for you.' Tamsin took them from Jamie and put them before her guests. 'If you don't feel like party food, Jamie can whip you up an omelette or something.'

'Thanks. But this is wonderful. It'll do very well. You're so lucky you have a gourmet cook in the house.' Leandra shot a meaningful glance at Nigel. 'I wish I did.'

Watching them eat, Tamsin became conscious of a current between herself and Leandra. She felt as she had often felt in Los Angeles that past summer, when she couldn't look at Leandra without getting wet. In fact, she was getting wet right now. She'd been with a woman very few times since she'd been home. Most of her energy had been focused on working out her relationship with Jamie and taking care of her now-numerous photography clients, especially Harry. He'd been a dream employer for a young photographer just starting out, referring her to friends of his when he didn't need her services. She'd seen Gina and Vanessa a few times each, but that was it. Now, seeing Leandra, she began to want what she'd been missing. But she didn't know how to approach Leandra – the six months of separation were a barrier in her mind.

While she was pondering her dilemma, Leandra spoke. 'Didn't you hear me, Tamsin? I was saying the smell is driving me wild.'

'Yes, of course. You said that, and I fed you.'

'I said it again. Singular, this time. *One* smell. You're wet, aren't you? I can smell you.'

Tamsin was a little embarrassed, but nevertheless her pussy got wetter at Leandra's words. Then she noticed that she, too, smelled sex along with the food, and it wasn't herself that she was smelling. Realisation hit her.

'You, too!' she proclaimed. 'You're wet, too!'

'I certainly am,' Leandra said. 'I've been thinking about this almost from the moment you left the States. I want some.' She put her hands on Tamsin's hips under her miniskirt and pulled down a sodden white silk thong. 'You really are ready for me, aren't you? Another minute and it would have been dripping down your legs.' Leandra stood up and spread her legs so Tamsin could reciprocate the gesture. Tamsin obliged, pulling down Leandra's tight black bikini. She saw Nigel's bulge was straining at his jeans.

'Let's get Nigel's trousers off so he'll be more comfortable,' Tamsin said. Both women turned to Nigel and helped him ease his jeans down over his stiff cock. He wasn't wearing underpants. Freed, his rigid cock rose into the air.

The doorbell rang, announcing the first of the party guests. Nigel tugged his jeans back up while Jamie went to answer the door.

'Just look at you!' Gina called from the kitchen door. 'What a touching reunion.'

Nigel continued to wrestle his recalcitrant cock back into the confines of his jeans. Tamsin made the introductions. She didn't feel shy in front of Gina. In fact, she felt rather pleased that Gina had caught a strange man in her kitchen with his pants down. Gina, after all, was the one who taught her all those good tricks before she left for California. She was happy to have Gina catch her in action.

The doorbell rang again. Nigel finally got his flies zipped, fumbling in his haste. At least her party wasn't off to a slow start, Tamsin reflected. She'd been a little worried about that, wondering if all her guests would be comfortable with each other. Apparently that wouldn't be a problem. Gina was already checking out Nigel, who wasn't objecting one bit.

Jamie returned to the kitchen with Vanessa and Harry in tow. There were hugs all around as the old friends greeted each other and began catching up on their news of the past six months. Talking non-stop, they drifted into the sitting room and mingled with the other arriving guests. Somebody put some music on and turned the volume down low. Nobody noticed that Gina and Harry were staring at each other as if transfixed. After a few minutes Gina excused herself and left the room.

When the CD ended, Tamsin rapped on the table for attention. 'Everybody is here now, I think. Let's adjourn to the play room.' She herded her guests to the back of the house into her well-appointed dungeon, in the centre of which was a small circular stage. 'Before you split up into small play groups, I have a special surprise for you. Gina?'

Gina danced onto the stage in a white tulle knee-length ballet skirt, leading Jamie by a white collar and leash. Jamie was wearing the standard men's full-body leotard – with one difference. His penis, almost majestic in its fullness, was rising from a slit in the front.

The audience gasped. Jamie did a slow pirouette so his viewers could see him from every angle. After everyone had a chance to admire him, he gracefully lowered himself to his knees, his back ramrod-straight and his cock straining towards Gina.

Gina unhooked the leash and danced around the stage *en pointe*, moving to music she must have heard only in her head. Then, on cue, music filled the room. It was wild music, assignable to no known genre. Drums throbbed in rhythms impossible to duplicate. Synthesisers wailed and sobbed. Jamie's erection expanded.

Suddenly Gina whipped off her skirt, revealing a plain white leotard. She spread her legs and slowly bent backward, gyrating with the music, until her hands touched the floor. She revolved in that position until her crotch was facing Jamie again.

The music was gradually accelerating as she pointed her sex towards Jamie's glorious erection. Jamie's face remained impassive as he waited, his eyes fixed on Gina's sex. Only the fire in his eyes hinted at his true feelings.

Gina moved toward him at a glacial pace, still maintaining her backbend. Her pelvis thrust at him as she inched forward. Just as she seemed about to touch him, she lay down flat on her back and raised her legs high above her head, spreading them wide in a split. She turned halfway around, propelling herself almost imperceptibly by her hands, and gradually lowered her feet to the floor just above her head. Her sex was so close to Jamie's that it seemed impossible that they couldn't feel each other.

Jamie didn't miss a beat. At a signal from Gina that was invisible to the audience, he shifted his body so that his cock was touching the crotch of her leotard. He moved forward on his knees. As he did so, he seemed to be entering her. She made no sound. The music was much faster now, but Jamie did everything in slow motion. Finally, with the material of Gina's leotard brushing his testicles, he bent over her bum and put his hands on the floor behind her.

Gina raised her legs off the floor, launching Jamie into a forward somersault. Without breaking contact or losing his rhythm, Jamie pulled up and Gina tumbled into a somersault. They rolled like this, sexes touching, around the entire periphery of the stage.

Watching, Tamsin felt herself getting damp. Gina hadn't allowed her to watch them rehearse. She'd had no idea that Jamie could dance, could be so – well – sexy. Judging from the moans around her, the spectacle was having the same effect on their other friends as well.

The pair on stage continued to roll. Jamie's pumping was becoming more frenzied. He no longer looked impassive. Rather, he seemed to have his whole being focused on his sex. His, and Gina's. The music got faster. Jamie thrust faster.

Gina let out a cry, followed immediately by one from Jamie. At the same instant the music stopped. Gina and Jamie collapsed in a tangle, their cries drowned out by those of the audience.

Tamsin made her way to the stereo to put on another CD that Gina had chosen beforehand. When the music started, Gina leaped up and tugged Jamie to his feet. Holding hands, they ran forwards and bowed, then bowed to the other side of the stage. Gina fastened the leash to Jamie's collar and led him away.

'Bravo! Magnificent! I know Gina's a professional dancer, but I had no idea Jamie could dance like that. I wonder what else I missed when he was my slave.' Leandra suddenly appeared behind Tamsin.

'You may borrow him if you like, while you're here. Discover his other skills for yourself.' Tamsin laughed at the look of surprise on Leandra's face. She hugged her friend.

Vanessa joined them just as the hug was about to evolve into something else. 'Look at that, Tamsin. Isn't it marvellous?'

'What on earth are you talking about?'

'Over there.' Vanessa pointed. 'Harry and Gina. He's groping her.'

'And she's groping him back. What's so unusual about that? Especially at a party.'

'Harry isn't like that. He never fondles strange women.'

'Well, he is now.' Tamsin took Vanessa's hand. 'Come on, both of you. We'll go find my bag of toys, and then it's time to party.'

24

'So, what do you think?' Leandra asked later, as she and Nigel were getting ready for bed. 'Are you proud of our protégés?'

'I certainly am. Watching Tamsin and Jamie tonight makes it worth the many painful hours I spent as Tamsin's guinea pig.'

'I still owe you for that, love. I had no idea she'd become that obsessed and would want to practise all the time. I still thought she was submissive at heart.'

'She was never submissive, Leandra, just inexperienced. Still, I'm glad we decided to be their mentors. It was great fun. But you're right. You do owe me. I may make you walk naked on a dog leash through the streets of London.'

'I don't owe you that much. I had in mind something a little more private. Tell you what. I'll be your slave for the next full month. But only when we're alone.'

Nigel laughed. 'You mean you don't want to go downstairs naked tomorrow morning and eat your breakfast from a dish on the floor? All right. But only because I'm concerned about what such a display would do to poor Jamie's psyche. I've got a better idea, though. I'll take you up on your month-long penance when we get back to California; we'll have more time alone there, and in the meantime I can enjoy the contemplation of the evil deeds I'll force you to commit. How does that sound?'

'Fine. It beats being your slave so publicly here. I have a reputation to maintain, you know.'

'So do I. Goodnight, my future slave.'

* * *

'You wanted to know about my success as a dancer?' Gina was sitting in full lotus position on the end of Harry's bed, sipping tea. It was two days after the party, and Gina still hadn't left Harry's house. 'What helps me the most is a rather esoteric Japanese discipline I've been studying and practising. It's a painting technique. Brush painting, actually. It's a form of meditation for me. It focuses me for my dancing.'

'What's it called?' Harry asked, almost interrupting.

Gina picked up on his eagerness. 'You really want to know, don't you?'

'Yes, of course. It's important. Everything you do is important to me.'

'I wasn't going to discuss it. I usually don't. Most people's eyes start to glaze over if I mention it. They've never heard of it, and they don't care. It's a very private thing for me. I don't know why I told you. It just felt safe, somehow.'

'It is safe. You're safe. I'm not most people. My eyes won't glaze. It's something *you* do, so it's important. It may be very important to me, also. What's it called?'

'You're babbling, Harry.' Gina smiled gently at him as she traced the heart-shaped birthmark on his penis. 'I'm not used to men telling me that what I do is important, so I just had to hear you say it again. Sumi-e is what I study. That's what it's called. Sumi-e.'

Harry burst into tears. 'I knew it! I love you! Forever!' he sobbed.

Vanessa pondered Harry's request for an appointment less than a week after the party. She was puzzled. Usually a big party like that took care of him for a while. Still, she was here, on time, bag of spanking paraphernalia in hand. She rang the bell.

Harry greeted her, fully dressed. This in itself was unusual. He liked to present himself in his underpants so she could punish him for being indecent and make him put on some clothes before she spanked him. Now not only was he dressed, his demeanour was different. Instead of cringing, he was fully in command.

'What's going on, Harry?'

'Thank you for coming, my dear. Sit down. I'll bring us tea. I have something to discuss with you.'

'Don't you want your spanking?'

'Not today. I'm sorry I misled you. I'll pay your usual fee, of course.'

'You're being awfully formal, considering what we've been through together over these last few months.'

'Sorry. I only have two emotional modes. Formal and naughty little boy. Today it's formal because we'll be talking business.' He poured tea into her cup and filled his own. 'Thing is, I want to hire you to train Gina.'

'Gina? Whatever for? Does she want to be a dominatrix, too?'

'Only for me. You see, Gina and I have a lot in common. She's the only person I've found, besides my sumi-e master, who shares my interest in sumi-e. This is very important to me. I never thought I'd find any-body who feels the way I do about it. And Gina does. We've formed a deep bond in a short time. I want her to spank me. She understands that it would bring us even closer together, and she's willing to do it. Problem is, she doesn't know how. If I show her, then I'm in command, which destroys the whole purpose. I want you to give her lessons.'

'I'll be glad to. Harry, I'm so happy for you. I assume you won't be needing my services any more, and that's all right. It would have been difficult to go back to our old relationship after having become friends, anyhow. Have Gina call me. And I won't accept payment. This will be fun.'

'This isn't goodbye. We're still friends, you know.

Perhaps later on you and Gina and I will have a group spank.'

'Perhaps. I'll look forward to it.' Vanessa started toward the door. 'Goodbye, Harry. And good luck.'

It was the Thursday morning after the party. Tamsin and Jamie were in their dining room having breakfast. They hadn't been alone together since the arrival of Leandra and Nigel who, this morning, were out scouting potential places to photograph Jamie. For a few minutes they ate without speaking.

Tamsin broke the silence. 'Would you like another kipper, Jamie?'

'If it would please you, Mistress Tamsin.'

'Come and get it, then.'

Jamie rose from the corner where he'd been squatting, crept to the table, seized the fish in his cuffed hands, and carried it back to his dish. 'Thank you, Mistress.' He squatted and resumed eating.

'I've been wanting to discuss something with you, Jamie. Or more accurately, I want to inform you what I've decided about our lives.

'An equal relationship won't work for us. We're not equals. You're my slave. I've been intensely aware of this since Leandra and Nigel have been here. We're not just role-playing any more. This is who we are, even in private. Look at us right now. Our guests aren't here to see. Yet there you are, naked, handcuffed, crouching in your corner, eating out of your dog dish. And you have a full erection. I'm very happy with the way your training has worked out.'

Tamsin waited a few seconds, giving Jamie a chance to respond. He said nothing.

'Very good, Jamie. I didn't give you permission to speak. But now I'm asking you, and I'll only ask you this once, if you're happy with our arrangement.'

'Yes, Mistress Tamsin. I am.'

'So be it, then.' She looked over at Jamie. He lowered his eyes.

She may have been about to say something else, but she heard the sound of Leandra and Nigel's hired car in the driveway. She picked up the end of Jamie's leash and, with him following on all fours, went to open the door for their friends.

Visit the Black Lace website at
www.blacklace-books.co.uk

LOOK OUT FOR THE ALL-NEW BLACK LACE BOOKS – AVAILABLE NOW!

All books priced £6.99 in the UK. Please note publication dates apply to the UK only. For other territories, please contact your retailer.

EVIL'S NIECE
Melissa MacNeal
ISBN 0 352 33781 8

The setting is 1890s New Orleans. When Eve spies her husband with a sultry blonde, she is determined to win back his affection. When her brother-in-law sends a maid to train her in the ways of seduction, things spin rapidly out of control. Their first lesson reveals a surprise that Miss Eve isn't prepared for, and when her husband discovers these liaisons, it seems she will lose her prestigious place in society. However, his own covert life is about to unravel and reveal the biggest secret of all. **More historical high jinks from Ms MacNeal, the undisputed queen of kinky erotica set in the world of corsets and chaperones.**

ACE OF HEARTS
Lisette Allen
ISBN 0 352 33059 7

England, 1816. The wealthy elite is enjoying an unprecedented era of hedonistic adventure. Their lives are filled with parties, sexual dalliances and scandal. Marisa Brooke is a young lady who lives by her wits, fencing and cheating the wealthy at cards. She also likes seducing young men and indulging her fancy for fleshly pleasures. However, love and fortune are lost as easily as they are won, and she has to use all her skill and cunning if she wants to hold on to her winnings and her lovers. **Highly enjoyable historical erotica set in the period of Regency excess.**

Coming in April

VALENTINA'S RULES
Monica Belle
ISBN O 352 33788 5

Valentina is the girl with a plan: find a wealthy man, marry him, mould
him and take her place in the sun. She's got the looks, she's got the
ambition and, after one night with her, most men are following her
around like puppies. When she decides that Michael Callington is too
good for her friend Chrissy and just right for her, she finds she has bitten
off a bit more than she expected. Then there's Michael's father, the
notorious spanking Major, who is determined to have his fun, too.
**Monica Belle specialises in erotic stories about modern girls about town
and up to no good.**

WICKED WORDS 8
Edited by Kerri Sharp
ISBN O 352 33787 7

Hugely popular and immensely entertaining, the *Wicked Words*
collections are the freshest and most cutting-edge volumes of women's
erotic stories to be found anywhere in the world. The diversity of themes
and styles reflects the multi-faceted nature of the female sexual
imagination. Combining humour, warmth and attitude with fun,
imaginative writing, these stories sizzle with horny action. Only the most
arousing fiction makes it into a *Wicked Words* volume. This is the best in
fun, sassy erotica from the UK and USA. **Another sizzling collection of
wild fantasies from wicked women!**

Coming in May

UNKNOWN TERRITORY
Rosamund Trench
ISBN 0 352 33794 X

Hazel loves sex. It is her hobby and her passion. Every fortnight she meets up with the well-bred and impeccably mannered Alistair. Then there is Nick, the young IT lad at work, who has taken to following Hazel around like a lost puppy. Her greatest preoccupation, however, concerns the mysterious Number Six – the suited executive she met one day in the boardroom. When it transpires that Number Six is a colleague of Alistair's, things are destined to get complicated. Especially as Hazel is moving towards the 'unknown territory' her mother warned her about. **An unusual sexual exploration of the appeal of powerful men in suits!**

A GENTLEMAN'S WAGER
Madelynne Ellis
ISBN 0 352 33800 8

When Bella Rushdale finds herself fiercely attracted to landowner Lucerne Marlinscar, she doesn't expect that the rival for his affections will be another man. Handsome and decadent, Marquis Pennerley has desired Lucerne for years and now, at the remote Lauwine Hall, he intends to claim him. This leads to a passionate struggle for dominance – at the risk of scandal – between a high-spirited lady and a debauched aristocrat. Who will Lucerne choose? **A wonderfully decadent piece of historical erotica with a twist.**

VIRTUOSO
Katrina Vincenzi-Thyne
ISBN O 352 32907 6

Mika and Serena, young ambitious members of classical music's jet-set, inhabit a world of secluded passion and privilege. However, since Mika's tragic injury, which halted his meteoric rise to fame as a solo violinist, he has retired embittered. Serena is determined to change things. A dedicated voluptuary, her sensuality cannot be ignored as she rekindles Mika's zest for life. Together they share a dark secret. **A beautifully written story of opulence and exotic, passionate indulgence.**

Black Lace Booklist

Information is correct at time of printing. To avoid disappointment check availability before ordering. Go to www.blacklace-books.co.uk. All books are priced £6.99 unless another price is given.

BLACK LACE BOOKS WITH A CONTEMPORARY SETTING

To find out the latest information about Black Lace titles, check out the website: www.blacklace-books.co.uk or send for a booklist with complete synopses by writing to:

> Black Lace Booklist, Virgin Books Ltd
> Thames Wharf Studios
> Rainville Road
> London W6 9HA

Please include an SAE of decent size. Please note only British stamps are valid.

Our privacy policy
We will not disclose information you supply us to any other parties. We will not disclose any information which identifies you personally to any person without your express consent.

From time to time we may send out information about Black Lace books and special offers. Please tick here if you do <u>not</u> wish to receive Black Lace information.   ☐

Please send me the books I have ticked above.

Name ....

Address ....

....

....

....

Post Code ....

Send to: Cash Sales, Black Lace Books, Thames Wharf Studios, Rainville Road, London W6 9HA.

US customers: for prices and details of how to order books for delivery by mail, call 1-800-343-4499.

Please enclose a cheque or postal order, made payable to Virgin Books Ltd, to the value of the books you have ordered plus postage and packing costs as follows:

UK and BFPO – £1.00 for the first book, 50p for each subsequent book.

Overseas (including Republic of Ireland) – £2.00 for the first book, £1.00 for each subsequent book.

If you would prefer to pay by VISA, ACCESS/MASTERCARD, DINERS CLUB, AMEX or SWITCH, please write your card number and expiry date here:

....

Signature ....

Please allow up to 28 days for delivery.